Praise for Joan Johnston

"Johnston's page-turner is replete with romantic angst, sizzling sex, and the promise of an enduring love." —*Publishers Weekly* (starred review)

"Joan Johnston continually gives us everything we want . . . fabulous details and atmosphere, memorable characters, a story that you wish would never end, and lots of tension and sensuality."
—*Romantic Times*

"A master storyteller . . . Joan Johnston knows how to spin a story that will get to the readers every time." —*Night Owl Reviews*

"Johnston has a keen eye for quirky circumstances that put her characters, and the reader, through a wringer. Laughing one moment and crying the next, you'll always have such a great time getting to the happy-ever-after."
—*Romance Junkies Reviews*

"Johnston is a writer who can combine romance side by side with tragedy, proving that there is magic in relationships and that love is worth the risk." —*Bookreporter*

By Joan Johnston

Bitter Creek Novels

The Cowboy
The Texan
The Loner
The Price
The Rivals
The Next Mrs. Blackthorne
A Stranger's Game
Shattered

Sisters of the Lone Star Series

Frontier Woman
Comanche Woman
Texas Woman

Captive Hearts Series

Captive
After the Kiss
The Bodyguard
The Bridegroom

Mail-Order Brides Series

Texas Bride
Wyoming Bride
Montana Bride
Blackthorne's Bride

King's Brats Series

Sinful
Shameless
Surrender
Sullivan's Promise

Connected Books

The Barefoot Bride
Outlaw's Bride
The Inheritance
Maverick Heart

Sullivan's Promise

A Bitter Creek Novel

JOAN JOHNSTON

DELL BOOKS · NEW YORK

A Dell Mass Market Original

Published in the United States by Dell, an imprint of Random House, a division of Penguin Random House LLC, New York.

DELL and the HOUSE colophon are registered trademarks of Penguin Random House LLC.

ISBN 978-0-399-17778-1
Ebook ISBN 978-0-399-17779-8

Cover design: Elizabeth Shapiro
Cover photograph: Rob Lang

Printed in the United States of America

randomhousebooks.com

2 4 6 8 9 7 5 3 1

Dell mass market edition: May 2019

This book is dedicated to
Nancy November Sloane,
whose cheerful, capable, and creative
assistance in all things book related
makes my life as a writer
so much better
in so many ways.

Sullivan's Promise

Prologue

RYAN SULLIVAN'S HEART jumped when he saw who'd finally gotten up the nerve to show her face at his ranch in Montana. An image of Victoria Grayhawk, stark naked, appeared in his mind's eye, her golden curls spilling across his pillow, her lithe body arched in ecstasy beneath him. He shook his head to dispel the disturbing memory and fixed his gaze on the unwelcome woman dressed in a denim jacket, jeans, and cowboy boots standing on his back porch.

"What the hell are you doing here, Lexie?"

Her striking blue eyes, concealed by shadows during their night together, looked wounded in the bright light of day. He noticed her hands were trembling as she stuck them in her back pockets. He realized she hadn't answered him and said, "I asked you a question."

Her chin lifted, and he saw a spark of the vibrant woman who'd attracted him when he'd first spotted her in the Million Dollar Cowboy Bar in Jackson Hole, Wyoming.

She looked him in the eye and said, "I made a mistake."

"Which mistake are we talking about here? The one where you lied about being on the pill? Or the one where you wanted me to give up parental rights to my son?"

"I didn't lie. I was on the pill. I don't know why I got pregnant. I only asked you to give up your parental rights because I wanted the child to be adopted by a loving family."

"Let me stop you right there. Cody isn't *the* child or *a* child. He's *my* child, since you gave up your right to have anything to do with him the day he was born."

She flinched, as well she should. He couldn't imagine any woman caring so little about her child that she would give him up to anyone, even his own father, and walk away without a second thought.

She met his gaze again, and he saw tears welling in her eyes. He hardened his heart. He didn't care what she wanted now. She'd had her chance to be a mother, and she'd thrown it away like a sack of trash. He wasn't going to let her back into Cody's life now. His son was a happy, healthy, six-month-old boy. He was doing fine without a mother. He had a doting father, a grandmother, an uncle, and a teenage aunt to give him all the love he needed.

"I know what I did was wrong," she said in a voice that grated like a rusty gate. "You can't say anything to me—or about me—that I haven't said to myself a thousand times over the past six months. I never should have walked away. It was the dumbest, most idiotic, utterly shameful thing I've ever done in my life. But I'm here now, and I want to see my son."

"He's *my* son," Sullivan shot back.

"I have visitation rights."

Sullivan remembered how surprised his lawyer had been when Victoria Grayhawk said she didn't want visitation rights, because she didn't plan to be a part of the child's life. It was her lawyer who'd insisted on writing in a clause allowing her to see their son "one weekend per month, from 5 p.m. on Friday to 5 p.m. on Sunday."

Sullivan remembered how she'd pursed her lips and shaken her head when her lawyer said, "You might change your mind." Sullivan had been tired of fighting and had agreed to her lawyer's terms, certain he would never see her again. They'd both signed the legal document, which was approved by a family court judge, making Ryan Patrick Sullivan the primary custodial parent and giving Victoria Alexandra Grayhawk visiting privileges one weekend a month.

For the past six months, he hadn't seen hide nor hair of her. Now, here she was at his back door on a Friday afternoon demanding to see *his* son.

"You can't see Cody. You can't hold him. You can't have him for the weekend. Get the hell off my doorstep. Get the hell off my property. Go away and don't come back."

"He's my son, too! You can't deny me the right to be a mother to him."

The flash of fire in her eyes reminded him of the look she'd given him at the bar, when he'd asked if she'd come back to his room at the Wort Hotel. The one that had turned him hard as a rock. The one that had made it impossible to swallow. The one that had caused him to capture her nape and touch his mouth to hers. A shiver of excitement skittered down his spine at the mere thought of that kiss.

He knotted his fists and forced the feeling down. "You're the one who walked away," he said in a voice made harsh by vivid memories he thought he'd put behind him. "You said you didn't want to be a mother. It's not something I'm ever likely to forget hearing."

"I told you, I made a mistake!"

"You sure as hell did!"

"I have legal rights," she protested.

"Good luck with that. Where were you planning to keep Cody for the weekend? You can't take him out of state without my permission, and I won't give it. Do you have a home here in Montana?"

"I've bought a cabin."

"Where?"

"On the edge of your property."

"Not the Wingate place," he said, horrified at the thought of having her so close.

"I think that was the old man's name."

Sullivan had been planning to buy that tiny log home on the edge of Glacier National Park, and the five hundred acres that surrounded it, for himself. He'd just been waiting for old man Wingate to lower his price, since he didn't think there was anyone else willing to buy such a shabby hovel so deep in the woods. Now the mother of his child was going to be living right on the edge of his property, day in and day out.

"What happened to your grand plans to save grizzlies and wolves from extinction?" he said with a sneer.

"I'm still working to save endangered species."

"I thought you had to travel to do your job. After all, that was the excuse you gave for not wanting to be a mother." That, and the fact that she didn't know him from Adam. He was just a guy she'd met in a bar. It had been good sex, she told him (great sex as far as he was concerned, though he hadn't bothered to contradict her), but that had been the extent of it. The pregnancy was merely an unforeseen, entirely unexpected consequence. At twenty-two, she wasn't ready to become a single mother, and she wanted the child to grow up in a loving home.

At twenty-four, he hadn't exactly been ready for parenthood, either, but he'd known he could never give his own flesh and blood away to someone else to raise.

"I still have to travel," she said defensively. "But I plan to be here at least one weekend a month to see my son."

"He's not yours. He's mine," Sullivan said. "And don't you forget it."

His gut clenched with fear for his child. He could probably put off the Grayhawk woman for a while, by bringing in social services to check out the living conditions in that old cabin in the woods. But eventually, she was going to get Cody one weekend a month. His little boy would be scared if he went off alone with some stranger. Which meant Sullivan was going to have to let that damned woman into his home to spend time with Cody, before she took him away and kept him by herself.

Not to mention making sure she knew how and what to feed Cody, how to change a diaper, what his bedtime ritual was, and how he sometimes woke up at night and needed a small light turned on before he would go back to sleep—for no reason Sullivan had ever been able to determine.

He studied the somber look on Victoria Grayhawk's face, so different from the bubbly smile and laughing eyes that had caught his attention at the bar. The air had shimmered with tension when he was still half a room away from her. It was as though she were tugging him toward her with an invisible rope, from which there was no escape. He felt the same attraction now and fought against it.

She wasn't the woman he'd imagined she was when he'd taken her to bed. That woman spoke of noble ideals and goals which, even though they ran counter to his personal feelings, still resonated with him. She wanted to save wolves and grizzlies from extinction—the same wolves and grizzlies that killed his cattle every year. She hadn't changed her tune, even when she'd found out they were on opposite sides of the fence. She'd simply cozened him with kisses to convince him to take a look at her point of view.

He'd been willing to sacrifice every cow on his ranch to feed hungry bears and wolves by the time she got done with him. He was well and truly lost, ready—if she'd just said the word—to tie the knot and take her home with him to Montana.

Except, when he'd woken up the next morning, she'd been gone. And he'd never gotten her last name. She'd simply called herself "Lexie." He'd only been in town for a two-day cattlemen's meeting, and when he'd asked about a "Lexie" in the bar the next evening, no one knew a woman of her description by that name. Nor had there been anyone in the lobby when they'd entered the hotel who might have known her. It was only later he discovered her name was Victoria Grayhawk, and folks in Jackson called her Vick. It was one more transgression to add to the growing list.

"Lexie" had been more careful than he was, asking enough questions to find out his full name, and that he lived on a ranch in Montana. She'd come looking for him when she found out she was pregnant, and that whole sorry legal mess had started.

He wondered if he would be so mad at Lexie now, if he hadn't felt so foolish for wanting more time with her, when she'd apparently forgotten all about him once the sun hit the morning sky.

"Rye? Who's at the door?"

"No one, Mom." That's what Lexie Grayhawk was and always would be to him and his son.

He could hear his mother—who was nosy, but in a good way—crossing the mudroom to see for herself who'd come to visit.

The sudden intense look of longing on Lexie's face told him something was amiss. Then he heard the screen door screech behind him and turned to see his mother stepping onto the back porch with Cody in her arms.

Cody leaned over and thrust out both arms, but it wasn't Sullivan he was reaching for. As Rye had turned to watch his mother's approach, Lexie had held out her arms to the child, her face lit with joy. Rye realized with a sudden pang that it was her smile he saw reflected on Cody's face each morning when he greeted his son—the same bow on the upper lip, the same fullness of the lower one, and the wide, inviting mouth.

Her arms reached for the baby, who was grinning toothlessly back at her.

Sullivan saw what was going to happen and intercepted the infant before the boy's mother—this stranger—could touch him.

He felt disconcerted because Cody was still straining to reach the woman, his tiny arms outstretched.

"Hello, Cody."

At the sound of Lexie's voice, low and husky, goosebumps rose all over Sullivan's body. That was the same mesmerizing voice that had coaxed *him* into her arms.

He tried to hand Cody back to his grandmother, to put him out of Lexie's reach, but his mom's arms were folded over her chest, and she had "that look" on her face that told him she knew exactly who was standing on their back porch. And that what Sullivan was doing—keeping a mother and her son apart—was wrong.

But he wasn't wrong. He knew it in his gut.

What if Lexie stepped into Cody's life and made the vulnerable little boy love her, and then changed her mind again? He wanted to spare his child that pain. Better she never became a part of Cody's life in the first place.

Lexie had dropped her hands, and her smile had faded, but her eyes still implored him to let her hold the baby.

Cody settled his warm body against Sullivan's heart and stuck his thumb in his mouth, but his eyes remained focused on the woman standing in front of him.

"Go away, Miss Grayhawk," Sullivan said in a calm voice that wouldn't upset the child in his arms. "There's nothing for you here."

"Except my son, whom I love with every fiber of my being."

He was startled by the fierceness of her voice as much as by the words she'd spoken.

"You can't stop me from being a mother to Cody," she continued. "The courts are on my side. Make up your mind that this is going to happen."

His heart was beating frantically, pushing against his ribs like a terrified animal trying to escape, knowing there *is* no escape. "Fine." The single word was harsh, and startled both her and Cody, who lifted his head and looked up at him with a tiny furrow between his brows.

"Fine," he repeated in a more moderate voice.

"I can take him?" she said, her arched eyebrows raised in question, reminding him that he saw her every day when he looked at Cody's face.

"No."

"Then what—"

"Cody doesn't know you. And you don't know his routine. If you're going to do this, you might as well start from the beginning."

"May I hold him?"

Rye felt an ache in his chest. Why couldn't she have asked that at the hospital? But the time for regrets was past. She was here now, and he was going to have to make the best of a bad situation. He would do what had to be done for Cody's sake.

"He might not want to go to you," he said as she took a step toward him.

Cody put the lie to his words, as Lexie smiled again and held out her arms and cooed, "Hello, Cody. I'm your mother."

The little boy eagerly reached out to her and left the safety of his father's arms for the far less certain ones of his mother.

She held the infant awkwardly at first, shifting him until she had him sitting on her hip, which God had apparently made for just that purpose. Her whole face was lit up so brightly it hurt to look at her. He saw before him the vivacious woman he'd met in a bar, who'd become his lover, and who was now the mother of his child.

He'd forgotten about his own mother. She pulled the screen door open wide with another loud screech and said, "Why don't you come inside?"

He stood helplessly by as Lexie Grayhawk, a woman he could never trust, a woman he both despised and desired, stepped into his kitchen . . . and into his life.

Chapter 1

MEET ME AT *the hospital.*

That cryptic message, stuck to Sullivan's back door, lodged Vick's heart in her throat and made her insides draw up tight.

Usually, Rye or his mother or his brother dropped Cody off at her cabin at exactly 5 p.m. on Friday for his monthly visit. When Rye hadn't shown up by 7:00, and hadn't returned any of her calls, she'd decided to come see what was wrong.

An enormous mutt with raggedy ears, which was sprawled on the back porch, thumped his tail when she looked in his direction but didn't bother to get up.

"What happened, Rusty?"

At the sound of his name, the dog rose and

stretched like an old man with rickety bones. By the time he'd taken a step in Vick's direction, she was already back inside her pickup. She punched up the number again, and heard Sullivan's phone go to voicemail again. She tried not to imagine the worst. She fought off the vision of her five-year-old son with a broken arm or a crushed foot or bleeding from some gaping wound.

"That horse is too damn big!" she muttered as she started the engine and headed down the dirt road leading from the Sullivans' Rafter S Ranch to the highway.

Her son looked tiny atop the buckskin he rode most often, but Cody loved the sixteen-hand-tall gelding. Although Dancer had never given Cody a bit of trouble, horses had instinctual responses to sudden movement, and Dancer could easily leap five feet sideways to escape a horse-eating rabbit. Even a good rider like Cody could be thrown.

Was he injured in a fall? Was he trampled by one of Sullivan's Black Angus cattle? Was it something even worse?

Cody was never far from Sullivan's side when he went out on the range, but he also rode the trails close to home by himself. It was March 10, early for grizzlies to be out and about, but she might be wrong about that, because grizzlies didn't actually hibernate. They merely had periods of dormancy and could awaken with little provocation. It had been a warm and dry winter, and there wasn't as much snow as usual on the ground. A roused bear might decide winter was over and be out foraging for food.

Could my precious son have been attacked and mauled by one of the animals I've spent the past six years of my life protecting?

Vick felt nauseated. She knew more than she wanted to know about the gruesome effects of a grizzly attack on human flesh. Lots of ranchers, including Sullivan, would be just as happy if the ferocious bears were erased from the face of the earth. Vick realized her heart was racing and her breath was coming in gasps.

Think about something else, or you're going to pass out.

But her thoughts were as out of control as her heart rate. Tears sprang to her eyes and her gut clenched as she raced south on busy U.S. 93, dodging cars and praying there wouldn't be one of those wrecks that tied up traffic for hours on the main road into Kalispell.

What if this accident had happened a year ago, when I was living at my father's ranch in Wyoming? Thank God I'm staying in Montana year-round now. Thank God I can be at the hospital with my son when he needs me most.

She might still have been residing in Wyoming year-round, with monthly three-day visits to Montana to see her son, if her father hadn't finally found the missing black sheep of the family running a cattle station in Australia and brought him home.

As an enticement to get his eldest son to return to

America, King Grayhawk had offered Matt full possession of the ranch where Vick and her three sisters, Leah, Taylor, and Eve, made their home, if he lived there for 365 consecutive days. Matt accepted the deal and immediately made it clear that, by the time that year was up, the four Grayhawk girls—better known as King's Brats—had better find another place besides Kingdom Come to live.

That had been the kick in the butt Vick needed to move herself—lock, stock, and barrel—to Montana. It was still an agony to say goodbye to her son each time she gave him back to his father, but she'd been able to see Cody far more often over the past year when he participated in school and church events that she could attend.

Unfortunately, living here had also meant more interaction with Cody's father. In the past, on days when Cody needed to be dropped off or picked up, Sullivan had either had someone else hand Cody over or, if he did it himself, maintained a stony silence. Since moving to Montana last year, she'd encountered Sullivan in situations, especially at Cody's school and at Sunday school, where they were forced to interact cordially.

It had been awkward, to say the least.

Whitefish was a small town, and she often ran into Sullivan shopping at the same grocery store, or out in the evening with his latest girlfriend at the same bar where she was getting together with Pete Harrison, a Flathead County deputy sheriff who'd recently turned into something more than just a friend.

Her accidental meetings with Sullivan always seemed to be fraught with tension. He spoke briefly and curtly to her, if he spoke at all. She figured too much had been left unsaid between them.

Or maybe, left unresolved.

Vick had never forgiven herself for giving away her child, so she couldn't very well blame Sullivan for begrudging her every moment she spent with Cody. She knew he only abided by their legal agreement for his son's sake, but that was good enough for her. She didn't need Sullivan to be her friend or even to be friendly. She just needed him not to interfere with her efforts to be a good mother.

Vick screeched to a stop near the emergency entrance to Kalispell Regional Medical Center and raced inside. She arrived at the reception desk, eyes wide with fright, and said, "Can you tell me the status of Cody Sullivan? I'm his mother."

The young woman hit some keys on the computer and said, "I'm not finding a Cody Sullivan."

"But he has to be here!"

"I have a Michael Sullivan admitted early this afternoon. Is he any relation?"

"No, but—"

"Then I can't give you any further information."

Vick shuddered with relief. Cody wasn't hurt. It was Sullivan's younger brother who'd been injured. She needed to hold her son in her arms, to reassure herself he was all right. "Mike Sullivan is my son's uncle. Can you tell me where his family might be?"

The receptionist hesitated, then said, "You can check the surgical waiting room."

"Where is that?"

"Second floor."

Vick's anger at Sullivan grew as she half walked, half trotted to the stairs, following the young woman's instructions to reach the waiting room. Why couldn't he have said in his note that it was Mike who'd been injured? Why couldn't he have called and told her Cody was all right? Refusing to have a conversation with her was one thing. This was something else entirely. He should have known she would be frantic with worry.

She saw Sullivan pacing as she entered the waiting room, but before she could say anything, Cody spotted her and came running.

"Mommy!"

Her arms opened wide to gather up her son, and she lifted him into the air—not an easy feat as large a five-year-old as he was—and hugged his warm, squirming body tightly against her own.

He leaned back, took her cheeks between his hands, and said, "Uncle Mike got eaten by a *bear*!"

She took one look at Sullivan's agonized eyes and realized Mike's injuries must be devastating. There had been two grizzly attacks in Montana the previous fall, against men out hunting deer and elk. Both victims had survived but with awful wounds to their arms and heads.

She set Cody down and clutched his hand as she approached Sullivan. "How's Mike?"

Sullivan gripped Cody's shoulder and said, "Go see if Gram needs anything."

Cody tore free and took off at a run toward his grandmother.

Until Sullivan had mentioned her, Vick hadn't noticed his mother, Darcie, sitting on the far side of the waiting room. While Vick's relationship with Sullivan had remained distant, she'd become surprisingly good friends with Cody's grandmother over the past five years. Darcie thought makeup was "tomfoolery" and her wardrobe could best be described as "comfortable." She was wearing worn-out jeans, a plaid wool shirt, and scuffed cowboy boots, with her silver curls escaping a frayed knot high on the back of her head. She was bent over with her forearms on her knees, her gaze focused on the floor.

Vick wondered if Darcie had called Sullivan's younger sister, Amy Beth, who was in Missoula finishing her senior year at the University of Montana, or whether she was waiting for the results of the surgery before contacting her.

Vick looked around the waiting room, expecting to see Sullivan's latest girlfriend—she couldn't remember her name—a long-legged redhead who wore enormous false eyelashes and very high heels, but she wasn't there. The pretty young woman, who was a very successful realtor, was probably out showing ranch property to prospective buyers.

"How bad is it?" she asked Sullivan.

"Bad." He shoved an agitated hand through sun-streaked chestnut hair that always needed a trim.

"Will he live?" She searched Sullivan's face and saw tears well in his moss-green eyes. He turned away and swiped at his eyes with his sleeve before turning back to her. Fury had replaced fear on his face.

"Are you happy now?"

"What is that supposed to mean?"

"One of your bears attacked Mike."

"*My* bears?"

"The ones you protect," he snarled. "Mike hiked into the forest hunting some cows that strayed across the Stillwater, where we don't have fence."

"Alone?"

"He had a shotgun."

Against a grizzly? Vick thought it, but she didn't say it. Sullivan was already crazy with grief.

"Mike was so badly mauled, he must have surprised the grizzly with one of our calves it had killed." Sullivan's voice broke as he finished, "He never had a chance."

"What happened to the bear?" Vick realized as soon as the words were spoken how insensitive they must sound. "What I meant—"

"I know what you meant," Sullivan interrupted. "You're worried about your precious grizzly. I saw a blood trail, but the bear was long gone. As far as I know, it's alive and well and out there waiting for some other poor, unsuspecting cowboy to come along, so it can take a swipe at him."

Vick didn't argue. She and Sullivan would never agree about the treatment of grizzlies. What had happened to Mike was a tragedy, and she understood Sullivan's rage and frustration. Because of the work she did, she also sympathized with the grizzly's plight. Because of the attack, it might very well be hunted down and killed, even if it had been surprised by Mike and was only defending itself and its kill. The fact that the bear had slaughtered a calf only complicated the situation.

Vick crossed to Darcie, sat down beside her, and put a comforting arm around her shoulders. "How are you doing?"

"I'm okay," Darcie replied in a tremulous voice as she gripped Vick's hand.

"How can I help?" Vick asked.

"The surgeon said Mike will need a lot of blood. I've already donated."

"I'll be glad to do that."

"Me, too," Sullivan said. "Why didn't you say something sooner, Mom?"

Vick caught the flash of panic in Darcie's eyes and wondered what had caused it.

Darcie opened her mouth and closed it again without speaking. "You two go ahead. I'll keep an eye on Cody."

"I want to give Uncle Mike my blood, too," Cody said.

"Next time, sport," Sullivan said, ruffling Cody's shaggy blond hair. "Your mom and I have this covered. You keep an eye on Gram and make sure she's okay."

As they headed for the nurses' station, Vick asked, "Do our blood types have to match for us to donate?"

"Mike's type O, so he needs the same type donor. My blood will work. Do you know your blood type?"

Vick shook her head.

"Even if you're not type O, the hospital will likely be grateful for the donation."

The nurse sent them to a lab on another floor, where blood could be drawn. Before doing so, the technician did a quick stick test to type their blood. "You're A negative," the technician told Vick. "You're also A negative," the technician announced a few moments later to Sullivan.

"I think you made a mistake," Sullivan said.

"The test is—"

"Check again," Sullivan interrupted. "Please."

"Why are you so sure he's wrong?" Vick asked.

"Mom is—and Dad was—type O. I know because I was required to ask for a tenth grade biology assignment. Two type O parents can only have kids with type O blood."

It took Vick a moment to process what it meant if Sullivan's blood type was *not* O. Sullivan's mom, or his dad, was not his biological parent. Or maybe neither was. She thought back to the momentary panic she'd seen in Darcie's eyes.

"A negative," the technician said smugly. "Told you so."

"Just take my damned blood," Sullivan said.

Vick tried to put herself in Sullivan's shoes. How awful to discover that one—or both—of your parents wasn't related to you. To make matters worse, someone he didn't much like—that would be her—was in on the secret. Should she reassure him that she wouldn't say anything to anyone? Or just keep her mouth shut?

She opted to stay silent.

Sullivan did the same, waiting without another word while Vick's blood was drawn, before he walked with her back toward the surgical waiting room.

"That's a kick in the head," he muttered.

"Are you going to tell your mom what you've found out?"

"No."

Vick couldn't believe Sullivan wasn't going to confront his mother and realized she was going to have to be careful not to let the truth slip out when she was talking with Darcie. "Don't you want to know . . ." Her voice trailed off.

He huffed out a breath. "What difference would it make now?"

Vick couldn't believe Sullivan was as indifferent to his astonishing discovery as he seemed, especially when he'd been so adamant about not giving away a child of his own blood. For the second time, she thought of that panicked look in Darcie's eyes when

Sullivan had decided to give blood. Maybe he was adopted. Or maybe Darcie had been pregnant when she'd married Sullivan's father.

Vick had been a baby when her mother ran off with one of her father's cowhands, and her father had been absent most of her childhood, living in the governor's mansion in Cheyenne, while she and her three sisters remained behind at his ranch in Jackson Hole. At least Sullivan knew he'd been loved. She opened her mouth to point that out to him and shut it again. They'd stayed out of each other's lives for the past five years. This was none of her business.

She was two steps past Sullivan before she realized he'd stopped in his tracks. She turned to face him and saw his brow was deeply furrowed.

He met her gaze and said, "I was seven when Mike was born and nine when Amy Beth was born, so I saw my mother pregnant with both of them. What happened? Why didn't they just tell me if I'm adopted?"

Vick couldn't believe Sullivan was sharing his thoughts—his very private and personal thoughts—with her, but she realized there was no one else. She was the only one who knew his secret. "I can't answer that," she said. "You'll have to ask your mother."

"Not happening," he muttered, striding off down the hall.

Vick hop-skipped to catch up to him. "What are you going to do?"

"Nothing. Not a damned thing."

"You're not going to ask your mother—"

"Ask her what?" he said, stopping again to confront her. "Why she and my father lied to me my entire life? Thanks but no thanks. I'd rather let sleeping dogs lie."

From what Vick could see, the hounds of hell were wide awake and howling. And the pitiless, unfeeling, unyielding man who'd kept her at arm's length for five years had suddenly revealed a very vulnerable underbelly.

Then she realized what else Sullivan's discovery meant. Maybe there was another reason to urge him to find out the truth from his mother.

Cody might have another set of grandparents out there somewhere . . . who didn't know he existed.

Chapter 2

"I'M NOT A babysitter, Rye."

"What were you planning to do if you moved in?" Rye asked his girlfriend, Sherry Franklin, who'd shown up at the hospital nearly seven hours after he'd called to tell her his brother was in surgery, fighting for his life.

"I never wanted kids of my own, much less yours."

"You didn't think it was important to mention that sometime during the past six months?"

"No. I did not."

Rye sighed. He'd given Lexie Grayhawk a cold shoulder over the past five years, but he had to hand it to her. The mere thought that Cody might be injured, and she'd broken land-speed records to get to the hospital. She hadn't hesitated to donate blood for Mike, and she'd sat beside his mother for hours offering comfort. At the moment, Lexie was distracting Cody, who was tired and cranky, with word games. That left Rye free to pace the floor with worry over his brother . . . and that other little matter that made him want to curl up in a ball and hide. Every so often he glanced at his mother, glad that he had an excuse not to ask her the questions that scrambled around untethered in his head.

"What bird lays eggs?" Lexie asked Cody.

"A chicken," Cody promptly replied.

"That was a trick question," she said, her blue eyes crinkling with laughter.

Cody cocked his head, then grinned and said, "*All* birds lay eggs! But we *eat* eggs from chickens."

She gave him a high five and said, "Right! Of course, people around the world eat eggs from other birds, too."

"Like ducks?" Cody asked.

"How smart you are," Lexie said. "Let's think of some more."

Rye realized she was teaching Cody as she played with him. When he compared the behavior of the woman he'd scorned for the past five years to the behavior of a woman who supposedly loved him, he realized he'd been fooling himself. Sherry would never make a good mother for Cody, much less a good wife for him. He took her aside and said quietly, "Thank you for coming, Sherry. I know you were busy today."

"It was time well spent," she said with an effervescent smile. "I made a sale—that forty-acre property that's mostly wetlands I haven't been able to unload."

"I think maybe we better call it quits."

"What?"

She looked shocked, and he had to admit this was coming out of the blue. He hadn't known himself until a few moments ago that he was going to break up with her. He did his best to let her down gently. "I think it's time we went our separate ways."

"You're breaking up with me because I won't babysit your kid?" she asked in a voice so shrill the surgical desk nurse looked up from her paperwork.

He kept his voice calm and level. "I'm breaking up with you because we obviously have different ideas about what's important to us. Do you want me to walk you out?"

The stunning redhead stood there for a moment, looking incredulous, her false eyelashes fluttering, then said, "I think I can find my way to the parking lot, Rye. And I know I can find a better relationship than this one." She marched away, her nose in the air, her very high heels *click-clacking* a brisk, furious farewell.

Rye watched her leave, surprised that what he felt first and foremost was relief. He approached his mother and said, "Do you have a friend who might be willing to help take care of Cody while you're here at the hospital with Mike? I've got cattle that have to be moved back across the river, and with Mike not available to help, I'll have to do it myself."

She frowned. "My friends all have busy lives. What about Vick?"

"What about her?"

"Have you thought about asking her to keep Cody?"

"Cody will be sleeping in his own bed, if I have anything to say about it," he replied. "And I do."

"Why not ask Vick to come stay at the Rafter S? She can bunk in Amy Beth's room."

"She's probably not available. She's got a job that takes her out of town pretty regularly. Or had you forgotten?" he asked with a pointed look.

"Ask her," his mother insisted.

Rye stalked off to stare out the window at the distant mountains, his right hip canted, his arms crossed protectively over his chest. Having Lexie stay at the ranch was the best solution for Cody. It irked him that he still couldn't get himself to call her Vick, even after all these years. Despite how her relationship with his son had started out, she clearly loved Cody now, and his son adored her. Rye sighed. It just stuck in his craw to ask Lexie Grayhawk for anything.

But his cows had all dropped calves, and he needed to keep an eye on them, especially considering the "endangered" wolves and bears ready to make a meal of his newborn livestock. He might as well bite the bullet and ask her to move in. The instant Mike was well enough to come home, she'd be out on her very attractive fanny.

Lexie was still sitting on the other side of the hospital waiting room with Cody in her lap, his son talking animatedly to her.

"Hey, Cody," he said as he approached them. "Gram needs you."

The little boy gave Lexie a hug, then slid from her lap and took off running.

Lexie's eyes stayed longingly focused on Cody until Rye spoke. She suddenly turned her gaze on him, and he felt a flood of desire that shook him with its intensity.

He swore under his breath. That was why he'd kept his distance over the past five years. That was why he'd done his best to avoid meeting her during those weekend handoffs. That was why every conversation he'd had with her over the past year since she'd relocated to Montana was awkward and uncomfortable. He'd never stopped wanting her. Not for one minute. He'd been afraid his hormones would overcome his good sense, so he hadn't put either one to the test. Every time Rye thought of how much he desired her, he reminded himself of the choice she'd made to walk away from their child.

He could never forgive her for that.

Rye had learned from his father— Shit! From whoever the hell it was who'd raised him from the cradle, that black was black and white was white and there was no room for anything in between. Lexie had been there for Cody once a month for four-and-a-half years, but who was to say whether she might take off and leave him behind if something more exciting caught her attention. The chances of that were probably slim at this point, but any chance at all of it happening wrung his insides. He just didn't know her well enough to be *sure*.

His muscles were taut as he fought his attraction to the mother of his son. How the hell was he going to get through several weeks, or months, of seeing her every morning at the breakfast table? Watching her read a book by the fire? Having her in his home every minute of every day?

But he didn't see a better solution to having a responsible caretaker for Cody while he was out on the range. Assuming, of course, that Lexie was willing to step in and help him out. After the way he'd treated her in the past, doing his best to avoid her entirely and speaking tersely when he couldn't, he wouldn't blame her if she spit in his face.

He balled his hands into fists, realized what he'd done, and let them hang loose at his sides. He made himself meet her gaze and felt his groin tighten. "Mom wants to stay in Kalispell until Mike can leave the hospital, which might be a while."

"Of course," she said, her eyes filled with concern he found disconcerting.

He gritted his teeth before continuing, "I don't have anyone to get Cody off to kindergarten in the morning or be there with him after school until my workday is done."

She looked at him with guileless eyes. "I see."

He kept his gaze locked on hers. "Do you?"

"Oh." Her brows lowered in confusion, then rose

in surprise. "Are you asking me to take him home and keep him while—"

"No." His voice sounded harsh in his ears. That was no way to solicit her help. He cleared his throat and began in a more conciliatory tone. "Actually, what I was wondering . . . What I wanted to ask . . . My mom suggested I ask . . ."

An amused smile grew on her face at his inability to say what he wanted to say. He felt flustered and realized this was exactly why he'd kept his distance from her. "Can you come stay at the ranch and take care of Cody while my mom keeps an eye on Mike here in Kalispell?"

Her mouth, her very kissable mouth, dropped open in shock. He resisted the urge to tip her chin up and cover her lips with his own.

"You want me to move in?"

He heard the distrust in her voice and resented it, even if he probably deserved it. "Yeah. If you're going to be around."

She looked down at her hands, which he noticed were twisted together in her lap. "I do have some travel scheduled." She looked up, pinning him in place with eyes the sort of blue that made you look twice, because they were so unusual. "But I'll rearrange it."

"You can sleep in Amy Beth's room."

"How long will you need me?"

He shrugged and realized how tense his shoulders were. "I have no idea. Mike's injuries are . . ." He swallowed over the sudden painful knot in his throat. *Devastating. Grisly. Likely to kill him.* "Bad," he managed to say. "I'll need you a couple of weeks at least. Maybe a month." He couldn't imagine what he would do if a month turned into six weeks. Or, God forbid, two months.

She lowered her long, dark, but very natural lashes to cover her eyes and caught her lower lip in her teeth, an affectation he'd learned she employed when she was thinking.

A moment later, her startling blue eyes were fixed on him, and he almost had to take a step back, the joy on her face was so radiant.

"So I'll be making all of Cody's meals and dressing him and tucking him into bed every night?"

Rye nodded. He felt his heart jump and took it for what it was: a warning that his feelings could quickly get out of hand if he didn't keep a tight leash on them.

"Then, yes! Of course I'll help. I'll have to go home and pack a bag, but I can meet you at the ranch later tonight. Shall I take Cody now?"

He realized that made the most sense. After all, it was her weekend to care for their son. "Sure."

She took a step forward and then backed up, and he realized she'd restrained herself from giving him an impulsive, and likely exuberant, hug.

Then she did it anyway.

Her arms surrounded his neck, and he felt her soft breasts pillowed against his chest and her smooth cheek against his stubble of beard.

His hands just naturally encircled her tiny waist

and held her close enough for his body to come to vibrant life.

"Thank you, Rye," she whispered in his ear.

He was surprised to hear her speak his first name, because she always called him "Sullivan." Maybe that was *her* way of keeping *him* at a distance. Then she almost yanked herself free and hurried over to say goodbye to his mother. A few moments later, she disappeared down thc hall, his son's hand tucked confidently in hers.

He waited for her to glance back, but she kept right on going. He was already having second thoughts, and she probably figured if she gave him a moment to reconsider, he'd change his mind.

"Sonofabitch," he muttered. Rye had no idea how he was going to survive having a woman he'd fantasized about for way too many years sleeping right down the hall.

Chapter 3

VICK ENTERED THE chilly Sullivan ranch house through the unlocked kitchen door, a vestige of frontier days, when travelers might seek refuge at the nearest home in bad weather, like the forty-below blizzards that threatened life and limb in Montana.

When she paused to look around, Cody tugged urgently on her hand.

"Come on, Mommy! I want to show you my room."

Vick was familiar with the Sullivans' enormous kitchen, which hadn't been updated for thirty years. A trestle table that seated eight in sturdy wooden chairs took up most of the room. Rose wallpaper had faded in the bright sun that streamed through a large, uncurtained window over the farm sink. She could see the Whitefish Mountains to the north and the Kootenai Range to the west. Most of Montana, Vick had discovered, was composed of lush green valleys and sky-blue rivers and lakes edged by colossal mountains.

The wide-planked pine floor creaked as she and Cody headed toward the back of the house, which felt as empty as it was. The ancient Coldspot refrigerator hummed behind her, and she heard the heater click on.

She'd stepped into the kitchen to pick up Cody on the few frigid winter days when no one could drop him off at her place. But after that initial, week-long period, while she'd learned Cody's routine as a baby, she'd never been beyond that room. Sullivan had made it clear she wasn't welcome in his home. She'd expected him to soften his attitude toward her when he saw how committed she was to being a good mother. He hadn't.

Vick was wide-eyed with interest, looking for any changes made over the past five years, as Cody led her through the living room. It still smelled of beeswax and was filled with the same rugged wood-and-leather furniture. A brindle cowhide took up most of the floor in front of the river-rock fireplace, while a new oil painting of a cattle drive held a place of honor above it. Sullivan's oak desk, messy with papers, faced the picture window, with a view of a forbidding—she wouldn't want to get lost in it—evergreen forest.

Cody led her down a long hall, and in the moments she had to peer into each bedroom, it was easy to tell which ones belonged to Mike and Amy Beth and Darcie, who'd been widowed seven years ago, when Rye's father, Patrick, had an embolism. The door at the end of the hall was closed, as it had been during her weeklong visit to the house four-and-a-half years ago, and she was left to wonder what Sullivan's room looked like. Cody pulled her into the small room next to it.

It was clear Sullivan had spared no expense for his son. The kitchen might not be updated, but this room was filled with everything a little boy might want or need. It looked strikingly similar to the room she'd prepared for Cody in her log cabin, except there were no frilly curtains covering the window, and the bedspread was more grown-up and masculine, while she'd bought one with Cody's favorite cartoon characters.

Vick sat on her son's bed and listened to him chatter excitedly as he showed her each toy and book, marveling that this moment had, at very long last, arrived. Her one weekend a month with Cody, while wonderful, was not enough. She'd missed doing all the normal things, like making her son a sack lunch, or dropping him off at kindergarten, taking him for his doctor's visits, or hosting a playdate with his friends, whose parents she'd only recently begun to meet.

Most of all, because their time together was so short, just Friday at 5 p.m. until Sunday at 5 p.m., she hadn't spent much time with her son when he was grumpy or exhausted, angry or petulant. She knew he must have all those moods, and she knew most people would say she'd been lucky to be spared them. But she'd felt like a visitor in her son's life, much as he'd been a visitor in hers.

Whenever she'd suggested to Sullivan that she would like more time with Cody, he'd reminded her that she was lucky to have any interaction with *his* son, and that her work schedule, that is to say, her travel schedule, was still both busy and unpredictable. Since she was one of the strongest advocates for protection of the grizzly, and the giant bears were within a year or so of losing their "endangered species" protection in Montana, she hadn't been willing to cut back on the time she spent working.

But for the next few weeks, or perhaps a little longer, the grizzly would have to wait. She was going to devote herself to being a mother. She was finally going to know what it felt like to wake up every day and perform all the tasks a mother would do for her son. She'd be combing mussed-up hair and taming a cowlick, coaxing her son to eat a healthy breakfast, urging him to enjoy his day at school, and finally, tucking him into bed at the end of each day and reading a storybook they'd chosen together.

"How's it going?"

Vick rose abruptly, feeling as though she'd intruded where she didn't belong, and turned to face Sullivan, who was standing in the doorway. His posture made it clear he didn't want her there, his arms crossed over his broad chest shouting the message:

Keep your distance. She couldn't help noticing the size of his biceps where his shirt was pulled tight, or remembering what it had felt like to have those very strong arms gently folded around her, gathering her close to a male chest that was ripped with muscle.

It took her a moment to realize she'd been invited here and hadn't done anything wrong. She lifted her chin and said in a cool, composed voice, "Cody was showing me his room."

"What about supper?" he asked.

"What about it?"

"Mom usually fixes it. Is that something you're willing to do?"

"I don't cook." As soon as she spoke the words, Vick realized how spoiled they made her sound. But she'd grown up in a home where either her eldest sister, Leah, or one of the maids prepared all her meals, that is, when she wasn't being fed at some Swiss boarding school. And she ate out whenever she was traveling for business, which was most of the time.

When Cody was visiting she made hot dogs on the grill or soup from a can or something from a package. "I mean, of course I cook. But just plain stuff, like steak and a baked potato or salad or macaroni and cheese."

"I love macaroni and cheese!" Cody piped up.

"Do you have a box of—" she began.

"There'll be some leftovers in the fridge I can warm up," Sullivan said, cutting her off. "Go wash your hands, Cody, and you can help."

To her surprise, Cody didn't jump up and race for the bathroom she'd seen halfway down the hall. Instead, he dropped the book he'd been holding on the bed and confronted his father. "I want macaroni and cheese."

"Gram isn't here to make it, and I don't know how," he said.

"You don't have the box kind?" Vick asked.

Sullivan shot her an irritated look. "Even if I did, and I don't, I've already told him what we're having for dinner. And it isn't mac and cheese."

Cody stomped his booted foot on the hardwood floor. "I want mac and cheese!"

"Too bad," Sullivan said. "Wash your hands and meet me in the kitchen."

To her amazement, Sullivan turned his back and walked away. To her utter horror, Cody threw himself facedown on his bed and bawled as though his father had beaten him with a stick.

She sat down beside him, desperate to soothe him, and patted him on the back. "Come on, Cody. Let's go help your father make supper. It'll be fun."

He rolled over and sat up, his face contorted, his lashes dewy with tears, and shouted, "Daddy doesn't like you here! That's why he won't make me mac and cheese. You need to go away. Now!"

Vick stared at her child as though he'd grown two horns and a tail. She'd rarely had any sort of altercation with Cody, and this one was particularly hurtful. But then, she'd always made it a point to do whatever she could to please him. Obviously, what was fine over a weekend once a month would result in a very spoiled child if he was indulged every day of the year. Vick suddenly realized she had a great deal to learn.

Sullivan must have made his feelings about her known to his mother and siblings, and her son—their son—had absorbed enough to know his father resented her. That situation had to be remedied, and would be, now that she knew about it. The question was what should she do now?

Vick was tempted to run away, to leave the house and stick to her monthly weekends with her son. If she did that, she'd be giving up the best, maybe the only chance she would have to get to know Cody better and perhaps convince Sullivan that she should have more time with him.

The fact that she still found Sullivan attractive was a complication she needed to leave on the shelf. He'd never shown the least bit of romantic interest in her since the single night they'd spent together, and she would only be letting herself in for heartache if he got even a hint that she regretted walking out of his life without a backward glance.

Why had she dressed and silently left the hotel the next morning without waiting for Sullivan to wake up?

Vick had thought a lot about that question. She'd guessed it was because she was afraid of getting more involved, of leaving more of herself behind than she already had. Based on her past experience, she didn't trust anyone to stick around for the long haul. The stranger with whom she'd shared a night of lovemaking, the likes of which she'd never imagined in her wildest dreams, was leaving Jackson the next day. So what was the point of being bitterly disappointed when he turned out to be uninterested in more than the night of pleasure they'd shared? It was better to simply walk away.

She had no idea what the result of spending so much time with Sullivan over the next few weeks would be. She felt a twinge of fear, a lot of anxiety, and yes, she admitted, excitement at the possibility of . . . Well, she wasn't quite sure what. She only knew she had to protect herself—mind, body, and soul—from getting mangled by someone who didn't care.

Vick shook her head, disgusted with her willingness to hope for any sort of fairy-tale ending to what had been an admittedly out-of-the-ordinary encounter with a stranger. Spending more time with Sullivan might end up being as much of a wake-up call as spending more time with her son. Maybe on closer inspection the rancher wasn't the appealing male that she'd painted him from a distance.

Vick followed Cody to the bathroom. She'd always kept an eye on him when he washed his hands. It was obvious that, here at home, it was something he did on his own. Maybe Sullivan had the right idea. She walked to the bathroom door and said, "When you're done, come to the kitchen. I'm going to go help your dad."

"Mac and cheese?" Cody asked hopefully.

"Sorry, buddy. I think tonight we're stuck with leftovers." Following Sullivan's lead, she turned and headed down the hall, her shoulders hunched, expecting to hear Cody throw another tantrum. There was nothing but silence.

Vick let out a relieved breath of air and then realized that, while she'd dodged one bullet, another one was waiting for her in the kitchen.

Chapter 4

RYE WAS BENT over, one hand on top of the refrigerator door, the other on his opposite thigh, staring into the abyss, but he wasn't seeing the meat loaf, mashed potatoes, and peas leftover from last night's dinner. He heard the sudden hum of the Coldspot over the sound of his heart pounding in his ears and realized he'd kept the door open too long. He felt trapped by the circumstances unfolding around him, and he couldn't think of a single move he could make to escape. He felt frozen in time and space. He stared at the shelves of plastic containers, his thoughts churning.

I should be waiting with Mom at the hospital. She'll need someone with her if Mike's surgery doesn't go well.

But he couldn't have sat down beside the woman he'd called "Mom" his whole life and not asked her the question that was all he could think about: *Who are my biological parents?* Darcie Sullivan had enough on her plate with Mike's life still at risk.

Don't die, Mike. Don't die. Don't die. The words sang like a mantra in Rye's brain. He couldn't imagine life without his younger brother giving him shit, grinning and tussling and arguing and sharing that bump and press of shoulders that was as much affection as they were willing to show each other as grown men.

It was because he knew Mike so well that he'd gone hunting for his brother when he hadn't shown up at the meeting they'd scheduled over lunch to discuss doubling the size of the calving barn. Ever since Mike's stint as a Navy SEAL, cut short by a gunshot wound that limited the range of motion in his shoulder, his brother paid close attention to time, and he never missed an appointment, especially one that involved food.

There had also been a feeling in Rye's gut that something was wrong. He would have said that feeling was the result of their blood bond. Except, as he now knew, he and Mike might not even be physically related.

Rye felt the cold wafting at him from the fridge, chilling his flesh. He should get out the leftovers and close the damned door. His position was strained enough to be uncomfortable, but he couldn't seem to move. His gaze was focused inward. As disturbing as it was to know Mike's life hung in the balance, it had been almost as upsetting to see Lexie Grayhawk making herself at home in Cody's bedroom. He'd never imagined having to deal with her in such close proximity. Never imagined having to resist the desire to touch.

He might have coped with both of those situations—Mike's life in the balance and Lexie's constant presence, one on top of the other—but it was the third looming cataclysm that had thrown him for a loop. It was hard to accept the fact that his father might not have been his biological father. Or that his mother was not his biological mother. Or that neither of them were his biological parents.

What made the whole thing so much more painful, almost unendurable, was the knowledge that his parents—*the people who'd raised him,* he corrected—had lied to him his whole life. Having faced the decision himself whether to allow his child to be raised by someone else, Rye couldn't imagine how anyone could give up their own flesh and blood. But one, or both, of his parents had done exactly that. What did that say about him? Or them?

If he was adopted, why hadn't Darcie and Patrick Sullivan simply told him so? Why hide the knowledge from him? What was the big secret? Was his biological father a murderer? His biological mother a drug addict? Were they teenagers too young to support a child on their own? Or had he been left on a firehouse doorstep like some unwanted burden?

Rye felt the angry flush begin at his throat and

rise to heat his icy cheeks. He gritted his teeth to control the rage that made him want to grab every container in the fridge and splatter them viciously against the wall. Which was more proof that he was going to have to come to terms with what he'd discovered, and get control of his emotions, before he confronted his mother.

Now that he knew a little of the truth, Rye was determined to discover the rest of the story, even if it was worse than anything he'd conjured in his imagination.

"How can I help?"

Rye jerked upright at the sound of Lexie's voice. She was standing on the other side of the ancient refrigerator door, leaning over the top to peer inside. He reached in for the meat loaf and peas and handed them to her. "Supper." Then he grabbed the mashed potatoes and followed her across the room to the stove.

"Should I turn on the oven?"

He shook his head. "I'll make up plates of food, and we can nuke them in the microwave."

"Where are the plates?"

He was surprised at how well they worked together, between his volunteering where the next thing was she might need, and her asking for what she wanted. He wondered if Lexie always wore jeans that hugged her rear end so lovingly. Her white Western shirt, tucked into belted Levi's, looked like it had been tailored to fit her, showing off a narrow waist and luscious, plum-sized breasts. She was wearing some kind of perfume, but he would have had to put his nose to her throat to get a really good whiff, and he wasn't about to do that, even if he found the idea nearly irresistible.

It was going to be dangerous having his onetime lover living in his home. It was really too bad his fascination for Lexie Grayhawk had never faded. To make matters worse, his physical attraction was now layered with admiration for the woman he'd come to know, despite his best efforts to avoid her company.

The twenty-one-year-old girl who'd picked him up in a bar was the same woman who'd argued with Congress to stop grizzlies from being delisted as an endangered species, who'd attended an infinite number of fundraisers to solicit donations for grizzly protection, who'd arranged to buy more land dedicated to grizzly habitat, and who had an unquenchable passion—and bulldog tenaciousness—when it came to protecting all endangered species. Finally, and perhaps most important, although he begrudged admitting it, she'd become a loving, caring parent to their son.

Rye had consciously kept Lexie at arm's length because he knew how easy it would be to do something he would regret. He didn't want the complications any sort of relationship with her, including a sexual fling, would cause. And honestly, what kind of connection could you establish with a woman you didn't trust?

Yeah, yeah, she'd come back after she'd walked

away from Cody, but the fact was that Lexie's first instinct had been to run. Who could say whether she might do that to him if they started a relationship and things got tough. Which meant that, however long Lexie Grayhawk remained a guest in his home, she was strictly off-limits.

Cody had arrived in the kitchen and, without being asked, went directly to the silverware drawer and collected what they would need for the dinner table. No signs remained of the crying fit he'd thrown in his bedroom.

Lexie shot Rye a shocked look, and he realized she'd had no idea Cody was the one who set the table each night, putting folded paper napkins, knives, and forks on the correct side of each cloth placemat, leaving room for the plates.

Rye finished pouring sweetened iced tea into three glasses and saw Lexie's raised eyebrows when Cody took one in each hand and headed back toward the table.

"Won't he spill those?" she asked.

"Hasn't so far," Rye replied.

"Isn't that too much for him to carry?"

"He's plenty strong. Kids need jobs if they're going to grow up to be responsible adults."

He saw her chagrin before she asked, "What other chores does he do?"

"Gathers eggs from the chicken house in the morning, measures grain for the horses in the barn, milks Daisy if I'm too busy."

"He's only five years old!" she protested.

"And lives on a ranch," Rye shot back. "Everyone does his fair share or he—or she—" he added, narrowing his eyes at her, "doesn't eat."

"But he's just a baby!"

She objected loudly enough for Cody to hear. He turned to her, thrust his chest out, pointed to it with his thumbs, and announced, "I'm not a baby. I'm a big boy!"

"Oh, lord," she muttered, shooting a look in Rye's direction. "Have I been buffaloed. I've been doing everything for Cody, thinking he couldn't manage for himself."

Rye grinned. "Now you know." He saw the disappointment in her eyes and said, "Don't worry. He still needs plenty of parenting."

"Like what?" she asked.

"He's a bear on taking a bath."

"I haven't had any problems getting him into the tub."

"How about getting him out of it?"

He watched her mouth purse into a shape that looked adorably kissable before she admitted, "He does like to spend a lot of time playing in the water."

He let his annoyance at himself for being so susceptible to Lexie's charms resonate in his voice as he replied, "There's five of us here need to use the same tub. He can't be spending all night in there. That goes for you, too."

It was plain as the pert nose on her face that she hadn't focused on the fact that they'd be sharing a bathroom, much less a bathtub. An image of Lexie naked, water streaming down the sleek lines of her lush body, rose before him. And caused the obvious response. He turned away, so she wouldn't notice, and cursed under his breath. He had to be more careful. He had to stop thinking of her in a sexual way. Unfortunately, that was easier said than done.

They were pretty much finished with their meal when a knock sounded at the back door.

"Are you expecting company?" she asked.

He shook his head. "Anybody looking for you?"

"Not that I know of."

When Rye flipped on the porch light and opened the kitchen door, he found a uniformed Flathead County deputy sheriff standing there with one booted foot perched against the top step. Rusty stood by his side, tail wagging, ready to slip inside if Rye wasn't careful.

"What's up, Pete?"

Deputy Sheriff Pete Harrison took off his hat and held it in his hands. "I'm sorry about your brother, Rye. I'm here to do my due diligence on Mike's bear attack for the Wildlife Human Attack Response Team."

"Meaning what?" Rye knew there was some sort of joint team that investigated bear attacks, but since no one he knew had been the victim of an attack, he wasn't quite sure how it worked.

Before Pete could answer, Lexie joined Rye at the door.

"Pete," Lexie said, a broad smile making her look

even prettier. "I didn't expect to see you today. We didn't have a date I forgot about, did we?"

"No. I'm here about Mike's grizzly attack." Pete's glance shot speculatively from Lexie to Rye and back again, before he said, "I didn't know you were here."

"I'm taking care of Cody while Darcie stays with Mike at the hospital."

Pete frowned. "You're *living* here?"

"Just for a month or so."

Rye could see Lexie's announcement didn't sit particularly well with Pete. It was common knowledge that Rye and Lexie had made a baby together, although no one knew much about how it had happened. Rye realized he wasn't willing to assuage Pete's concern by saying in plain words that he had no interest in Lexie Grayhawk.

Pete took a step closer to her, cutting off Rye's view, and said, "I did leave a message on your phone."

"Oh?"

"I have to work this weekend, but I wondered if you might like to go out dancing next Friday."

Without responding to his offer, Lexie said, "Come on in, Pete," gesturing him inside as though it were her kitchen and not Rye's. She stood back far enough that Rusty bounded inside.

Cody yelled, "Rusty!" and jumped up from the table. He raced after the dog, which Rye knew was headed straight for Cody's room, where it would hide under the bed, hoping not to be found and sent back outside.

Rye sighed. It was going to be a battle to get Rusty out of the house without an argument from his son, who never seemed to notice the mutt's dirty paws, the ticks that inevitably clung to its hide, and the drool that dampened Cody's sheets when the dog snuck up onto the bed—and under the covers—during the night.

Rye shot a perturbed look at Lexie, who was completely oblivious to the cardinal sin she'd committed by letting the dog in the house.

"Can I get you a cup of coffee?" she asked the deputy.

"That would be nice."

"Make yourself comfortable at the table. We were just finishing up supper."

Rye hid the spurt of irritation he felt at the knowledge that Lexie was dating the deputy. After all, he wasn't interested, so why not Pete? Harrison had movie-star good looks and a grin that had charmed a good many girls off a studded red-leather bar stool at Casey's in Whitefish. Besides which, he was a pretty good guy.

All these years, Rye had managed to avoid imagining the mother of his son in bed with another man. Which was foolish, of course, since he'd done his fair share of dating. According to his mother, who'd let a bit of information drop here and there, Lexie hadn't seemed to stick any longer with one man than he had with one woman.

"Cody, come finish your supper," Lexie said loud enough for the sound to reach down the hall.

Cody showed up in the kitchen a moment later and said, "I'm done, Daddy. Can I go play with Rusty?"

Rye had his mouth open to say, "Fine," when Lexie said, "You haven't finished your peas."

"Aw, Mom," Cody whined.

"One more bite."

To Rye's amazement, Cody crossed to his place at the table, picked up his fork, piled it high with peas, and stuck it in his mouth. He'd never insisted his son finish the food on his plate, not even because the starving children of some poverty-stricken nation were going hungry while his son had plenty. But Cody had obviously been through this with his mother often enough to know that he had to eat that last bite of food before he could escape the table.

He watched as Lexie caught Cody by the ears, leaned down to kiss him on the forehead, and said, "Don't start your bath until I'm done here."

As Cody scampered away to join the dog in his room, Rye said, "Can't he even take a bath on his own when he's with you?"

She looked startled. "He can. But it won't be much longer before he won't want me there. Until then, I intend to take advantage of every opportunity I can to spend time with him."

The response silenced him, reminding him that, so far, she'd only been seeing their son one weekend a month. She was right. Cody was growing like a weed, and it wouldn't be long before he didn't want or need his mother to be involved in a lot of the things he did. Rye had never let himself wonder too much about how Lexie felt about their arrangement. It was easier to pretend not to know her feelings on the subject.

It seemed having her here was going to wreak havoc in a lot of ways he hadn't expected. In any event, he was glad Cody was no longer in the room. Pete's arrival meant he was going to be forced to relive the moment he'd found the mauled body of his brother, in order to describe the gruesome scene for the deputy.

He turned to Pete and asked, "What is it you want to know?"

Chapter 5

VICK KNEW TOO much about grizzly attacks—male grizzlies could weigh upward of eight hundred pounds and have four-inch claws—to look forward to Sullivan's interview with the deputy. From the grim look on his face, Sullivan wasn't looking forward to recounting the moment either.

On the other hand, his answers to the deputy's questions would contribute to the Wildlife Human Attack Response Team's decision about the grizzly's fate. If the bear had been surprised and was defending its cubs or a kill, in which case it had been acting naturally, it would be left alone. If it had made an unprovoked attack on a human, it would be tracked and killed.

"Do you have any of the weapons Mike was carrying with him at the time of the incident?" Pete asked.

"I found his shotgun on the ground after the helicopter airlifted Mike out. It's in my truck. Whatever else he had with him would still be racked in his vehicle, which I haven't retrieved from the scene."

"What rifle does he use?" Pete asked.

"A Remington Model 700, .375 caliber. Why are you asking?"

Instead of answering Sullivan's question, Pete asked, "Had Mike's shotgun been fired?"

"I presume so, since the grizzly left a trail of blood."

"Did you look to see if it was fired?"

Sullivan's brow furrowed. "What are you suggesting?"

"Would you get his shotgun now, so we can check?"

Sullivan rose from the table and headed out the kitchen door without grabbing his coat. While he was gone, Vick asked, "What's going on, Pete?"

"Let's wait for Rye to get back."

He returned moments later breathing hard, a surprised look on his face, with the Remington 700 twelve-gauge shotgun broken in half, revealing that both barrels were fully loaded. "What the hell's going on, Pete? This hasn't been fired. How could you possibly know that?"

"I wasn't sure," Pete said. "But it was a possibility."

"I'd swear I saw a trail of blood," Sullivan insisted.

"I'm not questioning what you saw. I got a call from the hospital to come collect evidence of a gunshot wound."

"Mike was *shot*?" Sullivan blurted.

Pete held up a plastic evidence bag containing a crumpled 10mm bullet. "Mike was shot. Most likely before he was attacked by the grizzly, because the damage the grizzly inflicted concealed the bullet wound in his shoulder until the doctor got him into the operating room."

"How did that not kill him?" Sullivan murmured, staring at a bullet big enough to take down a grizzly.

"It hit the piece of metal the Navy put in Mike's shoulder to hold it together," Pete said. "Can you believe the luck?"

"I don't think there's anything lucky about my brother getting blasted by some idiot or torn up by a bear," Sullivan snapped.

"Sorry, Rye. You know what I meant."

Sullivan waved a hand to acknowledge the apology. "Any idea who did it?"

"Not yet. I'll be headed out to the site in the morning to see if I can find any spent casings or tracks from whoever was there with Mike."

Sullivan rubbed the back of his neck. "Who the hell would want to shoot Mike?"

Pete met Sullivan's gaze and said, "My best guess is he caught someone poaching, and not poaching just any game, but an endangered species."

"Someone was *hunting* a grizzly?" Vick interjected.

"I suspect whoever it was saw a target of opportunity," Pete said. "Most grizzlies won't be out and about for a couple more weeks."

Sullivan groaned in disgust. "I told Mike not to take that damned park ranger job, but I couldn't talk him out of it."

Vick knew Mike worked part-time as a Montana park ranger in the Flathead Lake District. Sullivan's brother was renowned for catching poachers. Apparently, this poacher had decided he wasn't willing to pay the stiff fine and perhaps face jail time for his offense.

Pete continued, "Either the poacher had already shot at the grizzly and hadn't managed to kill it, or Mike somehow got between him and the grizzly, maybe even protecting the man from the grizzly, or the grizzly from the man, and Mike ended up getting both shot and mauled. We won't know the truth until he wakes up."

Vick bit her lip to keep from saying, If *he wakes up*.

"Did the doctor tell you how Mike's doing?" Sullivan asked.

"Just that he survived the surgery and is in a medically induced coma until the swelling in his brain goes down."

"Did you see Darcie?" Vick asked Pete.

"She was in Mike's room when I spoke to the doctor," Pete said.

"How's she doing?" Vick asked, unable to imagine any reason for Darcie not to have called Sullivan to update him once Mike was out of surgery.

Then she remembered the results of Sullivan's blood test.

"Her eyes were pretty red from crying," Pete said. He shrugged uncomfortably and added, "Mike looked pretty bad."

Vick met Sullivan's troubled gaze. Had Darcie been crying for Mike? Or did her tears have something to do with what she feared Sullivan might have discovered when he gave blood? "Maybe you should go back to the hospital tonight to be with your mom and Mike," she said. "I can take care of Cody."

Sullivan's shoulders tensed, and his lips flattened to a thin line. "Let's wait until she calls." Then he turned to Pete and said, "I want to make the trip back to the attack site with you tomorrow. If you give me a ride, I can pick up Mike's truck. He left it on a logging road before he hiked into the forest after those cows."

"Sure, Rye. You should come along, Vick," Pete suggested. "You know the team values your opinion in these situations."

Vick regularly kept track of decision making that affected grizzlies in Montana, and she very much wanted to join the two men. The fact that the grizzly was wounded wasn't good news. Even though the bear might be innocent of wrongdoing, it would need to be hunted down and moved to a remote location. A wounded grizzly might not be mobile enough to stalk its usual prey, or hunt down the seeds and berries that were part of its diet. It could become a danger to humans when looking for easier pickings, including human garbage or ranchers' cattle, and might need to be killed.

Vick very much wanted to keep that from happening. "Do we know for sure the grizzly was defending a kill?"

"It made a pretty good meal out of one of my calves," Sullivan said.

That was more bad news for the grizzly. She wished she could go along and see the situation for herself. Normally, it was what she would have done. Not this time.

From the moment she'd committed herself to her life's work, it had consumed all her energy and emotion. Since Sullivan was Cody's custodial parent, he made all the choices where Cody's care was concerned, and her visitation had been strictly limited.

For the very first time, that wasn't true.

She could probably find a sitter for tomorrow and join the hunt for evidence. But she wasn't willing to give up even one of the precious moments she'd been offered to spend with her son.

Vick smiled apologetically and said, "I need to be here to take care of Cody. I think we'll be going to the hospital tomorrow to see how Mike is getting along and visit with Darcie."

"You're more than welcome if you change your mind," Pete said. As he rose and headed for the door, Sullivan followed to let him out. As Vick cleared the table, she heard them making arrangements for Pete to pick Sullivan up in the morning. When Sullivan returned to the kitchen, he picked up another stack of dishes from the table and brought them to her at the sink.

"I usually rinse mine before I put them in the dishwasher," she said.

"Don't have a dishwasher."

"What?" Vick couldn't imagine such a thing. Her father, King Grayhawk, was the richest man in Wyoming. Not only did their enormous ranch house in Jackson Hole have the most-up-to-date appliances, they always had a maid to help with the cooking and cleaning up. The first thing Vick had done in the tiny cabin she'd bought was install new appliances, including a dishwasher.

"Mom and Dad used to like doing the dishes together," Sullivan explained. "She'd wash and he'd dry. They enjoyed spending the time together talking about their day."

"So now that your dad's gone . . ."

"The three of us kids stepped in to take turns doing the washing and drying." He shot her a rueful glance. "Believe it or not, doing the dishes together provided the perfect opportunity for me to discuss ranch business with Mike."

With Mike hospitalized for the foreseeable future, Vick realized that she and Sullivan would be doing the dishes together each evening at the sink, shoulder to shoulder, hip to hip. She filled the sink with soapy water and watched as he grabbed a dishtowel from the horns of a ceramic steer attached to the wall next to the cabinets.

She washed and rinsed a plate, handed it to Sullivan, careful not to touch his hand, and said, "Well . . . What should we discuss?"

Chapter 6

RYE COULDN'T BELIEVE the situation in which he found himself. Imagine doing the dishes, like an old married couple, with Lexie Grayhawk. It was unbelievable. And unbearable. It was too much like what he'd imagined when he'd woken up the morning after their single, unforgettable night together. He'd wanted this, exactly this, with the woman he'd found in the most unlikeliest of places . . . only to find her gone without a trace.

He'd known, the day Lexie showed up out of the blue on his back doorstep, he was going to have to deal with all those unfinished feelings, those unrequited dreams, he'd left behind in Jackson Hole. Instead, he'd ignored them. Suddenly, the mess of emotions he'd been stuffing away like unwanted junk in an overcrowded closet came tumbling out.

"You realize this doesn't change anything," he said as he took a plate from her and began to dry it.

She shot him a wary look from blue eyes that reminded him of faraway oceans, but her voice was calm as she replied, "What do you mean?"

"I haven't forgiven you."

"You've made that plain."

"I don't trust you."

"Have I asked for your trust?"

He threw an arm out to encompass the kitchen, his home, his life. "You're here. Inside the walls I vowed you'd never breach."

The glass she was washing plopped back into the dishwater as she turned to face him. She leaned back, drying her hands on a towel hanging from a knob on the cupboard under the sink. "You're not being fair."

"I don't have to be fair. My job is to protect my son."

"Cody is *our* son," she quietly corrected. "And I resent the suggestion that I would ever do anything to harm him."

He felt a spurt of irritation because the truth was that since that first awful abandonment of their child, she'd proved herself a responsible and loving parent.

"I thought you'd quit," he said. "I thought you'd give up and go away, like a lot of weekend parents."

She lifted her chin, letting him see everything she was feeling. "I almost did."

"Why didn't you?"

"Because the joy of spending time with Cody outweighed the unbearable anguish of saying goodbye to him every time he left."

He hitched in a breath. He'd seen that ache of loss in her eyes more than once when she'd dropped Cody off on a Sunday evening. He'd pretended he didn't, because acknowledging her pain meant admitting his part in causing it. Now and again, she'd asked for more time with their son, but he hadn't allowed it. He'd wondered why Lexie hadn't taken him back to court and convinced himself she was probably relieved that he'd limited the time she had with their child. Otherwise, she would have fought harder to change their agreement.

Instead of being grateful that Lexie hadn't gone to battle with him, he'd been resentful that she made him feel like an ogre for not giving her more time with Cody, just because she asked for it.

He'd made a promise to her, when he was awarded custody of their child, that she'd never spend one more second with Cody than the law allowed. It was getting harder and harder to stick to it.

"You brought this situation on yourself," he said, feeling rotten for causing the sorrow he saw in her eyes.

She gave a short, sharp nod. "You've made sure I paid for my mistake. If you want me gone from here, just say the word."

There it was. He could banish the evil enchantress from his castle with a single word, or maybe two, since it took that many to say, "Get out." But he couldn't get anything past the horrible, swollen knot in his throat.

She waited another heartbeat, and when he didn't speak, turned back to the sink, finished washing the glass she'd dropped, and handed it to him without deigning to look at him.

He kept his gaze focused on the glass he was drying, but he could feel the electricity arcing between them. He'd accomplished nothing by speaking, just ratcheted up the ill will between them, which was, he realized, a defense mechanism. It was time he admitted what he'd been denying for years. He wanted her. Wanted her in the most primal way a man could want a woman.

Except, that was the problem, wasn't it? What he wanted was at odds with his good sense, which told him he should keep his hands to himself and his thoughts as far away from Lexie Grayhawk as he could get.

Rye's father had taught him that no excuse was good enough to justify doing something wrong. Mistakes weren't forgiven or forgotten. Rye had learned to judge people by their actions. Lexie had already hurt him twice, once by walking away after their night together without so much as a hail or farewell, and again by caring so little about the child they'd made together that she'd been willing to give him away to strangers.

When he was younger, and a lot more gullible, he hadn't agreed with his dad. He'd tried giving folks the benefit of the doubt. But a man who "accidentally" failed to deliver the amount of hay he'd promised had to be watched, because bags of feed often turned up short the next. Why put yourself in that position?

So no second chances. No wavering and giving in. No forgiveness, unless you wanted another dose of headache . . . or heartache.

It took Rye a moment to realize Lexie was draining the sink. "That's it?" he said, drying the last plate and stacking it with the rest in the cupboard.

"All done. I was going to supervise Cody's bath, unless you want to do it."

He saw the yearning in her eyes to do the job herself and told himself he was only giving in because she wasn't going to be around for long. "You do it."

He saw both relief and gratitude in her eyes and felt small and petty again. Which irked him because he wasn't the one who'd done wrong. She was.

He bit back a gasp when her breast made contact with his biceps as she brushed past him. He stood perfectly still as his body reacted in a way he would rather it had not. She paused and glanced up at him, before hurrying from the room.

He ached for her.

Rye grunted with disgust. At this rate, he'd be a wreck long before Lexie Grayhawk was out of the house.

You aren't the only one feeling a visceral response.

You saw the flush on her cheeks. You saw the flash of heat in her eyes when she looked into yours. Why not just go to bed with her? There's no way the sex will be as good as you remember it. When you realize that, you can get her out of your system once and for all.

Whenever their night of passion invaded his dreams, Rye saw Lexie's blue eyes shining up at him, remembered the salty taste of her skin, and imagined their sweat-slick bodies twined together as they slid over a precipice and fell into a well of pleasure so deep he had no desire to climb out. Rye had never felt more connected to another person. His feelings had been more than physical. Their night together had been . . . Hell. He had no words for what he'd felt that didn't sound sappy, especially considering how Lexie had walked away, like the whole experience hadn't been . . . He hesitated, stumbling over the word that came to mind. Then he sighed and savored it, even if he did feel like a fool for remembering every goddamn *transcendent* moment of their night together.

As the vivid memories rose, Rye's body hardened to stone. Hell and damnation! If he couldn't forget what had happened between them, it stood to reason she couldn't either. So maybe the idea of sleeping with her again wasn't so crazy.

And if pigs had wings, they could fly.

Chapter 7

VICK GOT CODY in and out of the bath with only a little trouble and a lot of laughs. But after she'd read him a story, he didn't want her to leave his bedroom.

"Stay with me, Mommy."

Vick's nerves were still ragged after her confrontation with Sullivan in the kitchen. The attraction was there; it had never gone away. She'd never tried to deny it. She'd simply done her best to ignore it. That wasn't as simple to do when they were confined under the same roof.

She sat down beside Cody and brushed a blond curl from his forehead. "It's time for bed, sweetheart."

"I know. But you're finally here in my own room in my own house. Pleeeeze."

Vick felt her heart squeeze at the thought that her cabin wasn't "home" to her son. What could she expect when he only stayed with her for two nights each month? She knew Sullivan didn't approve of what he called "coddling," but what could it hurt? She glanced at the empty doorway, then grinned and said, "Scoot over and give me some room."

Once she was lying down, she and Cody turned to face each other, nose to nose.

"This is nice," Vick whispered.

"Yeah," Cody agreed. "Can we do this every night from now on?"

Tears filled her eyes and blurred her vision. How could she tell her son this was only temporary, that in a month, or maybe less, this interlude would be over?

Cody put his palm against her cheek and said, "Don't cry, Mommy."

She blinked to stem the tears and ruffled his cornsilk-soft hair. "These are happy tears. I'm so glad to be here with you, in your own bed in your own room."

"Sometimes Rusty sneaks in to sleep with me," Cody confided. "When Daddy catches him, he makes him go back outside."

That was exactly what had happened this evening. Rye had needed to drag the dog out from under the bed, not an easy feat when the terrier-mix mutt weighed a good eighty pounds. Cody had found Rusty sitting on the back porch the previous fall and insisted he needed rescuing. The dog spent its time chasing rats in the barn in winter, lolled on the covered back porch in summer, when he wasn't chasing squirrels, and spent every other minute of his life being played with and petted by Cody.

Vick had invited Rusty to her cabin one weekend when Cody was visiting, and the dog had gifted her with a bloody, not-quite-dead, eight-inch-long pocket gopher he dropped on the kitchen floor. She'd decided Sullivan might have a point about keeping the dog outside.

Vick wondered if Cody's desire to have her lie down with him tonight meant he needed more time than he was getting with her, or whether all children simply wanted as much interaction with their parents as they could get. Or maybe, as Sullivan had once suggested to her, "Kids will do anything to postpone actually going to sleep."

She slid her arm around Cody's waist and pulled him snug against her, his head beneath her chin, and heard him sigh. Cuddling her five-year-old like this had to be all right. It felt too good to be wrong.

Suddenly aware of a soft touch on her shoulder, Vick lifted her head and looked around groggily. It took her a moment to realize where she was.

I fell asleep in Cody's bed. In Sullivan's house.

She carefully disentangled herself from Cody's embrace, so she wouldn't wake him, then rose and shoved a nervous hand through her long blond curls as she turned to face Sullivan. When he opened his mouth to speak, she put a fingertip to her lips and pointed to the open door. As they left the room, she hit the switch that turned off the lamp beside Cody's bed, and hurried down the hall toward the living room. A shiver careered down her spine as Sullivan followed in her footsteps like some stalking panther.

When she reached the flickering fireplace, she turned and confronted him. She wished he weren't so good-looking. His rangy body was all muscle and sinew and bone. She was tall; he was taller by a good half foot. She'd always found his green eyes mesmerizing, which was why she so seldom met his gaze. She fisted her hands to keep from reaching out to shove away the chestnut curl that fell over his forehead.

Vick felt her nipples tighten into buds. She couldn't *believe* this was happening.

You're feeling a simple (ha!) physiological response to an attractive person of the opposite sex. Don't make too much of it. Sullivan is not *Prince Charming. Far from it. And he wants nothing, whatsoever, to do with you!*

Vick knew there was no way Sullivan could want her, because she would never have been able to feel desire for anyone whose character she despised, as Sullivan did hers. She got the distinct feeling he would rather she were anywhere else. Too bad. He was stuck with her until Darcie came home. Nevertheless, she felt the need to explain why she'd fallen asleep in Cody's bed. "I know you don't like it when I—"

"Have I said anything that sounded like a complaint?"

"But you—"

"I realize you deal differently with Cody than I do. That doesn't mean my way is right and yours is wrong. It just means they're different."

"Oh." She shot him a crooked smile. "I guess I was figuring your house, your rules."

"Cody has grown up with two parents doing things differently. He's managing fine."

"But now that we're both in the same house—"

He interrupted her again. "You and I will have to work things out so Cody sees us as a united front. The main thing is not to let him get an answer from me he doesn't like and try to get a different answer from you."

"That sounds reasonable."

"I'm a reasonable sort of guy."

She shook her head and gave a rueful laugh. "Is that what you think?"

"About most things."

Not about her visiting rights with her son. Sullivan had been stubborn about keeping her out of Cody's life. Over the past year, she'd gone to as many of Cody's activities as she could manage, but being a part of her son's everyday life for this one evening had confirmed her need to share more time with Cody than her agreement with Sullivan allowed. She was finally ready to fight him, in court if necessary, to get it.

Vick settled into a padded rocker in front of the fire where she thought Darcie probably sat most nights, while Sullivan settled into an overstuffed leather chair next to it that had likely belonged to his dad.

"I have something I'd like to discuss with you," he said as he shifted to get more comfortable.

That couldn't be good. Vick shot Sullivan an uneasy look but said nothing.

"I think we ought to take advantage of the time you'll be living here to get to know each other better."

Vick frowned. "You've made it clear I'm not the sort of person you want to know any better."

"Maybe I've changed my mind." He lowered his gaze, making it difficult to perceive any glimmer of what he was thinking.

Vick waited anxiously for what was coming next, distrustful of his supposed change of heart.

When his green eyes suddenly focused on her again, Vick felt as though she'd been zapped with a thousand volts of electricity. She hitched in a breath. She couldn't be seeing in his half-lidded eyes what she thought she was seeing.

"I was drawn to you from the moment I spied you in that bar in Jackson," he said in a voice that made her quiver with anticipation.

She lowered her gaze to her hands, which she realized were knotted in her lap, before admitting, "The attraction was mutual."

"I remember how excited you were by your work."

She smiled. "I remember your groan when you found out what I do for a living."

He smiled back. "Protecting grizzlies and wolves? What did you expect from a cattleman?"

"You were surprisingly open-minded."

"You were a surprisingly good advocate."

"You had a lot of hopes and dreams of your own," she said. "Did you buy that champion Black Angus bull you wanted?"

He shook his head. "Couldn't afford him. I found one about as good the following year."

"I'm glad."

"You weren't sure you could handle all the travel for your job. How has that worked out?"

"It helped that my dad let me borrow his jet," she said with a wry smile. The smile disappeared as she continued, "I've learned to loathe hotel rooms. At least being busy helped keep my mind off what I was missing here."

"You mean Cody."

She nodded but didn't pursue the subject of custody, because it held too many hidden trip wires. Instead she said, "I remember your telling me the night we met how glad you were Mike came home safe from the war. And how much you relied on him to help you manage the ranch."

It was hard to look into Sullivan's eyes because of the pain she saw there. His voice was hoarse when he spoke. "I can hardly believe he made it home from Afghanistan mostly in one piece and is going to end up with hundreds of stitches from a bear attack."

Vick waited for Sullivan to complain about her

work saving grizzlies, but he didn't go there. "I've been praying he'll recover quickly," she said.

"It's going to be tough getting everything done on my own until he gets back on his feet," he admitted.

"Let me know if there's anything I can do to help."

"You can help me best by taking care of Cody."

"I'm glad for the chance to do it."

"That's another thing I liked about you when I met you. You're not afraid of hard work."

She wrinkled her nose and asked, "How could you possibly know that from one conversation in a bar?"

"You told me about all the chores your sister Leah made you do, so you'd grow up to be a responsible human being."

She laughed. "She set me to work in the barn because she knew I love horses. I complained every step of the way, but I experienced the satisfaction you get from a job well done."

"It seemed to me that you'd learned more from her than how to muck out stalls. You were chock-full of ideas for what I could do to put the Rafter S on firmer financial footing."

"I guess I absorbed more knowledge about the ranching business from Leah—she's the real financier in the family—than I realized."

"When I think about it now," Rye said, "it's strange how close I felt to you when we'd only shared a bit of talk and a couple of drinks. I just remember I was enjoying your company so much, I didn't want the night to end." He hesitated before adding, "I was glad you agreed to leave the bar with me."

"I hope you know that was unusual for me, something I'd never done before."

Sullivan met her gaze and said, "The night we spent together was a different experience for me, too."

Vick blushed as their night of lovemaking flashed in her mind. *Tangled, sweat-slick bodies, a soft mouth, an agile tongue, and strong, demanding hands.*

Before Vick had met Sullivan, she'd never gone to bed with a man mere hours after meeting him. She'd done it that long-ago night because she hadn't wanted her interlude with him to end, and because she'd known he wasn't going to be around for long, since he was only in town for a two-day cattlemen's conference.

"Why didn't you stay the next morning?" he asked. "Why did you run away?"

Because I liked you too much. Because it all happened so fast. Because I couldn't trust what I was feeling, and I didn't want to make a mistake like my mother did and fall for some cowboy with a pair of strong arms and a charming smile.

When Vick's mother had taken off with one of her father's cowhands, she'd left her four daughters behind. Vick had grown up feeling unloved and unlovable, which made her vulnerable to a man like Sullivan, who'd offered so much of himself to a woman who was virtually a stranger. Of course she'd run for the hills. What if she let herself love such a man and he abandoned her, as he was certain to do? That sort of pain would be unbearable. Better not to risk it.

Vick wasn't about to admit any of that to Sullivan, but he was waiting for an answer. She shrugged and said, "You were leaving for Montana the next day. What was the point?"

"I went looking for you the next morning."

She frowned and asked, "Why would you do that?"

"I wanted to spend more time with you."

"Why?"

He snorted. "You were in bed with me. Why do you think?"

"You wanted a nooner?" she said disdainfully.

His eyes narrowed and suddenly looked dangerous. "I wanted to get to know you better. I thought we'd found something extraordinary together. Something happened to me that had never happened before. Or since."

She shot a cautious glance in his direction. If all this was really true, why had he waited so long to say something? And why say something now?

"Imagine my surprise," he continued, "when I went looking for a girl named 'Lexie' and no one I spoke with had ever heard of her. Why did you give me that phony name?"

Vick wasn't sure why she'd called herself Lexie that night, except she'd been trying to find a more feminine name than Vick to use as she began her career supporting endangered species. She hated her regal first name, Victoria, and her middle name, Alexandra, was equally grand. Both could be off-putting, and she needed all the goodwill she could get to coax positive responses from supporters, like congressmen and senators.

Compared to her Hollywood-gorgeous fraternal twin, Taylor, and her blond and beautiful youngest sister, Eve, Vick was last and least of the three daughters her mother had borne King Grayhawk. She'd always compensated for her nothing-to-write-home-about face and equally average form with sparkling—sometimes not so sparkling, but at least intelligent—wit.

She'd toyed with the nickname Alex, but it felt too masculine, so she'd been trying Lexie out for the first time the night she met Sullivan. After doing something in that new persona so uncharacteristic as going to bed with a man she barely knew, she'd never used it again. Unfortunately, the name had stuck with Sullivan.

Vick focused her gaze on the man across from her and asked, "What would you have done if you'd found me?"

"Exactly what I want to do now. Spend time with you."

Her heart sank at the thought that if he was being honest, they could have started a life together a long time ago and been parents to Cody. Except, he'd been singing an entirely different tune when she'd shown up at his back door the first time. "You've had plenty of chances to get to know me over the years we've been co-parenting Cody," she pointed out.

His eyes looked troubled. "It was easier to nurse my grievance against you. And you weren't around much the first four years to remind me of what I was missing."

That was true. "And now, we're living under the same roof," she murmured.

He nodded. "We'll be seeing each other every day, bumping elbows, so to speak, with Cody witness to everything we do, everything we say to each other. I'd like to make this as stress-free for him as we can."

Her heart sank a little. Sullivan might have wanted a romantic relationship with her once upon a time in the past, but all he apparently wanted now was peace between them while they were living in the same house.

"Remaining cordial sounds like a good idea," she said. "Shall we shake on it?"

She reached across the distance that separated the two chairs and offered her hand. When he took it in his, she realized she'd made a serious mistake. All the hairs on her arm stood on end, and it was all she could do not to jerk herself free. She felt herself trembling from the simple touch of his callused hand.

She tried to stay cool and calm, smiling as she said, "Deal?"

"Deal." It took another moment before he released her hand, a moment in which she felt her whole body coming alive.

Suddenly, Vick realized what a rare opportunity Sullivan was offering her. She was perfectly willing to provide the amity he was seeking, but why not offer him something more? Over the past year, Vick had realized what a truly good man Sullivan was, aside from that whole black and white, wrong and right business that turned him into a stubborn jackass. Why not take advantage of this truce to give him a taste of what he was missing?

She'd been very careful not to give Sullivan even a hint that she'd come to admire him, not to mention still being strongly attracted to him. It would be the simplest thing in the world to let him know she would welcome a romantic relationship.

What then?

Then she'd let nature take its course.

Chapter 8

LEXIE HAD RETIRED to her room for the night, and Rye knew he should go to the hospital and check on his brother. But he still wasn't ready to confront his mother with what he'd discovered about his birth. She must be worried sick about Mike, and she didn't need to deal with another crisis. And after all, what difference did it make now? Patrick and Darcie Sullivan were the only parents he'd ever known. Neither parent had even hinted that Rye was not their biological child. There must have been a good reason to keep his past a secret, and he could wait to ask his mother what it was.

Rye settled for getting an update on Mike's condition by phone.

His mother picked up immediately and said, "I'm

not supposed to use my cellphone in Mike's room because he's receiving oxygen. That's why I haven't called you. I'm in the hall right now, so we can talk."

"I'll keep this short," he said. "Pete Harrison came by and told me Mike survived his surgery. I wanted to make sure you're both okay. How are you? And how is Mike?"

"I'm all right."

His gut wrenched when he heard the sob she was trying hard to repress.

"Just worried about Mike," she continued. "The doctor said his condition is 'extremely critical.' Did Pete tell you Mike was shot?"

"Yeah. I'm headed back to the site of the attack with Pete tomorrow to see if we can find anything to lead us to the shooter."

"How are things at the house?" his mother asked.

"Fine."

"No problems?"

He knew his mother was fishing for information, but he refused to make an issue of the fact that Lexie was sleeping under the same roof or give her any hint of their conversation tonight. "We're good here. Did you get in touch with Amy Beth?"

"She wanted to come home, but I told her there was no need, at least until Mike wakes up."

Which meant, Rye realized, he could probably expect his younger sister to show up a heartbeat from now. "Did you tell her Lexie is staying in her room?"

"I did."

"What did she say to that?"

"What you might expect."

Rye knew he'd infected his younger sister with his less-than-positive feelings toward Victoria Grayhawk. Having Amy Beth in the house was bound to wreak havoc with the truce he and Lexie had worked out. He'd call his sister first thing in the morning and encourage her to stay where she was.

"Get some sleep," Rye said.

"I've got a rollaway in Mike's room. I'll be fine. Rye, I think you should know that your father and I—"

He cut his mother off before she could start a conversation he wasn't yet ready to have. "Good night, Mom. I'll talk to you tomorrow." He hung up before she could say anything more.

Rye tried to sleep, but it was impossible to relax when he knew Lexie was right down the hall. He spent half the night wondering what his mother had been about to say and the other half wondering how he'd managed to screw up his conversation with Lexie so badly.

He'd told her how he'd felt in the past, all right. But he'd left her thinking those feelings had vanished the same way she had the morning after their night together. They'd ended up discussing the need to be responsible adults who didn't argue in front of their child.

He supposed he'd been saved from making a terrible mistake. What if she'd been open to a sexual fling? What if they ended up in bed together again? What if all those feelings they'd experienced together had somehow survived the hiatus he'd imposed on their relationship? Then what? Was he willing to take the chance that she wouldn't disappoint him again? Did he dare offer his heart to a woman who'd once done something so wrong there was no forgiving it?

He was tempted to do just that.

Needless to say, he was groggy and grumpy the next morning. It didn't help that Lexie had gotten up before him, put on the coffeemaker, and prepared his favorite breakfast, although he wasn't quite sure how she knew it was his favorite.

Then Cody padded into the kitchen wearing his footed sleeper, his blond hair askew, a huge smile on his face, and said, "You made my very most favorite breakfast!"

Mystery solved. Rye wolfed down the blueberry pancakes slathered in butter and drowned in huckleberry syrup, inhaled a cup of black coffee, and when Pete honked, jumped out of his chair and headed for the door.

"Wait!" Lexie cried.

He turned back and said irritably, "What is it?"

"You don't have to snap at me!"

"I didn't—" But of course, he had. This whole breakfast scene was just a little too homey, a little too perfect, a little too . . . much. He moderated his tone and met her gaze, carefully avoiding her dishabille in what looked like an expensive, full-length, navy-blue silk bathrobe.

The robe might have been sexy by itself, but she'd

spoiled the effect by adding a pair of fuzzy gray slippers with pink rabbit ears. It was not an outfit intended to entice a man, but he was nevertheless smitten. The paper-thin silk was snugged against her body with a belt that emphasized her tiny waist and defined her figure well enough for him to see she wasn't wearing a bra. He wondered what else she wasn't wearing under there.

His tongue was stuck to the roof of his mouth. He swallowed the drool he imagined someone would have drawn in a cartoon of the moment and said, "Pete's waiting. What do you want?"

"I'm planning to take Cody to Kalispell to shop for groceries. I thought we might go by the hospital and visit your mother. Would you like me to give her a message?"

"Tell her to give me a call if she needs me."

"I hope you find some evidence that leads you to the shooter," she said.

"Me, too."

"Will you be tracking the grizzly?"

"I don't know. Maybe. Probably."

"Be careful."

He was surprised at the warning, which sounded a lot like she cared. He just wasn't sure if she was more worried about what the bear might do to him. Or what he might do to the bear. He grinned. "Don't worry. I won't kill any grizzlies if it can be avoided."

"That bear is wounded," she reminded him. "That's likely to make it even more unpredictable."

He grabbed his coat and put it on and reached for the doorknob.

"Rye . . ."

Her voice saying his name—his first name—held him in place. He turned and waited for her to speak.

"Be careful."

"Don't worry about me. I'll be fine," he said.

"I wish I was going with you."

"To protect me? Or the grizzly?"

She opened her mouth to retort, but he was out the door before she could speak.

Chapter 9

VICK HAD HER hands deep in dishwater when her cellphone rang. With Mike's life in the balance and Sullivan out searching for a wounded grizzly, not to mention three sisters whose lives were fraught with calamity, she needed to answer the phone. She shook her hands free of soapy water and ran for her bedroom.

As she picked up her phone from the nightstand, Vick glanced out the window and saw snowflakes being driven sideways beneath a treacherous gray sky. With everything going on, she hadn't paid attention to the weather. A heavy snowfall was going to make tracking the grizzly difficult, if not impossible, and create a new set of problems. Since a wounded bear was more likely to attack humans, folks coming into the area to hike, or illegally hunt out of season, would need to be warned. Technically, that was the job of federal, state, and local authorities, but Vick believed you could never put out too many warnings. She had a network set up to make that happen. Making sure folks were careful in and around grizzly habitat, that they stayed on trails rather than bushwhacking, hiked in pairs, made plenty of noise, and carried lots of bear spray they knew how to use, prevented injuries like the ones Mike had suffered. Fewer bear attacks meant fewer sensational news stories suggesting grizzlies were a danger to humans and ought to be exterminated.

She glanced at her phone screen and realized her fraternal twin, who was also her best friend, was calling. Taylor had endured a harrowing experience the previous summer, when the Twin Otter she was piloting for smoke jumpers crashed in the middle of a raging forest fire in Yellowstone. The charred plane was found, but Taylor had remained missing and was presumed dead, along with the only other passenger, smoke jumper Brian Flynn.

The Grayhawks and Flynns, neighbors who were mortal enemies in the normal course of things, had searched together for nearly two weeks before Taylor and Brian were finally found, barely alive after their terrible ordeal. Taylor was now happily married to her firefighter husband, Brian, and they were eagerly anticipating the birth of twin girls in May.

Vick accepted the call and said anxiously, "Are you and the babies okay?"

"We're fine. Everyone's fine. Especially Leah."

Vick couldn't figure out what her half sister—they had the same mother, but King wasn't her father—had to do with Taylor and Brian's twins. "*Especially* Leah? What's going on?"

"Are you sitting down?"

"No, why?"

"You'll want to sit down for this."

Fearing something awful had happened to her eldest sister, who was the closest thing Vick had to a mother, she sank onto her bed. Her heart in her throat, she said, "I'm sitting."

"How long before Leah loses the ranch to Matt, and he kicks her out for good?"

Vick was expecting news of some physical injury, so it took a second for her to do the math in her head. "Beginning March 31 a year ago until now . . . Omigod! Just twenty days are left."

Since Matt had shown up, two of Vick's sisters, Eve and Taylor, had married and left Kingdom Come, and Vick had moved to Montana. Leah had stayed right where she was, swearing that, by hook or by crook, she would rid herself of Matt Grayhawk before the year was up.

"Kingdom Come is my home," she'd vowed, "and I'm not leaving."

Except, nothing Leah or any of them had said or done had made a dent in Matt's determination to own the ranch. He'd settled in with his twenty-year-old daughter, Pippa, and seven-year-old son, Nathan, and hadn't budged an inch, even when an unhappy, unwed, and pregnant Pippa had moved to Devon Flynn's cabin and refused to see her father. Since then, Pippa and Devon had married and were busy raising their twins.

"What is Leah going to do?" Vick realized that while she'd been distracted with her own problems, the sister who'd single-handedly raised her was facing a life-altering crisis. "She has less than three weeks to get him out of there."

"Matt's gone."

"What?" Vick exclaimed.

"That's why I wanted you sitting down. Matt left last night. Devon heard it from Pippa who told Brian who told me. Matt didn't say why he was leaving or where he was going. He just walked out and took Nate with him."

"What did King say to that? What did Leah say? Do you have any idea why he left? Or where he was going? This is great news! I mean, for Leah."

Over the past year, she and her sisters had learned that Matt wasn't the complete monster he'd seemed to be when he'd first arrived. But thanks to King favoring his son over his daughters, Leah had gotten stuck with the short end of a very ugly stick.

Suddenly, Matt was gone, like a puff of smoke. The fact that he'd taken his son with him spoke volumes. Clearly, he'd broken his contract with King.

"Does this mean Leah will get the ranch?" Vick asked.

"I think so. But who really knows? Remember that financial trouble King was in last year? I think there's still a chance he might need to sell the ranch to bail himself out."

"Poor Leah, if he does!"

Unfortunately, that sort of ruthless behavior was typical of King. Vick didn't exactly hate her father. She might even love him. She just didn't like him very much. "Wait a minute. Do you suppose King's financial woes have anything to do with Matt taking off like he did?"

"I hadn't thought of that," Taylor said.

"What if King is reneging on his promise to Matt? What if he *does* need to sell the ranch? Has Leah said anything?" Vick asked.

"She's as mystified by Matt's behavior as the rest of us. But ecstatic, of course."

"Unless King plans to screw them both," Vick muttered.

"What was that?"

"Nothing. Has King weighed in? What does he say about all this?"

"As far as I know, he hasn't made a peep."

"I can't imagine why Matt would leave at this late date."

"Obviously, something happened," Taylor said.

"Like what?"

Vick heard the silence on the other end of the line and imagined her twin deciding whether to share what she knew or, at least, suspected.

"Come on. Give. You must have some idea what sent Matt dashing off like that," Vick said.

"Actually, I do. I'll bet it has something to do with Pippa's mother."

"I thought Matt and Jennie weren't speaking to each other."

"As far as I know, they're not."

Matt and Jennie Fairchild Hart, Pippa's mother, had a long and torturous history together. But if they weren't talking, Vick couldn't imagine what Jennie might have to do with Matt's disappearance.

"What happens now?" Vick asked.

"I guess we wait for events to unfold."

Vick snorted. "I know you. You'll have the skinny on the whole situation before sundown. Call me when you find out."

Taylor giggled. "Will do. While I have you on the phone, what's new with you?"

Vick's heart was suddenly racing again. Her own news was every bit as momentous as Taylor's. Her twin, who knew her so well, would understand the ramifications of what she was about to reveal in the next few moments. She took a deep breath and said, "Sullivan's brother got mauled by a grizzly yesterday. He was also shot, probably by a poacher."

"Oh, no! Why didn't you call me? Is he going to be all right?"

"The doctors aren't sure. He's going to be in the hospital for a while, so I'm staying at Sullivan's ranch, in his sister's room, while Darcie stays at the hospital in Kalispell with Mike."

"You're doing *what*?"

Vick pulled the phone away from her ear, then put

it back again and said, "I'm sure you heard me the first time."

"Are you nuts? Out of your mind? Why would you put yourself in a situation where you have to interact with that bastard every day?"

"Please don't call him that. Sullivan is my son's father."

"Cody can't help that. You told me at Christmas you've still got a crush on the guy, but this sounds like an exercise in masochism."

Vick flushed. She'd forgotten she'd shared that tidbit with Taylor over the holiday. She remembered also mentioning that Sullivan didn't reciprocate her feelings, so she could understand why her twin might be upset.

"I'm happy I get to spend more time with Cody," she said.

"That lowlife should have offered to change your custody arrangements a long time ago."

Her twin was pushing. Vick needed her to back off. "Taylor, please. Don't."

Taylor sighed. "Fine. Be careful, Vick. You've already lost your heart. Don't lose your good sense. Keep your elbows out."

Vick giggled at the mention of a posture they'd used when they were dating to keep unwanted male attention at bay. No man could get close if they kept their sharp elbows extended from their bodies.

"Spend time with your son," Taylor said without taking a breath, "and stay away from that—"

"Taylor!"

"I wasn't going to say bastard. Or lowlife." She hesitated, then admitted, "I was going to say sonofabitch."

Vick smiled and shook her head. "Don't worry about me. I'll be fine. More than fine."

"If you say so."

"I do. Call me when you find out about Matt."

"I will."

Vick caught her lower lip with her teeth after she disconnected the call. She wasn't used to keeping secrets from her twin. But it was too dangerous to admit her hopes aloud. Taylor would have had a shit fit if she knew what Vick intended to do.

Tempt Sullivan.

Vick had to know, once and for all, if what they'd experienced together all those years ago had survived, or could be revived. If it couldn't . . . better to know for sure, one way or the other.

Chapter 10

"WHERE ARE WE going to live now, Daddy?"

It was a simple question, but Matthew Grayhawk had no idea how to answer his seven-year-old son. He only knew there was somewhere he had to be, and time was of the essence. The girl who'd stolen Matt's heart when he was sixteen, Jennie Fairchild—former U.S. senator from Texas Jennifer Fairchild Hart—was fighting for her life at MD Anderson Cancer Center.

"We'll be living in Houston, Texas, for a while," he told his son.

"Grandpa King told me lots of cowboys live in Texas," Nathan said.

"They do."

"Grandpa King said maybe I can ride a horse again someday."

Matt hadn't expected his father, King Grayhawk, to spend so much time with his grandson, when he'd spent so little time with any of the eight children he'd produced with his four wives. But King had clearly doted on Nathan. Matt fought off any guilt he felt about taking King's grandson so far from Kingdom Come.

The truth was he hadn't returned from his self-imposed exile in Australia a year ago in order to possess his father's Wyoming ranch. He'd come because he'd realized that the only woman he loved—would ever love—lived in America, and he didn't want to spend another moment of his life without her.

You really screwed up your chances of that, old buddy. You'll be lucky if Jennie ever lets you back into her life.

He simply couldn't give up hope that Jennie would forgive him for keeping the existence of their daughter, whom she believed had died at birth, a secret from her for nearly twenty years. Time had raced past without stopping, and he'd missed his chance to do the right thing. *Almost* missed it. As long as they were both still alive, there was still a chance to undo the wrongs of the past. That might not be true for long, because Jennie was deathly ill with cancer and might not survive.

Which was why he'd left Kingdom Come the instant he'd discovered she was in the hospital and flown to Texas in the family jet.

Matt met his son's sapphire-blue eyes in the rear-view mirror of the Lexus SUV he'd had waiting for him at Houston's William P. Hobby Airport and watched as Nathan swiped at the sweaty hair at his nape. It had been cold in Wyoming. Texas was sweltering. He turned up the AC, then asked his son, "Would you like to ride a horse again?"

Nathan made a face and admitted, "I'm still kinda scared of horses."

"No worries," Matt said, using one of the Australian expressions he'd picked up over the years running a cattle station in the Northern Territory. "Someday you won't be scared anymore."

Matt wanted to believe that. His son had been injured in a freak riding accident that Nathan's mother, Irene, had caused. Her horse had cut off Nathan's horse in an attempt to win an ill-advised race, causing Nathan and his mount to plummet over a ledge into a deep ravine.

When she reached their son, Irene had panicked at the sight of Nathan's two badly broken legs and the sound of his agonized shrieks. She'd put her hand over his mouth in an attempt to stifle his screams, which were upsetting his horse. The panicked animal, also badly injured, was writhing on the ground threatening to kick her. Unfortunately, she'd also covered Nathan's nose, accidentally suffocating him, putting him in a coma that had threatened his life.

Irene, now his ex-wife, was another reason he'd left Australia. A thoughtless and irresponsible parent, she'd been making noises about wanting custody of Nathan.

Nathan had ended up with one leg shorter than the other, resulting in a permanent limp, and he had a paralyzing fear of horses. That wouldn't have mattered, except Nathan had been born into a ranching family. Matt had remained patient, hoping that time spent around horses, if not actually on one, would eventually solve the problem.

Nathan's question reminded Matt that he needed a safe place in Houston for his son to stay after school, while he spent time with Jennie at the hospital. He hadn't left Nathan behind at his father's ranch, because he had no intention of ever returning, but he'd left so abruptly, he hadn't made any plans for Nathan's care.

Fortunately, he came from a large family. His niece, Kate, had a home in Houston with her husband, billionaire businessman Wyatt Shaw. With any luck, Kate would be willing to keep an eye on Nathan until he could make more permanent arrangements.

It surprised Matt to realize that he hadn't thought twice about leaving Kingdom Come only three weeks before he could claim it under his agreement with his father. He grinned, imagining King's expression when he realized the black sheep of the family had bolted again. His grin disappeared as he focused on the reason he'd been so willing to throw away a veritable fortune.

There was something a thousand times more valuable waiting for him in Houston.

Matt had never stopped loving Jennie, but at the moment, she wanted nothing to do with him. He couldn't blame her.

His teenage romance with Jennie Fairchild had seemed like a fairy-tale love story. When Jennie was fourteen, sixteen-year-old Matt had literally bumped into her in the Jackson Hole High School gym. Her long blond hair had been tied in a ponytail that trailed halfway down her back, and a fringe of bangs had covered her eyebrows, leaving him looking into a pair of soft gray eyes.

When he began checking out the rest of her, she took hold of his chin, forcing his gaze to meet hers. "There's more to me than my figure," she'd chided.

That simple touch was the moment he'd fallen in love with her. Deep and hard and forever.

They'd been each other's first loves, which might have been what made their attraction so powerful and lasting. Even though they were careful, Jennie got pregnant. When her parents found out, they left Jackson and hid Jennie away from him. Matt nearly went crazy searching for her. When his father told him Jennie had died giving birth to their daughter, who'd also died, Matt had raged against the world. But there was nothing he could do.

Until his uncle—King's nemesis, Angus Flynn—

told him the truth: both Jennie and the baby were alive.

Matt found their daughter, Pippa, with foster parents in Texas, and with Angus's help, secretly sought custody of her. Jennie was also alive, but he'd been forced to make a choice. Take the baby and run, or try to bring Jennie, who was only fifteen, along as well.

He'd chosen his daughter over the girl he'd supposedly loved more than life. At seventeen, he'd fled with Pippa to Australia, where neither Jennie's parents, nor his father, could find him to take the child away again.

During the years that followed, the time had never seemed right to contact Jennie and tell her they had a daughter. They'd both married other people. Before he knew it, their daughter was grown, and Jennie had remained unaware that Pippa even existed. Until finally, last year, an unwed and pregnant Pippa needed her mother. At least, that was the excuse he'd used to finally reach out to Jennie.

She'd been amazed to discover she had a grown daughter and devastated to learn that Matt had never corrected the lie her parents had told her. It had been the most gut-wrenching conversation of Matt's life. To make matters even worse, Jennie was a widow and had never had other children. Matt didn't know whether something had happened to her during the delivery of their child because she was so young, to make further pregnancies impossible, or whether Jennie had simply chosen not to have other children. Whichever it was, she blamed Matt for stealing her chance to be a mother.

Once Jennie and Pippa were reunited, they often spent time visiting each other. On the other hand, Jennie treated Matt like something unclean. It seemed the timing had always been wrong for them to make a life together. In the beginning, their parents had conspired to keep them apart, then fate had lent a hand, and his fear and foolishness had finished the job.

Now cancer was threatening to rob them of any hope of a future together. Matt had realized he couldn't bear to be apart from the woman he loved for one more moment. He was determined to get her back. He just had to convince her to forgive him first.

Matt felt the knot of emotion grow in his throat and swallowed over the pain. He was lucky to have found out Jennie was in the hospital. She'd told Pippa, of course, with orders not to breathe a word to him. Pippa had told her husband, Devon Flynn, who'd told his brother Brian, who'd told his wife, Taylor, who'd told her sister Leah, who'd told him. Matt couldn't discount the fact that Leah had spoken to him about Jennie's illness because she wanted him to break his agreement with his father by leaving the premises, so she would get the ranch instead of him. But he was grateful to have learned the truth in time to do something about it.

"Are we there yet?" Nathan asked.

"Not quite." Matt glanced at his watch. There

was no time to drop Nathan off anywhere if he wanted to make it to MD Anderson before Jennie went into surgery. His heart lurched when he thought of what she'd intended to face all on her own.

A double mastectomy.

Matt couldn't imagine what Jennie must be feeling at the thought of having both breasts removed. And surgery was only the preliminary step. She was also facing a course of adjuvant chemotherapy, which just meant it followed within thirty days of the surgery. She'd forbidden Pippa to come to Houston, since their daughter was still nursing her twins. That left him.

He parked the SUV in the MD Anderson garage and headed inside, holding Nathan's hand firmly in his own. One whiff of the hospital corridor, and his son stopped dead. He looked up at Matt with anxious eyes and said, "Why are we here, Daddy?"

"A friend of mine is sick."

"I don't like hospitals."

Who could blame him? Nathan had spent far too much time in one for a kid his age. "It's okay, Nate. We're just visiting. You don't have to come back after today."

He watched the tension visibly leave Nathan's narrow shoulders before he said, "Okay."

Matt continued his journey to Jennie's room, hoping and praying they hadn't taken her somewhere else to prep her for surgery. His heart was beating fast, but he wasn't sure whether it was the prospect of seeing Jennie again, or the result of scooping Nathan into his arms and taking the stairs two at a time. He was pretty sure seven-year-olds weren't allowed on Jennie's floor, but he hadn't seen a nurse at the desk nearest the stairs, and since he'd done a search online and knew exactly where he was going, he hurried along, hoping he'd get away with what he was doing.

He paused outside Jennie's door to take a deep breath and let it out.

"Are you okay, Daddy?"

He gave his son a reassuring smile. "I'm fine." *Scared to death that Jennie will send me away, but otherwise, just fine.*

"Are we going in?" Nathan asked when he didn't move.

His feet felt like they were rooted to the floor. Suddenly, he wasn't sure he should have dragged Nathan here. What if Jennie yelled at him to "Get out!"

Then he reminded himself that she'd spent her life as a politician's wife before she became a politician herself. She would take one look at Nathan and be calm and cool and collected. Was that why he'd brought his son? Because he knew Jennie wouldn't make a scene with a little boy standing there and throw him out on his ass? He flushed with guilt. But it was too late to leave Nathan somewhere else. He had no choice except to bring him along for the ride.

He knocked, heard no response, and knocked louder.

"Come in."

Did she sound weak? Scared? Upset?

He opened the door, his heart in his throat. It had been a gamble to come here, but one he'd had to take. He watched her face closely as she looked up from rearranging the sheet around herself and met his worried eyes.

She looked surprised. No. *Stunned.* Her gaze shot to Nathan and then back to him.

"This must be Nathan," she said, smiling at his son.

"I'm Nate," Nathan replied as Matt set him down.

"I'm Jennie," she said, extending her hand.

Nathan reached out and took it, shook it, then stepped backward until he hit Matt's legs. Matt put a hand on his son's shoulder and aimed him toward a chair in the corner. "Why don't you have a seat and get comfortable while I talk to Jennie?"

Nathan glanced up to remind his father that he would *never* be comfortable in a hospital but did as he was told.

Jennie shot another look at Nathan, then narrowed her gray eyes as she focused them on him. "What's going on, Matt?" she said in the carefully controlled voice he'd expected her to use. "Why are you here?"

"I heard about your surgery. Not from Pippa," he hurried to say. "I'm here to offer whatever support you might need."

"You're twenty years too late."

His heart sank at the bitterness in her voice.

"Don't send me away," he heard himself pleading,

then added almost belligerently, "I'm not letting you send me away. You don't have to forgive me."

"No need to worry about that."

"Just let me help."

"I don't want or need anything from you."

He felt her rejection like a stab to the heart. But even wounded and bleeding, he kept on fighting. "You wouldn't let Pippa come, and you don't have anyone else. There's only me, Jennie."

"And me," Nathan piped up from the corner. He hopped out of his chair and crossed to Jennie's bed.

Matt had thought they were speaking too softly, if intensely, for Nathan to overhear. Obviously, he'd been wrong.

"It's no fun to be in the hospital," Nathan said. "I know. It's better if someone comes to visit and brings you books and games and stuff. Daddy and I can do that."

Matt could see Jennie was torn. She could easily say no to the man who'd stolen her child and run away. She was having a much harder time saying it to a little boy with his father's sapphire-blue eyes and a terrible limp.

"All right," Jennie said, addressing herself to his son. "I accept your offer."

Nathan grinned. "Good. 'Cause, you know, you never win when you argue with Daddy. We could have been here all day." He turned to Matt and said, "Can we go now?"

Astonished, Matt met Jennie's eyes, which were crinkled with laughter. Before he could say anything to mess things up, a nurse opened the door, spied him and Nathan, made a disapproving face, and said, "You shouldn't be in here."

"We were just leaving," Matt told her, grabbing Nathan by the hand. Before they got out the door, he turned to Jennie and said, "See you after your surgery. I love you."

He hurried out the door before she could reply. He hadn't meant to blurt it out like that, but the truth was the truth. She might as well get used to hearing it, because he intended to keep saying it for the rest of her life . . . however long that turned out to be.

Chapter 11

LEAH GRAYHAWK STEPPED off her horse on the edge of an evergreen forest, where she couldn't be seen from the main ranch house at Kingdom Come, and waited for her husband, Aiden Flynn, to arrive. Leah smiled inwardly. Poor Aiden. Not only was he not living under the same roof as his wife—he lived and worked on his father's ranch, the Lucky 7—but as far as anyone except her sister Taylor and his brother Brian knew, they were merely *dating*.

Part of the reason for the deception was practical. Aiden's father hated her father. For nearly forty years Angus Flynn had done his best to make King Grayhawk's life miserable. It was Aiden's potential courtship and marriage to Leah that had convinced Angus to take his foot off King's neck last summer, because it presented him an even sweeter revenge for his sister's death than King's financial ruin. Quite simply, Aiden had promised that he and Leah would name their first child, King Grayhawk's grandchild, after its *other* grandfather, Angus Flynn.

Meanwhile, Leah and Aiden had agreed that the best way to end the feud between their families once and for all was to merge the two ranches into one, so the two angry old men could no longer use those assets as weapons against each other. To make that happen, Aiden had to get control of the Lucky 7, and Leah had to get control of Kingdom Come.

Until that happened, Leah was unwilling to move away from home, which meant she and Aiden had to live separately, so they could manage their respective ranches. Their living situation gave both of them a lot of incentive to make the merger happen.

Although Matt was gone, that was only the first hurdle Leah had to leap. There was the small (Ha! Ha!) matter of getting her father to deed the land to her, a daughter who wasn't even related to him by blood.

"The news is all over town," Aiden said as he stepped down from his horse. "Congratulations, Leah."

Aiden was wearing a wide smile, a twinkle in his blue eyes, and worn Levi's with a heavy wool sweater. When he opened his arms, Leah stepped into them. Even when she'd hated Aiden, after discovering he'd bet his brother Brian that he could get her to fall in love with him, she hadn't stopped loving him. Since then, she'd forgiven him, but she still didn't quite trust him. Every time she allowed herself to be held by him, every time she allowed him to show his love, the hurt faded a little more.

As Aiden pulled her close, she leaned into his strong body. She wanted him, and it was obvious, once he embraced her, that he felt the same desire. She tipped her head back and took his face between her cold hands.

"I wish I could take credit for Matt being gone. All I did was inform him that Jennifer Hart is in the hospital. He was gone within hours. I feel sorry for both of them."

"It's too bad about her cancer. But it's past time he went after her. He's loved Jennie nearly all his life."

Matt had left home and lived with his uncle and cousins after a pregnant, fifteen-year-old Jennie was hidden away from him by her parents, with help, Matt believed, from King. Aiden had firsthand knowledge of how distraught Matt had been as he made a futile search for her.

Aiden covered Leah's cold hands with his warm ones and leaned down to kiss her gently on the mouth. "It's been a long wait, baby. But it's almost over."

Aiden knew how she felt about his calling her "baby." Babies had to be taken care of, and she stood on her own two feet. Allowing the endearment, gracefully accepting it, was a sign of her willingness to let Aiden carry some of the burden she'd always shouldered herself, a surrender to his love, and evidence of her growing confidence that he would never hurt her again.

"How soon can you ask King to put you in charge of the ranch?" he asked.

"Once Matt left, I became foreman by default," she said. "What I need is a piece of paper from King making it clear that all future decisions about the ranch are mine."

"What are the chances of that?" Aiden asked.

"King can't want the ranch too badly for himself," Leah said wryly. "He was going to give it to Matt in three weeks."

Aiden grinned. "There is that. The question is will he give it to you instead?"

Leah lowered her gaze and pressed her cheek against Aiden's chest, where she could hear the steady beat of his heart. When his arms tightened around her again she said, "All I can do is ask."

"When are you going to do that, exactly?"

She knew he was eager for them to live as man and wife, but she wasn't as certain they would be living happily ever after as he seemed to be. She put the focus back on him. "How are things going at the Lucky 7? When is Angus going to hand his ranch over to you?"

Aiden sighed. "I thought he would have done it by now. I've been persistent about asking. He counters with 'When are you going to make that Grayhawk girl your wife?' "

Leah smirked. "What do you say to that?"

"I'm working on it." He pressed his forehead against hers and said, "I don't know how much longer I can go on like this, Leah. I want to wake up with you beside me in the morning. I want to start a family with you. I want—"

She kissed him to cut off his entreaties, which made her heart hurt. His response took her deep, and she gladly followed where he led.

Leah wanted the same things Aiden did, but she was willing to wait until they'd done what was necessary to end, once and for all, the feud between their families. Or at least, that made a convenient excuse other than her fear of being abandoned by him. Leah had deep scars from being left behind when her mother ran off with one of her father's hired hands. If a mother could abandon her daughter, how certain was a husband's love? Leah knew her fear was unreasonable. That didn't mean she wasn't terrified all the time.

Breathless, she broke the kiss and put her fingertips against Aiden's lips to keep him from speaking. "I'll ask King today."

He kissed her fingertips, then twined his fingers with hers. "What if he says no?"

"Let's see what answer he gives me before we borrow trouble."

"I won't wait forever, Leah."

"I know King loves me, Aiden, even if he's never said the words. Surely—"

"Nothing is certain where that sonofabitch is

concerned." He sounded as angry and frustrated as Leah felt herself.

She caressed the too-long hair at his nape, not correcting his unkind, but generally held to be accurate, description of her stepfather. Instead, she said, "You need a haircut."

"Don't change the subject."

She smiled. "I wasn't. You need a wife, Mr. Flynn."

He laughed. "I do. I do." His face sobered. "When can we meet again? Where can we meet?"

She knew what he was asking. It was as though they were teenagers still in high school. Or illicit lovers. They'd made love in his truck. In hers. In horse stalls. In barn lofts. Even in hotel rooms in town, when it was too cold outside. But not in his home. Or hers. There was too much chance of getting caught.

"I don't understand why we can't just tell them," he argued.

"We'd lose the leverage we have with your dad. And with mine." She pulled his head down to kiss him, in an attempt to assuage him, but he wasn't satisfied anymore with just the taste of her. He slid his hand inside her coat, inside her shirt, inside her bra to the warm flesh of her breast.

"Hmm." He made a hungry sound. His callused hand was equally greedy.

Leah realized that in a moment he would have her naked and they'd be down on the frozen ground. Aiden didn't care. He would take her anywhere, anytime. She shared his desperation, but she was still rational enough to call a halt.

"Aiden," she whispered. And then, more urgently, "Aiden."

"What?" He lifted his head, and she saw shining blue eyes, radiant with passion.

"We can't."

He jerked his hand free, accidentally popping the first button on her blouse, which went flying. "I'm done with this, Leah."

For a moment she thought he meant he was done with her. Her heart skipped a beat and then threatened to stop altogether.

Then he continued, "Don't ask to see me again until you can take me home to your father and introduce me as your husband. To hell with this pretense of dating. Nobody needs that sort of charade, least of all us."

"I don't understand."

"I think you do. You just don't like what you're hearing. No more furtive lovemaking. I'm cutting you off cold."

"Cutting off your nose to spite your face is more like it," she retorted.

"Maybe so. But if you're suffering as badly as I am, maybe you'll get this thing done."

"I told you I'm doing the best I can," she protested.

"Do better." He turned and marched toward his horse.

"Aiden!"

He paused and glanced at her over his shoulder. He didn't speak, just waited for whatever it was she had to say.

"I love you."

She hadn't said it in a very long time. She wasn't sure what reaction she expected. Maybe that he'd turn around and march right back and take her in his arms.

He just stood there staring at her. At last he said, "I love you, too." He mounted and spurred the gelding to a gallop, its hooves slinging mud and snow as Aiden raced across the pasture.

Leah's throat was swollen so thick she could hardly swallow. She'd lied to Aiden. The real reason she hadn't asked King for the ranch yet was because she'd been too afraid. What if he said no? What if he said hell no? It would break her in half to lose the ranch. It would break her heart to discover her stepfather didn't love her enough to do whatever it took to make her happy.

She trudged toward her horse. She might as well get this over with.

Chapter 12

LEAH KNOCKED ON King's office door and, as she always did, entered without waiting for him to respond. She caught him with his head back, holding a bloody handkerchief to his nose. "What happened? Are you all right?"

He sat up and dabbed at the last of the blood. "Don't fuss, Leah. It's just a little nosebleed."

She hurried to his side and examined a sun-and-wind-ravaged face that was gaunt and pale. "You're getting a lot of them, lately."

"It's nothing."

She noticed a bruise on his forearm that hadn't been there earlier, and all he'd done was work in the office today. "When was the last time you saw a doctor?"

"Don't like doctors."

"That wasn't what I asked."

"Haven't seen anyone since MD Anderson gave me a clean bill of health after that cancer scare."

That had been years ago. Leah's heart skipped a beat at the thought that King's leukemia might have returned. Nosebleeds were a symptom, along with bruises and unexplained loss of weight. King had exhibited all of those warning signs and one more. Fatigue. He'd given her a lot more responsibility lately. She'd taken it as a good sign. Now she wasn't so sure.

Because of Matt's departure, they were shorthanded, putting even more stress on King. That was partly her fault. She was the one who'd told Matt about Jennie's cancer. She was the one who'd sent him haring off to Texas. She could handle most of the slack left by Matt's departure, but she'd been counting on King to pick up the rest of the burden until she could hire extra help. Right now, he didn't look well enough to swing a loop.

She stuck her hands on her hips and said, "You should hand this place over to me and get some rest."

"The hell I will!" He shoved his coffee cup away, causing it to spill, and swore as he jumped up to get out of the way of the steaming liquid dripping over the edge of his desk. He turned on her and bellowed, "Don't go putting me in my grave before I'm dead, young lady."

Leah's jaw dropped. She'd come here intending to

ask for control of the ranch, but not in the awkward, insulting way she'd done it. "I didn't mean— How could you think— Don't be an old fool!"

"So now I'm an old fool?"

Leah flushed when she realized what she'd said. "Damn it! I'm worried about you."

"You've been hinting that you want control of Kingdom Come for the better part of a year. You've made no secret what you thought about my deal with Matt, and you've done everything in your power to thwart my intentions. Well, Matt's gone, but I'm still here, alive and kicking."

"And you aren't about to give this ranch to some girl who's no relation to you," Leah said bitterly.

"Don't go putting words in my mouth."

"It's true, though, isn't it? When I was a little girl, I was afraid every minute of every day that you'd realize my mother had left me behind, and I didn't belong here. First, I made myself invisible, so you wouldn't throw me out. Then I made myself indispensable, so you'd keep me around."

"Leah, I—"

Her body was trembling with rage and frustration. "You're not getting rid of me! I won't let you. You need me, old man. And don't you forget it!"

She whirled to flee, but he caught her arm and flung her back around so she ended up imprisoned in his arms. She struggled not to cry, battled the weak, female tears as she resisted his enfolding arms, which cinched tight around her. Her heart was thumping so hard it hurt, and she was having trouble catching her breath.

"Leah, Leah, calm down. Be still. Let me speak."

She dropped her forehead against his chest, hiding her moist eyes, and swallowed the sob that threatened to break free. But every muscle in her body remained taut, warding off whatever dirty trick this unfamiliar embrace represented. She'd never seen King hug any of her sisters, who were his blood relations, which left her suspicious of his motives now.

"Are you ready to listen?" he said in a quiet voice.

She didn't answer. She had fists full of his shirt and was hanging on for dear life, afraid that if she let go, she would splinter into a million pieces.

"Of all your mother's children, you've always been my favorite."

Her head snapped up, and she stared into his blue eyes, not believing what he'd said or the fact that he'd made such an admission. She opened her mouth to speak, but her throat was too swollen with emotion for any sound to get out.

"I've watched you grow into one helluva businesswoman. I know you could run this ranch with one hand tied behind your back."

When he stopped there, she cleared her throat and said, "But . . ."

"I've always dreamed of my eldest son running Kingdom Come. I'm not willing to give up on Matt. Not yet."

"He broke his agreement with you," Leah cried.

She let go of King's shirt, put both palms flat on his chest, and gave a tremendous shove. He let go, and she stumbled backward. She quickly found her footing and put herself toe-to-toe with him. "Matt left! He walked away without looking back. I'm here. Why not give the ranch to me?"

"I've already answered that question."

"You're not being fair."

"Never said I was."

"What can I do to change your mind?"

He smiled crookedly and shook his head. "That's what I love most about you, Leah. You never give up. You never give in. Keep up that attitude, and someday this place may be yours."

"How is that possible?"

His eyes looked bleak. "Matt might not come back."

What good did it do to be his favorite daughter, when what King really valued was his eldest son?

"What I should do is move in with Aiden Flynn at the Lucky 7 tomorrow," she muttered.

"Now, just a minute," King said. "Don't be hasty."

"There's nothing for me here. From the start, Matt has made it clear that once he owned Kingdom Come we girls had to move on. If you're determined to give the ranch to him, you won't be seeing any more of me."

"Matt never said anything like that to me," King protested.

"He never said much of anything to you."

King made a face. "Matt still blames me for something that wasn't my fault. I only told him what Jennie's parents told me. I had no idea either Jennie or their baby was still alive."

"Have you told him that?"

"He never gave me a chance. He ran straight to Angus, and Angus did his best to separate me from my son. It was one of the cruelest things that sonofabitch ever did to me. I didn't kill his sister. Jane was mentally unstable long before I divorced her. I believe Angus fixated on punishing me for her death, because he feels guilty for not keeping a closer eye on her himself. She was living with him when she swallowed the pills that took her life."

Leah's brows lowered as she shook her head in disbelief. "Oh, my God. I see everything so clearly now. Giving Matt the ranch has nothing to do with loving your eldest son. It's really about shoving Angus's nose in Matt's return to the fold and undoing a bit of his nasty revenge. You two bitter old men deserve each other. I don't know why I've wasted so much time worrying about you."

"I can take care of myself," he blustered.

"Fine. See a doctor or don't. Just leave me out of it. I've got plenty of work to do until Matt shows up again." She stopped at the door and turned to say, "And I'll be here if he doesn't."

Chapter 13

LEAH LAY NAKED in Aiden's arms in his bed at the Lucky 7. She'd known he was glib-tongued, but she hadn't realized how susceptible she was to his entreaties. She hadn't wanted to tell Aiden on the phone that she'd failed in her quest to get possession of her father's ranch, and today was the first chance she'd had to meet up with him in person. He'd accepted her news with such a downhearted look, it made her want to weep. Was it any wonder she'd let him talk her into bed?

"We're going to get caught, Aiden."

"By whom?" He kissed her throat, sending a thrill through her body, and she turned her head so he could reach her tender flesh more easily.

"Your father."

"Angus is on a business trip."

"So is King. Do you suppose they're meeting up somewhere in secret?"

"I seriously doubt it." He raised his head and met her gaze with heavy-lidded eyes. "I don't want to talk about them, Leah. I want to make love to you."

"Again?"

He laughed and kissed her on the nose. "We've always been in such a hurry there hasn't been time for seconds. Or thirds."

"Thirds?" she said breathlessly.

"Unless you have somewhere you have to be."

She shook her head. "I hired a foreman yesterday to take Matt's place. He seems to know his business. Who's managing things here while you're in bed with me?"

"No more talk about work, Leah."

"But—" His mouth seized hers and cut her off. She didn't say another word for the next hour, but she contributed quite a few moans and groans and sighs, culminating in some animalistic cries she couldn't quite believe had come out of her mouth.

They lay in each other's arms, their sweat-slick bodies still connected, their lungs heaving, and Leah knew this was where she belonged.

King just *had* to give her the ranch.

Or you're going to have to give up your dream of owning it. Push was coming to shove. Time was running out. It wasn't fair to ask Aiden to wait forever to live as husband and wife. If she had to make a choice between spending the rest of her life with Aiden or owning the ranch . . .

"What are you thinking?" Aiden asked.

"How much I love you."

Enough to give up her lifelong dream of owning Kingdom Come for a future that included him? Leah wasn't willing to give up the fight. Not yet. Not while there was still a chance that she and Aiden could accomplish something that would help not only them, but also their fathers and brothers and sisters, live a lot more happily ever after.

"Leah," Aiden murmured in her ear.

"What?"

"We forgot about using a condom."

"If I haven't gotten pregnant after all the times we never used a condom—" Leah cut herself off. And separated her body from Aiden's so she could lie on her back with her arm across her eyes. When was the last time she'd had a period? She did a mental calculation and realized that she, who was as regular as clockwork, had missed the last one. How could she not have realized it sooner?

"I wouldn't mind if you got pregnant," he said, kissing her ear.

"Because that would force us to tell everyone we're married," she said, swatting at her tickled ear, letting her irritation at herself leak into her response to him.

"You'd look beautiful pregnant with my child," he said, brushing an errant curl behind her shoulder so he could press a kiss there.

Leah sat up abruptly and reached under the covers in search of her bikini panties.

Aiden, his head perched on his hand, held them up on a forefinger. "Is this what you're looking for?"

She reached for them, and he snatched them away. "Aiden, hand them over."

"Uh-uh. We have a lot more loving to do today."

Leah was no longer in the mood. She wanted to get to a drugstore and buy a pregnancy test kit and find out whether she was going to have Aiden's baby. At least, that was her last thought before Aiden began to kiss and touch and kiss some more, arousing her to a point where she could no longer think, she could only feel.

She let her fingertips roam in return, looking for places she knew were sensitive, reveling in Aiden's guttural groans of pleasure. She sought to give as much pleasure as she took, tantalizing and tasting, loving the feel of his rough beard against her belly and lifting her hips as he slid his hands beneath her and raised her up to be teased and tasted in return.

He forgot the condom again. But she had a horrible, wonderful feeling that it really didn't matter.

Chapter 14

RYE WAS FILLED with dread as he approached the place where he'd found his brother lying in a pool of blood the previous day. He looked for the red stain on the grass, but it was already covered by a sparse layer of snow. The grizzly had killed and partially eaten one of Rye's seven-hundred-pound Angus calves, but the carcass was gone. Either this bear or another scavenger had dragged it away somewhere.

"I found blood in the grizzly's right forepaw print," Rye told the deputy. "Which suggests the bear was hit in the shoulder, or maybe his leg. I also found splashes of yellow-brown fluid."

"So he was shot in the stomach or intestines as well," Pete said. "Why isn't that bear lying here dead?"

"Maybe the shots only grazed him," Rye said.

"Likely that grizzly crawled off and died," Pete replied. "What I want is the idiot who shot your brother."

Rye wondered what had brought the bear, his brother, and the poacher, who had to be trespassing, into this clearing all at the same time? With any luck, Mike would have the answers to all his questions. He sent out a silent prayer that his brother would get well and refused to imagine anything else.

"We'll need to work fast if we're going to find evidence that'll lead us to that poacher," Pete said, eyeing the large flakes of snow threatening to cover everything up. "Where was Mike's body when you got here?"

Rye showed the deputy the spot between a blue spruce and a lodgepole pine where he'd found his brother.

"Face up?" Pete asked.

"Face down." Before he'd moved Mike, Rye had pressed two fingers into the sticky blood on his brother's throat and shuddered with relief when he found a thready pulse. He'd been shocked when he turned Mike over and saw the horrific damage to his chest and scalp. Mike's eyes had remained closed, but he'd groaned. Rye's insides had clenched at the thought of the pain he'd caused his brother by moving him.

"Based on the angle of Mike's body when you found it, and knowing the bullet struck him on the right side of his chest, where would the shooter likely have been?" Pete asked.

Rye drew a line of sight with his arm. "Anywhere along that trajectory." He'd found Mike in a small clearing within the dense forest, just off the logging road where he'd left his pickup. The shooter couldn't have been too far off. Otherwise, the bullet would have been deflected by the surrounding trees and shrubs.

"Let's hope he didn't hang around to collect his casings," Pete said.

The two men got down on their hands and knees to sift through the snow as cautiously as paleontologists uncovering a rare dinosaur skeleton. Rye thought their effort was an exercise in futility, but finding a casing or something else the shooter might have dropped in his haste to escape was their best chance of holding him accountable. The bullet that had hit the metal plate in Mike's shoulder was too badly crumpled to be of any use for comparison purposes.

"Holy shit!" Pete exclaimed.

"What?"

"I found something." Pete reached inside his sheepskin coat, grabbed a pen out of his shirt pocket, and carefully slid it beneath a golden aspen leaf that was covered with snow. He grinned as he pulled the pen back out with a bullet casing balanced on the end of it. He slipped the casing into a plastic bag he'd brought along for that purpose. "It stayed dry enough under that leaf," he said excitedly, "that we might even be able to get a print off it, if the shooter loaded his own ammo. When we catch the sonofabitch, we can compare this to other casings from his rifle."

"Do we keep looking?"

"There's at least one more casing here," Pete said, "since it seems likely that grizzly had two separate wounds."

They kept at it for another half hour as the blowing snow blanketed the trees and the temperature fell another thirty degrees.

"No chance of following that grizzly's trail today," Pete said as he stood and dusted off his trousers and then his gloved hands. "Likely this snow will send the bear back into its den for another couple of weeks. We'll post grizzly warnings at the trailheads in the park and get back out here as soon as the snow melts to look for both the bear and the shooter." He met Rye's gaze and said, "With our luck, we'll get all the snow that didn't fall this past winter over the next two days."

"Let's hope not." Rye was tired and irritable. He hadn't slept well last night, and it was hard not to be discouraged by the one measly bullet casing they'd found. The snow had also covered the tracks of the poacher. Rye wondered whether the guy had walked in or come on horseback. He hadn't seen any sign of another person's presence when he'd found Mike, but then, he hadn't been looking. The poacher hadn't driven, because there had been no other vehicle or muddy vehicle tracks on the logging road, other than his own and those from Mike's truck.

"So what's the deal with you and Vick?" Pete asked.

Rye's heartbeat ratcheted up a notch, but he kept his eyes straight ahead and his voice even. "What do you mean?"

"Don't play coy with me, Rye. You guys have a kid together, and now she's living at your place. What gives?"

Rye felt his neck flush. "She's helping me out with Cody while my mom's staying with Mike in Kalispell."

"That's all?"

"That's all. End of story."

"So it won't be awkward if I take her out dancing Friday night?"

"Would you care if it was?"

Pete shot him a wry grin. "Nope."

"There you go. Be my guest."

Pete's eyes looked troubled. "Look, Rye, if I'm butting in on something—"

"You're not."

"Can I ask another question without you biting my head off?"

Rye grimaced. "You can ask." That didn't mean he was going to bare his soul or anything close to it.

"I thought at first you'd adopted Cody, until your mom let it be known around church that he was your flesh and blood. No word about who the mother was. Then Vick buys that cabin." He put up a hand to stop Rye from speaking and said, "I make it my business to know who's living in these woods."

He continued, "Nobody realizes Vick is Cody's mom until she shows up at Sunday school and she's playing with him and he calls her 'Mommy.' Why all the secrecy? Why not just introduce her to the congregation and tell everybody the truth, instead of making us guess what's going on?"

Rye did his best not to heave a long-suffering sigh. He'd known questions would be asked when Lexie moved in at the Rafter S. Whatever story he told Pete would get around—in a good way. He chose his words carefully as he explained, "Lexie's pregnancy wasn't planned."

Pete raised a curious brow when Rye called Vick by a different name, but he didn't interrupt.

Rye debated how much to tell the other man. Pete could have asked Lexie for answers. Which made Rye wonder, why hadn't he? Maybe he had, and Lexie had told him to go fly a kite.

Rye decided not to beat around the bush. "What is it, exactly, you want to know?"

Pete kept his eyes on his feet, which might have been because the footing was uneven. Or might have been because he was leery of prying further into Rye's personal life. He hesitated, then said, "What's your relationship with Vick? Exactly?"

"We don't have one."

"But—"

"We're parents of a little boy. Lexie has visitation one weekend a month."

Pete whistled. "That sounds a little on the stingy side."

"She's lucky to have that!" Rye snapped.

Pete eyed him sideways, and Rye swore under his breath. "Look. It's complicated. I don't love her. Never did. We were strangers who hooked up. Get the picture?"

"You're not strangers anymore," Pete said. "She's been coming and going about as long as you've had Cody, and last year she moved here for good."

"Yeah. So?"

"You're still just . . . acquaintances?"

"For lack of a better word. Sure."

"You never wanted to tap that again?"

Rye shot him a look through narrowed eyes. "Leave me out of this. Do what you want. I'm not her father, her brother, or her uncle. I'm just a guy who fucked her once."

Rye hated himself for explaining his unforgettable night with Lexie in such crude terms. But if he didn't shut Pete up, he was liable to coldcock him, which would reveal a hell of a lot more about his real feelings for her than he wanted the deputy to know.

Why not just tell him to keep his hands to himself? Why not stake your claim? Why give him a free hand to move in on a woman you want for yourself?

Rye spied Mike's truck and the deputy's pickup through the evergreen trees and restrained an audible grunt of relief.

"I'll keep an eye out and let you know when the snow melts enough to do some tracking," Rye said.

"Don't go hunting without me, Rye."

Rye stopped abruptly and met Pete's gaze. "That sounds like a warning."

"I don't want you going after that shooter on your own, and there's a team of folks who'll want to be in on tracking down that wounded grizzly."

Rye bit the inside of his cheek to keep from speaking. Mostly, the Wildlife Human Attack Response Team was composed of experienced trackers and woodsmen, but their focus was the bear. He wasn't going to let some poacher get away with what he'd done to Mike. He wasn't looking to kill the guy, just to make sure he didn't get away with what could easily have been murder.

Might be murder, if Mike doesn't recover.

Rye pushed those thoughts away. Mike was going to get better. He had to get better.

"See you later," Rye said as he stepped into Mike's truck.

"See you Friday," Pete replied with a grin. "When I pick up my date."

Rye sat and seethed as Pete started up his county vehicle and drove away. He made up his mind in that moment to hire a babysitter on Friday night. Maybe he'd do a little dancing in Whitefish himself.

Chapter 15

RYE CAME IN from the range long after dark, long after dinnertime, dead tired. He used the boot jack at the back door to rid himself of his muddy boots and let them drop on the kitchen floor. The house was dark and quiet, and he supposed Cody and Lexie had long since gone to bed. He found a note on the kitchen table and read it by the light from the back porch that streamed through the window in the door. It said his supper was on a plate in the oven.

He was too tired to eat. His stomach growled a protest, but he ignored it.

In the five days since Mike had been attacked, his brother's condition hadn't improved. Rye had been doing double duty on the ranch, and he wasn't sleeping well. It felt like the weight of the world was on his shoulders. He was juggling too many balls, and he wasn't sure how long he could keep from dropping one of them. Or all of them. He was so exhausted he could hardly keep his eyes open.

Rye considered tumbling into bed, but he'd pulled a cow out of a bog, and he was filthy. He dropped his Stetson on the antler rack by the back door, left his sheepskin coat on a chair in the kitchen, and padded down the dark hall toward the bathroom in his stocking feet. He ripped at the snaps on his Western shirt, then stripped it off and dropped it behind him, along with his long johns shirt.

He unbuttoned his Levi's and paused long enough to shove them down and hopped from one leg to the other yanking them off. He shoved his underwear down and pulled off his socks, leaving them in a heap by the bathroom door. He'd be awake first thing in the morning and pick up everything then. Right now, he just wanted to feel gallons and gallons of hot water streaming over his sore muscles.

He had no trouble finding his way to the bathroom in the dark. He'd done it all his life. A yellow glow from the night-light he kept on for Cody seeped into the hall. He shoved the bathroom door the rest of the way open and stood gaping at what he found.

Flickering candles scattered around the bathroom provided enough light to see that Lexie was lying naked in the claw-foot tub. She'd apparently fallen asleep. He saw a container of bubble bath on the floor beside the tub, but whatever bubbles had kept her body concealed from sight had long since popped.

He couldn't take his eyes off her. She looked angelic lying there with her blond hair floating on the water, her slender body, with its ripe breasts, the perfect image of a woman. As his body reacted eagerly and ardently to the naked woman in his tub, Rye's mouth twisted wryly.

Must not be as dog-tired as I thought.

The last thing he wanted to do was embarrass Lexie. He would have turned around and left, except he really needed that shower. And from the way her head was canted along the edge of the tub, if she slid down the wrong way, she could drown. What the hell was she thinking, falling asleep like that?

He had to wake her up, which meant she was going to find out he'd seen everything there was to see. Between his fatigue and his arousal, it was hard to think what to do. He stood there for another moment admiring her, then slid a towel off the rack, wrapped it around his waist, and tucked it in tight to cover his nakedness. He grabbed a second towel to hold outstretched to her, so she could protect what little modesty she had left.

Now all he had to do was figure out how to wake her up. Should he touch her shoulder? Or call out to her? Better to keep his distance, which meant calling her name.

He had to clear his throat before he could get any sound to come out. "Lexie."

She didn't move.

Louder, he said, "Lexie, wake up."

She moaned and started turning onto her side. In a moment her nose would be in the water. Rye grabbed her wrist and yanked her up and out of the water, wrapping the towel around her as best he could. Unfortunately, it slid down to her waist, and her naked breasts were plastered against his naked chest.

When she started to shriek, he covered her mouth with his hand. He wrapped a hand around her waist and did his best not to drop her. "You're okay. It's just me. You fell asleep in the tub. I grabbed you because I thought you were going face-first into the water."

She froze in his arms and her eyes, wide with dismay, met his.

He took his hand off her mouth and said, "I'm sorry. I didn't know what else to do. Will you be all right if I let go?"

"The towel," she gasped, reaching down to grab the towel to pull it up to cover herself.

He leaned back so she could reach it, but she caught both the towel he'd intended for her and the towel that was wrapped around his waist, pulling both free. Leaving him standing there, mud-streaked and stinking, in his birthday suit.

Rye realized the ridiculousness of the situation and chuckled.

"Don't you dare laugh at me!"

"I'm not laughing at you. I'm laughing at us." He arched a brow. "It's not as though we haven't seen all of this before." He held out a hand toward the towels she had clutched against her body and said, "Can I have one of those?"

She fumbled with the towels, hanging on to one, which she hugged to her chest, and holding out the other to him. Rye took it and wrapped it around his waist, but it did nothing to hide his aroused body, which tented the terry cloth. He shook his head and said, "Nothing I can do about that. Your body's beautiful, and my body's definitely interested in doing something about it."

He saw her pupils were dilated, but he wasn't sure whether it was from desire or fear. "I'm not going to make a move on you," he said. "I desperately need a shower and some sleep." He couldn't resist adding, "I'm just too tired to do that body justice."

She wrapped the towel around her so it covered both her front and back, then sidled toward the door. She stopped halfway there and said, "I'm sorry I fell asleep in the tub. I was tired, too. Cody was fussy all day. We went for a horseback ride, but he was too scared to follow any of the trails that led into the forest. He was terrified of getting eaten by a bear."

"Good lord. I hope you told him that won't happen."

"Of course I told him! It didn't do any good. He missed you. He missed Gram. He missed Mike. He didn't care that I was there."

Rye slid a wet curl behind her shoulder as a way

of touching her, not sure how to deal with the despair he saw in her eyes. "I'm sorry you had such a hard day." He shrugged and said, "Sometimes kids fuss. It goes with the territory."

"I'm a terrible mother."

He pulled her into his embrace, tucking her head beneath his chin in an effort to comfort her. "You're a wonderful mother."

She sniffled and said, "You're just saying that because you feel sorry for me. Here I am trying to be a full-time mother, and I'm failing at it."

He kissed her temple, fighting the urge to find her mouth and put his tongue inside and taste her and maybe see where it would lead.

It seemed he had a conscience, because it was speaking loudly in his ear: *She doesn't need sex. She needs reassurance.*

He brushed the bangs from her brow and said, "What you're experiencing is plain old everyday, frustrating, exasperating, maddening parenting."

"Is that all?" she said with a choked laugh.

He kissed the tears from each of her cheeks and said, "That's all. It'll get easier. I promise."

She sniffed again, wrinkled her nose, and said, "You smell. Like cow, I think."

He put his hands to her shoulders to separate their bodies. "Which is why I came in here in the first place. Beat it, so I can shower and get to bed."

She quickly crossed back to the tub and pulled the plug, unaware that when she bent over, he got a good look at two rosy cheeks attached to a pair of luscious legs. She went around snuffing each of the candles and hurried back toward him again.

"Thanks for waking me up. I would have been a prune by morning."

"Or drowned."

She smiled and said, "Or drowned. Good night, Sullivan."

"Good night. Don't get discouraged. You'll get another chance to do it better tomorrow."

"Thanks. I needed to hear that."

She whisked past him, careful not to touch. He leaned back a half inch himself to make sure their bodies stayed separated.

But it didn't do much good. His body ached with wanting her.

He made the shower icy cold and stood under it until he'd washed away all thought of Lexie Grayhawk.

Chapter 16

EXCEPT FOR WORRY about Mike, whose condition hadn't improved, and concern about the wounded grizzly, which had disappeared, Vick had just spent one of the happiest weeks of her life. The naked encounter with Rye in the bathroom had been awkward, but his encouragement had helped her get back on the horse, so to speak. She'd picked up the role of mother with even more determination the next morning.

The vast emptiness inside that had kept her from feeling truly happy whenever she wasn't with Cody had been filled to overflowing with her son's laughter and tears, his grouchiness and sulks, his curiosity and creativity. She savored every moment of her time with him and tried not to think about how she would feel when Darcie returned, and she was forced back out of Cody's life.

Much of what she was experiencing was new, and tonight Vick found herself in yet another strange situation. In the past, she'd simply gone about her business during the endless weeks she didn't have custody of her son. So why did she feel so guilty for leaving him with his father for one evening to go on a date with Pete Harrison?

Vick would have canceled at the last minute, but as she was about to call Pete, a fresh-faced young woman showed up at the kitchen door.

As Sullivan let her in, she said, "I know I'm a little early."

"No problem," he replied.

"Who is that?" Vick hissed. The girl looked too young to be Sullivan's date, but Vick couldn't imagine why else she would have shown up at his back door.

"Teresa!" Cody yelled joyously from the living room.

As Vick stared with wide eyes, her son raced across the living room all the way to the kitchen and threw himself at the young woman. Her hands slid under his arms as she lifted Cody and swung him in an exuberant circle, while the sound of Cody's laughter rippled across Vick's spine.

"Daddy didn't tell me you were coming," Cody said.

"Teresa babysits for Cody," Sullivan said.

Vick stood frozen like a deer in headlights. Because she only had her son one weekend a month, she spent every moment of that time with him. Naturally, there would be occasions when all the Sullivans were busy at the same time; hence the need for a *babysitter.*

Vick released a silent sigh of relief that the young woman wasn't Sullivan's date, and that he hadn't sandbagged her date with Pete by taking off and leaving her with no one to care for Cody.

Obviously, he'd had this planned.

"Where are you headed tonight?" she asked.

"Out."

Vick pursed her lips. What could she say? Where Sullivan went, and with whom, was none of her business.

He grabbed his black felt Stetson and a shearling coat and scooted backward out the kitchen door without another word to her or the babysitter.

Which was when Vick realized he hadn't given the babysitter any instructions. She turned to the girl and said, "Teresa, is it?"

"Yes, ma'am."

She smiled and said, "Please, call me Vick."

"All right, ma'am." The girl grinned, revealing a gap between her two front teeth. "Vick."

"I take it you've done a bit of babysitting for Cody."

"Sure have," she said, then put her mouth against Cody's neck and made a buzzing sound with her lips, making him giggle and hide his head under her chin.

Vick had mixed feelings watching her son interact with the babysitter. While she'd been worried about how Cody would feel if she "abandoned" him for an evening with Pete, he seemed delighted at the chance to spend time with someone else. Was she that easily replaceable? Or did his willingness to cheerfully let her leave mean, contrary to her own experience as a child, that her son was confident his mother would return?

"I presume you know Cody's schedule," Vick said.

"Yes, ma'am." The babysitter smiled an apology. "Vick."

"And you have the phone numbers for—"

"I do. Including yours. Mr. Sullivan texted it to me today."

Vick wasn't sure where to go from there. She heard a knock on the kitchen door and hurried to let Pete in.

"Ready?" he asked, his dark eyes crinkling as he smiled at her from the doorway. He looked around and asked, "Where's Rye?"

"He left a little while ago."

"Hmm."

She was glad he didn't ask any more questions, because she didn't have any answers for where Rye had gone. She grabbed her coat and was surprised when Pete took it and held it for her. They'd only been out a couple of times before, and she'd put her coat on before she'd answered her door.

"Who's taking care of—"

"Sullivan hired a babysitter."

"Is there a time we need to be back?"

The fact that their evening might be curtailed by the need to take a babysitter home by a certain hour had never occurred to Vick. She'd never babysat herself, and had no experience being cared for by a babysitter. Her father had hired a series of housekeepers who lived on the property. Vick felt a flare of anger at Sullivan for not speaking with her before he'd made his arrangements.

"Sullivan will take care of it," she said at last. He'd hired the babysitter; he could make sure she got home on time, whatever time that was.

"You mentioned dancing," she said as he helped her into his pickup.

"I thought Casey's, unless you have a better suggestion."

Vick was about to suggest they drive farther south, to Kalispell, where they had a lot more options, but she didn't know where Sullivan had gone, and she didn't want to be too far away in case there was any kind of emergency. "Casey's is great."

She wondered if other mothers worried when they were away from their children as much as she did. Because Vick had kept Cody's existence a secret from everyone except her twin, she hadn't been able to ask the rest of her sisters those sorts of questions.

Looking back, Vick knew why she hadn't immediately told Leah, who'd been a surrogate mother to her, that she was pregnant and asked for her advice. Partly, she'd been ashamed. Who got "accidentally" pregnant in this day and age? Partly, she'd been afraid of being judged for the choice she'd already made to give up her child. Partly, she hadn't wanted to burden her sister with one more problem, when she already had enough difficulties of her own.

Mostly, she'd kept her pregnancy, the birth of her child, and her small part in his life a secret from her sisters because she was pretty sure they would have urged her to take Sullivan back to court and demand more visitation, visitation she hadn't believed she deserved.

Over the years, her attitude had changed. Now, not only did she believe she was entitled to more time with her son, she believed he deserved more time with his mother.

"You're awfully quiet," Pete said.

This was supposed to be a fun evening out. Vick didn't want to spend it recounting the past or complaining about Sullivan, first hiring a babysitter without saying a word to her, and then skipping out without telling her where he was going or when he would be back.

She put a smile on her face and unclenched her hands, which she'd stuck in her coat pockets. She would be double-damned if she let Sullivan ruin her night out.

She'd first met Pete at a local government meeting, where she was arguing the county should commit to protecting more grizzly habitat, and talking to him had always been easy.

So why was she having so much trouble coming up with something to say?

"No word about the grizzly that attacked Mike?" she asked.

Pete shook his head, then shot her a hangdog look. "I thought we had an agreement about bear talk."

Ten minutes into their first date, all of which she'd spent talking about grizzlies, Pete had laughed and said, "If it's all the same to you, I'd rather talk about humans—us—than bears."

Vick wrinkled her nose, to acknowledge the subject of bears was off-limits and said, "Fine. How was your week?"

"I spent the whole of it hunting for that wounded grizzly."

Vick laughed and shook her head. "Now who's breaking the rules?"

Pete grinned. "You asked."

"What *else* did you do?"

Pete spent the rest of the journey to Casey's relating the various incidents that kept a deputy sheriff busy in Flathead County, a lot of which concerned auto accidents, domestic disputes, missing tourists, and teenage vandalism. When they arrived, she resisted the urge to get out of the truck on her own, waiting instead for Pete to come around and open the door. When he put his hands to her waist to lift her down, her heart fluttered. His touch was strong and sure. And the littlest bit possessive.

That sudden burst of sexual awareness was enough

to make her realize that, if Sullivan weren't in the picture, she would have been happy to pursue a more serious relationship with Pete.

So why don't you? If Sullivan hasn't changed his mind about you in all this time, what makes you think he's ever going to seek you out?

Her twin would say she'd been flying in a holding pattern, waiting for a place to land. After that incident in the bathroom, Sullivan had been a ghost. What was she waiting for? When was she going to allow herself to move on with her life?

Vick had automatically put her hands on Pete's shoulders when he lifted her, and she kept them there as he slid her down the front of his body. She could feel the strength in his arms, but with their coats separating them, not much else. When her feet touched the ground, she tilted her head slightly and focused her gaze on his eyes, which were mostly in shadow.

He hesitated, searching her face, and she felt his gaze shift from eyes to cheekbones, to nose, and land, at last, on her mouth.

Vick wondered if there was something she was doing with her face or her body that caused so many of the men she dated to seem unsure that she would welcome their kisses. She didn't move forward or back, just continued to watch. And wait.

She kept her eyes focused on Pete's as he lowered his head, letting them slide closed as their mouths met. His lips were warm and supple and . . . tentative. She was shocked at how much she wanted him to deepen the kiss. When his tongue finally slid between her lips, she leaned her body into his, needing to be closer, hoping to feel more.

She was left wanting when he suddenly stepped back. She looked up at him through lazy, half-lidded eyes, wondering why he'd ended the kiss.

She bit back a gasp when she saw a huge shadow at his left shoulder.

Then Sullivan said, "You two are going to freeze your asses off out here. See you inside."

Vick felt a flare of fury that he'd interrupted their kiss. She saw a muscle jerk in Pete's jaw as he clenched his teeth and knew he was equally annoyed at the interruption. His eyes followed Sullivan, and if looks could kill, Sullivan would have dropped stone-cold dead before he reached the door.

Vick stepped back, forcing Pete to release her. The mood was broken. Whatever might have happened, if they'd been left to themselves, wasn't going to happen now.

Chapter 17

RYE HAD FOUGHT the urge to come to Casey's, knowing Pete and Lexie would likely wind up there. He'd driven around for a half hour, looking for somewhere else in Whitefish he wanted to go, then muttered, "To hell with it," and headed for the bar, which had first been opened as the Sprague Saloon in 1905. The wide plank floors and brick walls were remnants of the taverns and billiard halls that had made their home there ever since.

He made a point of staying downstairs, rather than heading to the bar that served the dance floor up one flight, where he supposed Pete and Lexie would spend their evening. He slipped onto a backless leather-padded stool and ordered a Jack Daniel's neat.

The female bartender, someone new, gave him a million-watt smile and said, "Are you sure you wouldn't rather have our special?"

The girl didn't know he was a regular at Casey's, or she wouldn't have suggested he have a huckleberry margarita. It was hard for Rye to believe that hunters and fishermen who came to Whitefish actually drank such a concoction, but since Montana was known for its huckleberries—purple and sweet, but half the size of a small blueberry—he supposed it gave them something to talk about when they got home.

He shot her a look that was all the answer she needed, and shortly had his drink in front of him. Rye stared at it without picking it up. He didn't want a drink. He wanted to go back and live the past week over again and do a better job of it.

Dealing with Lexie had been stressful, because every interaction, especially since their naked encounter in the bathroom, was layered with repressed desire. He winced when he thought of the immature way he'd dealt with having her in his home, avoiding her as much as possible, then pulling that stunt tonight, setting up a babysitter without telling her and stalking out.

He'd done no better with his mother. Every meeting between them at the hospital had been fraught with undercurrents. He'd confined his conversations to questions about Mike's condition, his gut wrenching every time he looked at his brother, whose features were unrecognizable, a horror mask of bruised and swollen flesh, and ragged lines of stitches sewing him back together. He'd sat beside Mike, touching a small spot on his brother's arm that wasn't covered with stitches and told him to fight for his life, that he was needed and loved. All the while, he was wondering whether he was Mike's half brother or no relation at all.

His mother sat on the other side of Mike's bed looking too wrung out, too overwhelmed, to handle one more burden. Rye kept putting off the confrontation about the discovery he'd made, because something else lurked in her faded hazel eyes. Something more than fear for Mike. Panic.

So he hadn't asked the questions that begged for answers. And the tension he felt simmered and bubbled beneath the surface, threatening to boil over.

It was no wonder, with his emotions so close to the surface, he'd overreacted when he saw Pete kissing Lexie in the parking lot. The surge of jealousy he felt was so powerful it had been all Rye could do not to smash his fist into Pete's mouth. He'd felt a flare of roaring heat suffuse his body when Pete's hand slid around Lexie's nape. His heart had lurched when it dawned on him what he was seeing.

She's kissing him back.

He had no rights where Lexie was concerned. None. He'd gone for years without seeking her out. Why this sudden rush of possessiveness? What was it about seeing another man kissing her that made him want to claim her for himself?

Perhaps his change of heart was tied up with the

knowledge that his world was no longer merely black or white. That he'd been holding her to a standard that was unrealistic. People made mistakes. There was a great deal of gray out there. Otherwise, how could he explain his father keeping such a secret from him?

Unless his father hadn't known the truth.

Rye growled. It was impossible to imagine his mom lying to his dad. He'd seen how much they loved and trusted and respected each other. Could their whole marriage have been built on a lie? Had his mother been pregnant with some other man's child when she married his father? What other explanation was there? His blood type required the existence of at least one other person.

Unless he was adopted and had two unknown parents out there somewhere.

Rye heard a mellow voice and a quiet guitar and realized that the entertainment tonight was just a guy singing ballads in the corner. He heaved a sigh of relief. Pete wasn't going to be putting his arms around Lexie on the dance floor upstairs. There was no need to hang around with his knuckles dragging to protect his woman like some caveman. In fact, he'd better get himself out of here before he did something he'd regret.

Rye tossed down his whiskey and pulled out a bill to pay for his drink. When he turned to leave, he realized Pete and Lexie were sitting at one of the dining tables near the front window.

Leave, Rye. Get your butt out the door.

Instead, he turned and walked across the room. "Too bad about the dancing."

"There's dancing later," Pete said. "The DJ doesn't come in until ten. We decided to get something to eat first."

"Mind if I join you?" Rye was already pulling out the wooden chair next to Lexie before Pete could answer.

Pete pursed his lips ruefully. "Sure. Why not?"

Lexie shot Rye a sideways look and said, "Is your date meeting you here?"

"I don't have a date."

"You came all the way to Whitefish to have one drink?"

"And dinner."

"You were about to leave," she pointed out. "I saw you pay your tab."

So she'd been watching him. Was that a good thing? He smiled and said, "I suddenly realized I'm hungry." He kept waiting for one or the other of them to tell him to leave, but neither one did.

So he stayed.

Every so often, Lexie's jean-clad thigh would brush against his under the table. She quickly moved it away, but he watched a flush rise on her throat each time it happened. He was careful not to touch her on purpose, not to let their elbows or their hands meet, but he was aware of every move she made, every word she spoke, every glance she exchanged with the other man.

Rye wasn't the least bit hungry, and he had to

choke down the hamburger he ordered. He used eating as an excuse not to talk. He didn't have anything to say. He just listened. And learned a few things he would rather not have known, because they made Lexie seem more fallible, more human.

"I can't believe your father and Angus Flynn are still fighting over something that happened forty years ago," Pete said.

"He blamed my father for his sister's death, and he's been trying to ruin him ever since," Lexie replied. "Unfortunately, it wasn't only our fathers who ended up feuding. My three sisters and I spent a lot of our youth figuring out ways to make the lives of Angus's four sons—Aiden, Brian, Connor, and Devon—miserable. We did everything from poking a hole in a gas tank so a couple of 'those awful Flynn boys' would have to walk home from a hunting trip in the wilderness, to gluing their boots to the mudroom floor. We shaved the hair on one of their 4-H calves, and they retaliated by putting salt in Leah's 4-H cherry pie."

Pete laughed. "That just sounds like good fun."

"I agree. If it had stopped at that. But Eve's cinch was cut before a barrel racing competition, and when the saddle rolled, she ended up with a broken arm. So Leah sliced Aiden's cinch during the calf roping, and he ended up with a broken leg."

"Whoa. That sounds a lot more serious."

"It gets worse."

"Worse?" Pete asked. "How?"

"Aiden bet Brian he could make Leah fall in love with him."

"Uh-oh."

"He won. When Leah found out the truth, she was heartbroken."

"That's too bad," Pete said. "Did the Flynns make their bet public as revenge for one of those tricks you played on them?"

"Taylor—my twin—is married to Brian Flynn, who made the bet with Aiden in the first place. She told me about it."

"There's another one of you out there?" Pete asked, his eyebrows rising nearly to his hairline.

Lexie has a twin? There are two women like her out there in the world? Rye was appalled at his ignorance.

"We're not identical," Lexie said. "Taylor and I don't look much alike. She's far more beautiful."

"I find that impossible to believe," Pete said, taking her hand in his.

Rye gritted his teeth and bit the inside of his cheek.

Lexie smiled. "We were best friends growing up. Taylor's expecting twins, and I was planning to be there when she delivers." She shot a look at Rye. "Now, I'm not so sure that'll be possible."

"We can make arrangements for Cody's care while you're gone," Rye interjected.

She looked Rye in the eye and said, "I'd love to take him with me. So my family can meet him."

"They've never met him?" Pete said. "He's five years old!"

Lexie pulled her hand free of Pete's and knotted it with the other on the table in front of her. "They would have needed to come to Montana to meet him, since the custody agreement doesn't allow me to take him out of state."

Rye felt Pete's eyes on him, making it clear what a sonofabitch he thought Rye was for keeping Cody from meeting his Wyoming relatives. He felt his ears getting red, but he wasn't about to make excuses to Pete Harrison. What Lexie had told Pete was the truth, but not the *whole* truth.

Rye had given Lexie permission to take Cody to Jackson Hole to meet her family the previous Christmas, only to discover that she hadn't yet told them about Cody's existence. He'd reneged on his promise, because he didn't think it was fair to Cody to put him in that situation. Rye had insisted she break the news to her family *before* she showed up with Cody in tow.

"You've told your family that you have a son living here in Montana?" Rye asked.

She lifted her chin. "Taylor knows. And she's the one I plan to visit."

He bit his tongue, unwilling to argue with her.

Pete's phone rang. As he retrieved it from his jeans pocket he said, "Sorry, but I have to keep it on." He looked at the screen, answered, and said, "Where? I'll be there as soon as I can." He wore an apologetic expression when he turned back to Lexie. "We'll have to cut this short. There's a five-car pileup on U.S. 93 south of Kalispell."

Rye said, "I can take Lexie home. That'll save you time."

Pete looked torn. He focused his gaze on Lexie and said, "Would you mind?"

She took her lower lip in her teeth for twenty full seconds before she said, "Not at all. Your job is important. Do what you need to do."

Pete threw enough money on the table to cover the check and the tip and said, "I'll make it up to you another time."

Rye was feeling relieved knowing that Pete wouldn't be holding Lexie in his arms while they danced or holding her hand during the drive home or maybe kissing her and doing a little petting in his truck before she headed inside.

She must have read his mind, because when Pete rose to leave, she did, too. She intercepted Pete on his way to the coatrack and twined her arms around his neck, pressing her body to his from breasts to hips. She whispered something in his ear that made him smile, then kissed him, all the while watching Rye with one eye over Pete's shoulder, making sure he was seeing what she was doing in explicit detail.

It was hard to miss the fact that her tongue was in Pete's mouth, and his was in hers. Rye wouldn't have watched, except it was like passing that five-car pileup on the highway. He couldn't seem to turn away.

Pete finally broke the kiss, his fingers sieving

through Lexie's hair before he said something Rye couldn't hear that made her laugh. Then Pete grabbed his coat, slung his arms into it, and hurried out the door.

A moment later, Lexie was back at the table, but she didn't sit next to Rye. She took the spot Pete had vacated. She looked him in the eye and said, "I think it's time we had a talk."

Chapter 18

VICK FOCUSED HER narrowed gaze on Sullivan. "I don't appreciate your tagging along on my date." He didn't look the least bit repentant. She arched a brow and waited. "No apology?"

Sullivan met her gaze with lazy-lidded eyes. "I'm not sorry."

She hitched in a breath. "What's going on, Sullivan?"

"My name is Rye."

The sound of his voice, rough and low, sent a shiver down her spine. Vick shook her head, confused by what she saw in Sullivan's eyes. Or rather, not believing what she saw. Tension always flared between them whenever they got within ten feet of each other. This was something else. Something more compelling. Something more powerful. Something that had lain dormant for years and been reignited during their naked encounter in the bathroom.

Vick rose abruptly, her chair screeching on the wooden floor. "I want to go home."

"Sure. Let's go."

Then she realized that leaving the bar wouldn't really solve her problem. She was going to be trapped with Ryan Sullivan in the cab of his pickup for the entire time it took to get back to his ranch north of town. She grabbed her coat, but he took it from her and held it until she slipped her arms inside. He turned her around and zipped her into it, an act she found surprisingly intimate, before shoving his arms into his own coat. She hurried away from the masculine hand she felt at her back, guiding her toward the door.

When she got outside, Vick realized she had no idea where Sullivan had parked.

"Around the corner," he said, aiming her in the opposite direction from the one she was headed.

She grabbed the door handle as soon as she reached his pickup, in an attempt to avoid the courtesy he'd been showing her so far. The door was locked. She turned to him in exasperation. "Who locks their doors in Whitefish?"

"I have a rifle racked in the back window and a Glock in the glove compartment."

"Oh." So maybe locking the door made sense. She waited impatiently for the click that signaled the door was unlocked and managed not to jerk when he put an arm under her elbow to assist her into his pickup.

Frosty plumes rose inside the cab, which was how she knew she was hyperventilating. She forced herself to take a deep breath and let it out. Sullivan wasn't going to do anything she didn't want him to do. But that was the problem, wasn't it? She wanted him to kiss her and hold her and touch her . . . and put himself inside her.

The danger of that was obvious. She didn't want to get hurt. And she didn't trust Sullivan's motives where she was concerned. Why now? She'd dated other men, and he hadn't made a peep. What was different about tonight?

She gave Sullivan a sideways glance. His jaw muscles flexed, as though his teeth were gritted. "What's going on, Rye?"

She hadn't intended to use his first name. She had too many memories of using it the night they'd spent together. Calling him "Sullivan" all these years had kept him at an emotional distance. But something had happened tonight to bring down the wall he'd put up between them.

He huffed out a breath and said, "I'm tired of fighting this . . . thing . . . between us."

She angled her body to focus on his face, but he stubbornly refused to look at her, keeping his eyes on the road. "Why now?"

"Why not?"

"That's not an answer."

"Life is short. Anything can happen. There are no guarantees."

"So this—" She gestured a hand between them. "Is what? A response to the grizzly attack on Mike?"

"That's certainly part of it."

She felt the hairs prickle on her arms as she realized what else might be involved. "Does this change in attitude toward me have anything to do with what you found out about yourself at the hospital?"

"You mean that my parents may not be my parents? If somebody could give me away, I'm thinking what you did wasn't so bad. At least you realized your mistake and did something about it."

"I thought you didn't give second chances."

"I've been rethinking that whole black-and-white philosophy my father taught me. Especially in light of the colossal lie I was told my whole life."

He swore as the truck skidded on black ice and veered toward the sturdy trunk of a very large pine. Vick reflexively grabbed the dash. Her heart rose to her throat before the pickup finally slithered to a stop, leaning perilously over the berm and threatening to roll into a gully beside the road. She was afraid to move, for fear her weight would be all that was needed to tumble them the rest of the way over.

Sullivan was out of the truck an instant later standing on the highway, grabbing her hands as she scrambled past the steering wheel, and pulling her out of the pickup. His arms folded tightly around her, and she clung to him, marveling that they'd survived unhurt.

He exhaled a shuddering sigh. "That was close."

Too close. End of the line close. No more chances close, Vick thought. It could have been all over for both of them. She met Sullivan's gaze in the moonlight and saw that he'd experienced the same terror as she had—and was feeling the same aftershocks.

A moment later, his mouth sought hers, his tongue finding its way inside, insisting she catch up and take the dangerous curves along with him, then appealing for more, enticing her to join him on a wild ride of passion.

He twisted his hands in her hair, holding her head so he could slake his thirst, as she twined her arms around his neck, but their bodies were robbed of further touch because of their bulky coats. Their breathing was laborious, their tongues dueling as they mimicked the sex act, until a blaring horn and a pair of bright headlights forced them apart.

It's still there, Vick thought with despair as she stared up at Sullivan, her chest heaving, the blood racing in her veins. Everything that had been there that long-ago night was still there. But now those memories were mixed with new sensations. The smell of a different aftershave. The callused pads of Rye's fingers hot against her cold skin. The scratchiness of a two-day-old beard against her cheek, when he'd been clean-shaven. The supple play of his lips against hers, more desperate and demanding. The strength of his embrace, which promised a surely elusive safety from all harm.

Everything about Ryan Sullivan appealed to her.

Why him? Why this man above all others? What was it about Ryan Sullivan that made her come alive in his arms?

Vick wondered if the look in her eyes was as unsatisfied—and guarded—as his.

He moved her out of danger from traffic and said, "Let me get my truck back on the road, so we can get out of here."

He didn't say where they were going, whether back home or to a hotel in Whitefish or her lonely cabin in the woods. She didn't really give a damn.

Once he'd eased his pickup onto the highway, he reached across the cab and opened the door for her. She quickly climbed in and shut the door and buckled herself in.

She saw he was headed the same direction and asked, "Where are we going?"

"To hell probably," he muttered, keeping his eyes on the road.

So much for getting a direct answer. When he took the turnoff for the Rafter S, Vick soughed out a breath she hadn't realized she'd been holding. Was that it? Was he going to pretend nothing had happened? Were they going back to their separate rooms at his ranch?

"Rye . . ." Vick wasn't sure what to say, because she wasn't sure what she wanted. Or rather, she knew what she wanted, she just wasn't sure whether she ought to ask for it. What if having sex caused a rift between them, and she had to move out? She would lose this precious chance to spend time with her son. Was one night of passion worth the price she might have to pay?

What if it's not just one night? What if it's the rest of your life?

What if it wasn't? What if Sullivan was merely satisfying his curiosity? What if he just wanted sex because he was . . . How had he put it? *Tired of fighting this . . . thing . . . between us.*

He pulled his pickup to a stop at the back door, unsnapped his seat belt, and angled his body toward her. When he opened his mouth to speak, she pressed her fingertips against his lips.

"No, Rye. As much as I want . . . this . . . I don't think it's a good idea. So I'm saying no."

She fumbled to get her seat belt loose, then shoved open the door, and ran for the house.

He caught her before she'd taken five steps and turned her around. "You didn't give me a chance to speak."

"I had a pretty good idea what you were going to say."

"All right. Let's hear it." He made a "come on" gesture.

"You want to finish what we started."

"I do. Absolutely. But not what we started tonight."

She frowned in confusion and waited for him to explain.

Sullivan yanked off his Stetson and shoved a frustrated hand through his hair, before putting it back on and tugging it low on his forehead. "I want a chance to finish what we started in Jackson."

Vick's frown grew deeper, putting creases in her forehead and between her brows. "What we started? Nothing got started in Jackson."

He shook his head. "Our chance for a future together. Our chance to spend our lives together. You cut that short by running away. I want a chance to see what might have happened if you'd stuck around."

Chapter 19

RYE DIDN'T KNOW where he'd gotten the nerve to speak, but he wasn't sorry he'd poured out his guts. He wasn't sure what he'd expected Lexie to say or do, but he was stunned by her response.

She laughed.

The burble of sound was more amused than hysterical, Rye thought, but still disconcerting.

Her laughter stopped abruptly, and her voice was harsh when she spoke. "It's too late, Rye. You can't turn one night of bliss into more than it was. You know nothing about me."

"I know one very important thing," he said. "Cody is the center of your life, its beating heart. Do you deny it?"

"No." She lifted her chin defiantly, as though it

was a shameful thing to admit, when she was supposedly so dedicated to her work.

"And you can't discount what we feel when we're together."

"Lust?" She said the word like an epithet.

Unfortunately, he couldn't deny he felt lust. And he wasn't in any position to suggest his feelings for her might be something more lofty. Love wasn't even a glimmer on the horizon.

"Lust isn't a bad thing."

"Unless it's the *only* thing," she snapped.

"Like I said, we need time to see whether we're compatible in other ways besides sex."

The frown was back between her brows. "What is it you're suggesting?"

"I'm not sure, exactly. Dating seems absurd when we're living in the same house."

"I'm not going to have sex with you."

"Did I mention sex?" He'd been thinking plenty about it, but the fact was he hadn't put it on the table. At least, not since she'd taken it off in no uncertain terms.

"I'm listening," she said.

He had no idea where to go from here. "We could commit to having meals together."

"We're already doing that."

"And washing dishes together."

"Also doing that."

"And spending time together doing things with Cody."

"I would love that," she admitted.

"Let's try that for a week, and see how it goes. Agreed?" he said, extending his hand.

She set her gloved hand in his, met his gaze, and said, "Agreed."

He pulled her close and leaned down, waiting to see if she was willing to seal their deal with a kiss. She'd just turned her face up to his, when the back porch light flicked on, blinding him.

Rye held up a hand against the glare as the screen door opened, and his sister stuck her head out. "You can send Mizz Grizzly Bear home," Amy Beth said. "I'm here to take care of Cody."

Rye almost groaned aloud. He'd completely forgotten about making that phone call to Amy Beth. He loved his little sister, but sometimes she was a real pain in the ass. He caught the stricken look on Lexie's face and grabbed her hand to keep her from bolting, as he tromped up the steps and forced Amy Beth back into the kitchen. "What are you doing home? Mom told you to stay at school."

"I was worried about Mike," she said. "And Mom."

"Mom?"

"She sounded . . . funny. Strange. Not like Mom."

Rye knew what Amy Beth meant, because he had a pretty good idea *why* their mom sounded "strange." She was holding on to a pretty big secret, and the longer she kept it, the heavier it weighed on her soul.

Amy Beth's intuition was correct, but her timing couldn't have been worse. The problem was how to get rid of her, now that she was here.

Rye could feel Lexie tugging on his hand, trying to edge backward out the door. He met her gaze and said, "Don't go," then turned to Amy Beth. "You'll have to stay in Mom's room tonight, since Lexie is using your room. You can head back to Missoula tomorrow."

"I'm staying here till Mike's well."

"There's nothing you can do for Mike that isn't already being done. There's no sense getting behind in your studies. It'll just be one more thing Mom has to worry about, and that Mike will feel guilty about, once he's well enough to come home."

"Mike would—"

"Mike wouldn't want you to fuss over him," Rye said flatly.

Amy Beth dropped her chin, acknowledging the point. When she lifted her head again, tears had brimmed in her eyes.

Rye's gut twisted. He couldn't stand it when his little sister was hurting. He let go of Lexie and pulled Amy Beth into his arms, holding her close and rocking her. "Mike is going to be fine," he said in a soothing voice. He wanted to believe that. Had to believe it. "We need to keep doing what has to be done. Mom will keep an eye on Mike and let us know if we need to be there."

"School seems so unimportant with Mike in such bad shape," Amy Beth said, her voice muffled against his chest.

"It's going to take Mike a long time to get well." *If he gets well at all.* "It doesn't make sense to put our lives on hold. You need to finish up your classes, so you'll be available to help over the summer, if Mike needs you."

Amy Beth heaved a sigh. "I suppose you're right." She looked up at him, her mouth twisted in a rueful smile. "You always are." She freed herself from his arms and looked over his shoulder. "At least *she's* gone."

Rye glanced over his shoulder and saw that Lexie had taken off. He let go of his sister, shaking his head in frustration as he turned to stare at the door. "Damn it all to hell!"

"Were you really about to kiss her when I turned on the light?"

"What?" Rye turned back around in time to see the speculative look in Amy Beth's hazel eyes, so similar to their mother's. He felt an embarrassing flush heating his throat and stuck his hands in his back pockets.

"Because it looked to me like the two of you were getting pretty cozy. What's going on, Rye?"

"Lexie's been helping out with Cody while Mom's gone."

"I thought you hated her guts."

"I never hated her. I just—"

"Really?" Amy Beth interrupted. "Then why have you never had a good word to say about her?"

"I haven't said much of anything about her."

"Exactly! So why did you invite her to move in? And don't say it was because you needed her help with Cody."

"But I did—I do—need her help."

"You could have asked me."

"You need to be in school."

"You know I would have come at a moment's notice."

"She's Cody's mother."

"Yeah, and I'm his aunt." She stuck her hands on her hips. "Spill. What's going on, Rye?"

Rye knew Amy Beth wasn't going to stop until she got an answer. So he gave her one. "I want to get to know her better."

"Why?"

"Give me a break, Amy Beth." When she arched an inquisitive brow, he added, "This is none of your business."

"Holy crap! You want to jump her bones." She leaned back against the sink and crossed her arms. "You sly dog. What happened to make you cross the Waterloo?"

Of course Amy Beth had gotten to the crux of the matter. Rye shrugged. He didn't owe his sister an explanation. He couldn't tell her the truth anyway. Not until he knew it himself.

"The point is you're not needed here," he said. "The sooner you return to school the better."

"Are you sure Grizzly Girl will come back?" She held up a hand when he opened his mouth to object to that description of Cody's mother and said, "Vick lit out of here the first chance she got."

"She'll be back because she wants to spend time with Cody."

"And with you?"

"Yes, pest. With me, too."

"This is too delicious! I can't wait to share it with—" She cut herself off. Tears welled in her eyes again, and one spilled over. "With Mike," she whispered.

He took her in his arms again as she sobbed. He didn't reassure her that everything would be all right. Things were pretty damned messed up right now, and there was no telling what might happen with Mike or what the fallout might be from the secret Rye was privy to now. Besides, his own throat was too painfully swollen to speak.

Amy Beth sniffed, then pushed herself away. "You better go after her tonight. If you wait until tomorrow, you're liable to change your mind about having her around. Or she's liable to change hers. I don't want to be responsible for ruining the romance of the century."

"You won't be ruining—"

"Anything," she finished for him. "Just go. Tell her I'll be out of here by tomorrow, and she's welcome to use my room."

"You're a pretty great sister," Rye said softly.

"It's easy to be a great sister when I have a seriously stupendous brother like you."

Rye croaked a laugh, because speech was impossible. He grabbed Amy Beth's arms, kissed her on the forehead, then leapt back as she tried batting him away. A moment later, he was on his way to find Lexie and talk her into coming back.

Chapter 20

VICK WAS HALFWAY home when she realized she was going in the wrong direction—away from Cody and Rye. She heaved a sigh of vexation. She shouldn't have run away. She should have stayed and fought for her right to spend time with Cody. And with Rye. For a long time, she'd felt like she deserved to be punished for her decision to give up Cody. She'd considered the restricted access she had to her son as a penance and had stoically endured it.

She'd also wallowed in regret after bolting like a scared rabbit from the powerful—and frightening—feelings for Rye that had emerged during the single night they'd spent together. Loving a man was simply too risky. Easier not to get involved. Except, in both instances, her attempts to avoid pain had left her without a child she'd loved from the moment of his birth and a man she might have loved forever.

Vick believed she'd finally forgiven herself for making two such monumentally bad decisions and moved on, stronger than before. But look what she'd done. At the first sign of resistance from Rye's family, she'd bolted.

Vick shook her head in disgust, slowed her pickup, and looked for a place to turn around. Unfortunately, the narrow, rutted dirt road that led to her cabin didn't have a lot of space for maneuvering. Considering the consequences if she got stuck in the mud and snow, she decided to drive the rest of the way home, pick up a few things she'd forgotten when she'd first packed, and head straight back to the Rafter S.

Vick was in her bedroom when she heard a knock at the back door. Her first thought was that Pete must have been released from the scene of the accident sooner than he'd expected and had come to see if she wanted to spend more time together. As she headed for the kitchen door, she realized it wasn't Pete's face she wanted to see when she opened it. Which meant she needed to tell the deputy how she felt. It wasn't fair to string him along to avoid facing her feelings for another man.

"Pete, I—" Vick cut herself off when she discovered someone else standing on her back porch. Her heart jumped. "Rye. What are you doing here?"

"May I come in?"

She hesitated, then took a step back to make room

for him. She shivered, closed the door to keep the cold air out, then put her back against it. "I was just picking up a few things before I head back to your place. Don't tell me I'm not welcome. I don't care what Amy Beth says. I'm Cody's mom, and I intend—"

His kiss cut her off.

Rye's arms tightened around her, and he took possession of her mouth as though he'd been waiting a thousand years to taste her. All the longing, all the unrequited need she'd thwarted were there in the urgency of his seeking tongue. Passion rose with startling speed, and it was hard to catch her breath, impossible to catch up with the overwhelming wave of emotion that threatened to knock her off her feet. His hands tangled in her hair, and she gasped as he angled her head and took her deep again.

She craved his kisses. Trembled at the feel of his hands on her face. Shivered as his hot breath trailed along her throat. She wanted it all too much. Wanted it enough that, if she lost it, she would be devastated. The more yearning she felt to have Rye finish what he'd started, the more fear she felt that she was making yet another mistake.

She braced her palms against his muscular chest and whispered, "Rye."

Vick didn't know why she hadn't said "No." That single word would have stopped him cold. Saying Rye's name in a throaty voice had the exact opposite effect. It was another sign of the ambivalence she felt. She wanted Rye, had yearned for his touch ever since she'd left his bed in Jackson. But then, as now, fear warred with desire.

Tonight, desire was winning the battle.

She froze at the sound of a heavy knock, and they both turned to stare at the kitchen door.

"You expecting company?" Rye asked.

"No."

He met her gaze and said in a husky voice, "You want to answer that?"

Considering how isolated her cabin was, they both knew whom it had to be. "Not really," she said. "But I think I should." Sure enough, when she opened the door, she found Pete standing on her back porch.

Before she could speak he said, "Rye's truck is here."

"He came over to . . ." *Make love to me.* She didn't speak the rest of the sentence, but she was sure Pete got the gist of it.

"May I come in?" he said.

A shadow appeared at Vick's shoulder, and she felt the shimmering tension as Rye took a stand at her right hip. The two men squared off like barnyard dogs, stiff-legged, neck hairs hackled.

"Guess you changed your mind," Pete said to Rye.

"Guess I did," Rye replied.

Pete's shoulders squared and his leather-gloved hands fisted, while Rye's stance widened. Vick realized that if she didn't say something, they would likely go for each other's jugulars. "I'm sorry, Pete."

She saw the flicker of disappointment in his dark eyes, watched his lips flatten and a muscle jerk in his jaw, and realized he was more invested in the possibility of this relationship than she'd thought.

"You sure about this?" he said, his gaze shifting from her to Rye and back again.

She would have spoken, except her throat had suddenly swollen closed. She gave a jerky nod.

"Good night, Vick. See you 'round." He turned his attention to his rival, touched a forefinger to the brim of his Stetson, and ducked his chin in acknowledgment of defeat. "Rye."

Rye nodded and said, "Pete."

Vick stood frozen, struck numb with disbelief at the ultimate civility of the encounter between the two men, as Rye shoved the door closed. Before she could say a word, he swept her into his arms with a curt, "Bedroom?"

To the victor goes the spoils.

Vick just had time for that thought to flash in her head before Rye followed her pointing finger down the hall, his long strides eating up the distance and giving her no time to change her mind.

He dropped her on her feet beside her perfectly made bed, in a room lit by a tiny night-light along the wall, and threw back the covers. He was already reaching for his belt buckle as she shoved his sheepskin coat off his shoulders. He popped several buttons on her wool shirt, and she heard them clatter across the wooden floor, creating raucous music along with the jingle of his belt buckle and his zipper coming down. She wasn't far behind Rye, toeing off her Ugg boots and unzipping her jeans.

He yanked his wool shirt off over his head along with the long johns shirt under it, then shoved her bra up out of his way, his mouth latching on to a nipple as his hand slid inside her unzipped jeans to claim her sex, which was already hot and wet.

He murmured his approval in the brief moment before his mouth found hers again.

She thrust her hands into his hair and returned his kiss with an urgency that shocked her. He fumbled as he shoved her jeans and scrap of underwear completely out of his way, but his hands were sure as he grasped her bare ass and pulled her tight against the pulsing length of him. Their breathing was harsh as her nails dug into his shoulders, and her breasts molded themselves to his chest.

He toppled her onto the bed, unwilling to wait, shoving his own jeans and hers down far enough for their bodies to mate. He was inside her in a single thrust. She whimpered, lifting her hips as she struggled to be closer, urging him deeper inside.

He suddenly stopped and looked into her eyes. "Are you protected?"

"The pill."

He smiled wryly.

That hadn't worked the first time, but the chances of it failing again had to be infinitesimal. For a moment she thought he would speak, but he merely tucked a stray curl behind her ear before his mouth found hers again, his tongue mimicking the sex act, while his body held still inside her.

She felt inner muscles clench at the feel of him throbbing and fought not to come. She didn't want this to end. She didn't want him to leave. She didn't want to face the decisions that would have to be made when this was over and done.

Rye made a guttural sound in his throat and began to thrust again, long, deep strokes that reached inside to her core. His mouth found her breast, and he sucked and bit to the edge of pain.

She clasped his shoulders and hung on for dear life, feeling her body reach for the bliss they'd experienced once before. For something exceptional. For something that had never happened before or since.

At long last, when she thought she couldn't bear the pleasure anymore, he spilled himself inside her with a primitive cry of satisfaction. A moment later, her orgasm rolled over her, tumbling her like waves crashing against a rocky shore.

He held her close for only a moment before he separated them and rolled onto his back, his arm stretched across his forehead hiding his face.

She felt bereft. And suddenly afraid. Where were they supposed to go from here? Why had she let him in the door? Why had she let him into her bed? Why had she let him into her body?

Vick had often wondered if she'd imagined the magic she'd felt with Rye, how his touch was different from any other man's, how his kisses made her insides quiver. She'd forgotten the exhilaration she'd felt caressing the ribbed muscles in his chest, forgotten the feel of his buttocks in her hands as she wrapped her legs around his hips. Most of all, she'd forgotten the joy she'd experienced in the moments afterward, when their lungs heaved and he slid away, pulling her close to hold her next to his heart until their breathing was quiet again.

She remembered what he'd murmured before he'd slipped into sleep. *"I don't want this night to end."*

Tonight he wasn't speaking. It seemed a lifetime before he turned onto his side, perched his head on his palm, and stared down at her.

Vick felt self-conscious being half naked under Rye's intense gaze and resisted the urge to remove the bra twisted across her upper chest or otherwise cover herself.

"This is a hell of a thing," he said.

Vick sat up and turned her back on him, realizing with absolute and horrifying certainty that this had been another mistake. A really bad one. "You can leave anytime. There's nothing keeping you tied here." She flinched when she felt his hand on her shoulder and realized he was sitting up behind her.

"I wish that were true," he said.

She glanced over her shoulder. "Cody is—"

"This has nothing to do with our son."

He unsnapped her bra, and she pulled it down and off her arms and threw it aside. "Then what are you talking about?"

His hands slid around her and possessively cupped her breasts. "This."

She put her hands over his and lowered her head as he nosed her hair aside and kissed her nape. "This is just sex," she said.

"I wish that were true," he murmured for a second time, his breath heating her flesh.

"If it isn't just sex, what is it?" she demanded, doing her best not to succumb to his lovemaking before he explained himself.

Rye stopped kissing her, and his hands slid down to frame her waist. "Hell if I know."

She pulled herself free and bent to grab her shirt from the floor and pull it on before turning to face him. Unfortunately, it was missing enough buttons that she had to hold it closed with one hand. "Then I suggest you take yourself home until you figure it out."

She wasn't sure what she'd been hoping for when she'd given him the ultimatum. Maybe that he would give her a better explanation, to clear things up between them. Instead, he stood, pulled up his jeans, and tucked himself in—not easy in his surprising state of arousal—zipped his jeans, buckled his belt, and went hunting for the rest of his clothes. He found them and was dressed a few moments later. He grabbed his coat off the floor and turned to face her.

When he reached for her, she took a step back.

"I want to kiss you."

She shook her head, not trusting herself to speak over the knot of pain that had formed in her throat.

"I've tried to get over you," he said almost angrily. "Tried for years. It didn't work. Now that I've had another taste of you, I know what I feel isn't going to go away."

"This can't happen again." She met his gaze, her stomach in knots. "It's dangerous to get involved. Right now we're able to parent Cody without friction. But the truth is you've never forgiven me for the choice I made all those years ago."

He made a face, but he didn't deny it. He opened his mouth but closed it again without saying anything.

"Until that happens, I don't see a relationship between us going anywhere." She wanted to ask him why he'd come to her door tonight and what it meant that he had. She wanted to savor again the feeling of being cherished in his embrace. She wanted to rub her cheek against the whiskers that had burned her tender flesh as they made love.

"I better go."

She didn't say anything to stop him as he headed for the door to her bedroom, his cowboy boots, which he'd never removed, thumping on the hardwood floor.

He stopped when he got there and turned to face her. "I came here to tell you Amy Beth is heading home first thing in the morning. I'll need you to take Cody to kindergarten tomorrow and pick him up afterward."

It took her a moment to realize he was inviting her back into his home, despite what had just happened between them.

He hesitated before adding, "You might as well come for breakfast. I told Amy Beth she owes you an apology. You should be there to hear it before she leaves."

When Vick heard the kitchen door snap closed, she sank back onto her bed, pulled the covers up to her neck, and whispered the questions she should have asked Rye before he left: "What do you expect from me? What happens between us now?"

Chapter 21

RYE HAD THOUGHT long and hard for the past week about Lexie's claim that he didn't really know her. He was missing a lot of meaningless information, like her favorite color and her favorite food. But he was also missing information about important stuff, like whether she wanted more kids and whether more kids—which he wanted—would fit with her career. If their relationship was to move forward, he had to ask her about those things.

Rye's stomach was churning, and he realized he was afraid of the answers he might get. What if they had differing views that couldn't be compromised? What if they were sexually compatible but their lives didn't fit in any other way? What would he do then?

Stop it, Rye. Don't borrow trouble. Ask your

questions and listen to her answers. If you want Lexie Grayhawk in your life, you'll figure out a way to make it work.

At least, that was what he hoped. The memory of their night together—how it had begun and how it had ended—had also been on his mind. He took it as a good sign that Lexie had given Pete his marching orders. On the other hand, while he hadn't begun to slake his thirst for her, she'd made it clear sex was on hold until they knew each other better.

Which was why he'd suggested a family picnic today along the banks of the Stillwater River, which bordered his property.

Rye had figured he and Lexie would have a chance to talk while Cody played with Rusty. And since Cody was along, Rye wouldn't be tempted to try and seduce Lexie.

As the three of them stood on the edge of the swollen river, engorged by the melted snow from the mountains that crowded its banks, Rye made a point of telling Cody, "Be sure you and Rusty don't play too close to the edge."

"Okay, Daddy." Cody bounded away with Rusty on his heels.

He watched Lexie catch her lower lip in her teeth and asked, "Did you want to say something to him?"

She shook her head. "Cody needs to play without me hovering over him every minute. The only danger I see here is the river, and you've warned him about that."

"You're not worried about a grizzly leaping out at us from the forest?" he said with a wry smile.

"We're picnicking in a meadow, where a bear can see us in plenty of time to avoid us."

Rye spread a blanket on the grass, and once the food was set out, he called Cody to come eat his lunch. After they'd all consumed their ham sandwiches and potato chips and sodas, Cody took off to play with Rusty again, while Rye and Lexie relaxed on the blanket in the warm spring sunshine.

Rye never really took his eyes off his son, but his gaze kept sliding back to Lexie, who focused her attention on him as he peppered her with questions.

"Favorite color," he said.

"Blue. Yours?"

"Green. Favorite food?"

"Pizza."

"Mine's Black Angus steak. Rare," Rye volunteered.

"Of course it is. Music?"

"Anything country. You?"

"Me, too." She sat up and wrapped her arms around her knees. "Does this stuff really matter to you?"

He shrugged. "You said I didn't know you. I'm trying to find out . . . things . . . about you. What should I be asking?"

"Are you okay with me being rich?"

He'd been lying on his side and was startled into sitting up. "You've never acted like you had money. Are you rich?"

"I have a trust fund. It's how I bought the cabin."

"I thought you had a mortgage."

"Nope. I don't have as much cash as I would have had if my father hadn't gotten into financial trouble recently. But together with what I've earned at my job, I have a nice nest egg."

The Rafter S Ranch had been in Rye's family for so many generations there was no longer a mortgage on the house. But they'd borrowed money from time to time for improvements using the ranch as collateral. He was making payments on a loan right now to finance the construction that would double the size of the calving barn.

"I don't mind that you have money," he said, "if you don't mind that I don't."

She laughed. "Touché. What about kids?"

"I want more, if that's what you're asking. How about you?"

"I'd like at least one more," she admitted.

"How about three more?"

"Whoa! That's a lot of kids."

"Too many?" he asked.

"I'd have to think about it," she said. "My work is important to me. I wouldn't want to completely abandon it."

He realized this was the sort of revelation Lexie had been talking about, where they had differences in their hopes and dreams for the future that would have to be worked out.

The discussion felt too serious, too perilous, and

he opted for asking another trivial question. "Cats or dogs?"

"Dogs," she said with a twinkle in her eyes that set frogs jumping in his stomach.

"Whew!" he said, wiping imaginary sweat from his brow. "Rusty will be glad to hear that." He shook his head. "I can't believe I let Cody talk me into adopting that mutt. He sleeps the day away on the back porch, and if I don't keep an eagle eye on him, sneaks into the house to sleep the night away in Cody's bed."

She laughed and glanced toward the Stillwater, where Rusty was racing after a stick Cody had thrown.

He followed her gaze to the rough-haired terrier. The stick had landed in the rushing water. The dog leapt in after it and was quickly swept downriver by the current.

Cody ran hell-for-leather along the bank after the dog, yelling "Rusty! Come back! Rusty!"

"Cody! Watch out!" Rye yelled as he jumped to his feet and raced toward the river.

Cody turned toward him, but as he did, the bank crumbled under his boots. He shrieked, his arms pinwheeling as he tumbled backward into the water.

"He can't swim!" Lexie cried as she leapt up and sprinted after Rye.

"Cody's a strong swimmer," Rye shouted back.

At her shocked look he said, "He learned last summer. But the water's freezing, and his wet clothes will be heavy." Which just meant she was right to be scared shitless. Rye was running full tilt, and Lexie was keeping up with him, but Cody seemed to be moving farther away from them.

Lexie had obviously noticed the same thing. She whimpered and said, "Please, God. Please, God."

Rye saw a sopping-wet Rusty running along the bank. He'd obviously escaped the roaring water. To his amazement, the dog suddenly jumped back in. It took Rye a second to realize what he was seeing. Apparently, Cody had called Rusty to him, and when the dog swam close enough, his son grabbed Rusty's collar. A moment later, the big dog began swimming toward a tree trunk that had fallen partway into the water, hauling Cody along with him. Cody snagged a limb and hung on, while Rusty climbed his way up onto the rotted log.

"We're coming, Cody!" Rye shouted.

"Don't let go," Lexie called out.

It took a lifetime to reach his son, and his heart was in his throat the whole way.

"Be careful," Lexie warned, as Rye scooched his way out to the end of the rotten log on his belly. It seemed to take forever to get close enough to grab Cody's sleeve. But once he had a good hold, he quickly hauled his bedraggled, shivering son into his arms and hugged him tight.

"You're squishing me, Daddy," Cody protested.

Water rushed across Rye's feet, threatening to throw him off the log, and he realized his position was still precarious. He saw Lexie's outstretched hand and realized she'd crawled out along the fallen tree far enough to reach for Cody. He handed his son off to her and the two of them inched their way back along the log until they reached dry land.

Rye joined them just in time to be splattered with water as Rusty shook himself. Rye felt an ache in his throat as he sank to his knees and hugged the dog. "Thank you, Rusty," he muttered. The mutt that had been nothing but a nuisance, the mutt he'd resented having in the house, had just saved his son's life.

The picnic could have ended in disaster. It actually ended in a stony silence from Lexie that felt every bit as catastrophic. She was avoiding his eyes, avoiding his touch, avoiding him. He had no idea what he'd done wrong.

Or maybe he did. How could he not have told her about Cody's swim lessons? What was the big deal? He couldn't remember what he'd been thinking at the time. It was merely part and parcel of his efforts to punish Lexie for the mistake she'd made, a mistake she'd apologized for again and again.

He really was a bastard.

After Cody was buckled into his car seat, but before they stepped into the pickup to go home, Lexie pulled Rye aside so they were out of Cody's hearing.

"You should have told me," she said, her voice sharp as a razor.

"Told you what?"

"That Cody could swim. I was terrified he was going to drown. What else don't I know, Rye? What other knowledge about my son have you been keeping from me?"

"Nothing. I swear," he said, holding up one hand like a Boy Scout taking an oath. "I figured Cody would have mentioned the swim lessons. I won't let it happen again."

"You better not."

"That sounds like a threat," he said, his heart pounding. How had things gone so far sideways? He'd never seen Lexie so angry. His friendly family picnic was turning into something dark and dangerous.

"Which reminds me," she continued, "our custody agreement has to change. Whether we end up together or not, I need more time with my son."

"Wait a minute," Rye said, feeling his universe spinning out of control. "Where is this coming from?"

"From years of being deprived of my son's company, that's where," she snarled. "I guess it's a good thing I've got money and you don't, because however much it costs, I'm going to take you back to court and get my visitation rights revised."

"Take it easy," he said, reaching out to lay a hand on her shoulder. "We can do this without going to court."

"We can?" She jerked her shoulder so his hand dropped away. "How much more time are you willing to give me, Rye? How much time with Cody are you willing to give up?"

None. That was the word that came to mind. Obviously, that wasn't the answer she wanted to hear. Rye suddenly had some inkling of how horrible it must be for Lexie to have so little time with Cody. The thought of seeing his son even a minute less in a single day left him gutted. And Lexie had been living with that reality for four and a half long years.

"You're right," he said, his throat aching and his stomach in knots. "I've been unfair. Things have to change. But please, Lexie, give us a little time to work things out ourselves before you involve the courts."

She looked him in the eye and demanded, "How much time?"

"Until Mike comes home from the hospital. Okay?" Rye didn't know whether that was going to be two days, two weeks, or two months. He wanted his brother to get better, but he dreaded the confrontation he was sure to have with Lexie when Mike finally came home.

Chapter 22

RYE UNCLENCHED HIS fists and shook them out as he headed down the sunlit hallway toward the hospital room where Mike was fighting for his life. Rye's breathing was erratic and his heart was racketing in his chest. He wasn't a man who feared much of anything, but he dreaded confronting his mother about the secret he'd learned about his birth.

He just couldn't put it off any longer.

After the calamitous picnic yesterday, Rye was being forced to reevaluate his behavior toward Lexie Grayhawk. He would never have made the choice to give up his own flesh and blood for adoption, but he understood now why Lexie might have thought it was the best solution, and it was past time he stopped punishing her for it. If his biological parents could give him away, was what she'd done so awful? In the end, Lexie had realized the enormity of what she'd given up and taken steps to recover what she'd lost.

Not only that, but she'd continued being the best parent she could be, in spite of the obstacles he'd put in her path. Because of his behavior, not only was Rye farther than ever from any possibility of a relationship with her, but his rights to sole custody of Cody might be in jeopardy as well.

Until Mike returned home, they were going back to being cordial co-parents. Between now and then he had a lot of fast talking to do.

Shit.

Rye would have groaned, except he'd reached the door to his brother's room, which was open, and he didn't want his mother to hear him and ask what was wrong. He'd persistently ignored her not-too-subtle hints that Lexie was not only a good mother but would make a good wife. He didn't need or want his mom's advice on his love life.

Rye was shocked when he entered his brother's room to see that Mike was awake. His bed was cranked up so he was nearly sitting upright. Rye felt a flush of euphoria along with a ration of disbelief. "Mike?"

"Rye." The whispered word was raspy, and a pained expression flashed on his younger brother's face. Mike reached up to touch his throat with a hand covered in white tape, which was being used to connect a needle to a tube running to a clear bag of liquid. "Hurts to talk," he said in a strained voice.

Because it would be hard for Mike to answer, Rye asked his mom, "When was the breathing tube removed?"

"Early this morning."

"Why didn't you call me?"

"I did call. Amy Beth answered. She said you told her to go back to school."

He saw the questioning look in his mother's eyes but didn't explain, because he couldn't without telling her that he'd taken Lexie's side over his sister's.

"You just missed Amy Beth," his mother continued. "She came by to check on Mike on her way back to Missoula."

"And got good news, I see," he said, smiling at Mike. "I'd ask how you feel, but you might kick my butt."

"Would if I could," Mike said slowly and with difficulty. He tried to smile but winced when stitches in his face that made him look like Frankenstein's monster resisted the movement. "Mom said . . . I got shot . . . before I got mauled."

"You don't remember?"

Very carefully, Mike shook his head. "Just the bear . . . coming at me . . . and his godawful bad breath."

Rye chuckled. His brother was definitely on the mend if he could joke about the attack. He wondered if the shooter had been trying to kill the bear to protect Mike and missed. But if that was the case, why not call 911? Something was off about the whole thing. "Has anyone from the sheriff's office been by to talk to you?"

Mike started to shake his head again but moaned instead.

Rye turned to his mother for an answer.

"I haven't called to tell Pete that Mike's awake," she said. "I wanted to give your brother some space before he has to answer a lot of questions."

When Rye turned back to Mike, his brother's eyes were closed, but his chest rose and fell reassuringly. Rye took a step closer and lowered the bed so Mike could rest more easily. He smoothed a hand over Mike's mussed hair, then found a tiny spot without stitches, and kissed his brother's forehead.

When he rose, he turned to his mother and said, "I think it's time to talk."

He saw a myriad of emotions in her hazel eyes. Fear. Regret. Love. Compassion. None of which did anything to relieve his anxiety. "Maybe we should go get a cup of coffee."

When she rose from the chair she'd occupied beside Mike's bed, she did so sluggishly, as though she were an old, old woman with creaky bones and achy muscles. Her shoulders sagged and her chin had dropped nearly onto her chest. She obviously didn't want to have this talk any more than he did.

He waited for her to leave the room first and followed her down the hall to the hospital cafeteria. She walked like a prisoner on the way to the guillotine, which didn't bode well for the coming conversation. He worked to control his breathing, which had become patchy.

Once they reached the cafeteria, he didn't speak except to ask if she wanted coffee. She nodded, and he got a cup for each of them, black for him and sugar and cream for her. He carried the ceramic mugs to a table in a private corner and set them down. He pulled out a chair for her and waited until she sat before taking the seat across from her, so he could see her face while they were talking.

He took a sip of coffee and hissed when it burned his tongue. Her coffee sat before her untouched. He waited for her to speak, until it became plain she was waiting for him to say something first.

"Who are my parents?"

She looked shocked. "How can you ask me that? Your father and I are your parents. We raised you. We loved you. We—"

He interrupted her. "My biological parents."

For a moment, he saw defiance, but it didn't last. Like a balloon pricked with a very sharp needle, her body shriveled in on itself. Her hands slid from the top of the table to her lap, and her eyes focused downward as though she couldn't bear to face him.

Acid rose in his throat, and for a moment he thought he might vomit. His stomach churned, but it didn't erupt. "Mom?" He realized what he'd called her at the same moment she did.

Her head came up and she met his gaze and said, "I'm your biological mother."

The fact that she'd only mentioned herself meant

he had another father than the one who'd raised him. "Who was he?"

"Does it really matter?" she asked plaintively.

"It does to me. Not his name, really, but the fact of his existence. Why didn't you tell me?" The words seemed torn from his marrow.

"I wanted to, but . . ." She met his gaze with bleak eyes and whispered, "Your father didn't know."

Rye was appalled. "Dad didn't know? How could he not know?"

She made a small movement with her shoulders that might have been a shrug but said nothing.

"What kind of man gets a woman pregnant and doesn't marry her?" he ranted.

"A married man."

Everything Rye believed about his Madonnalike mother was being shot to hell. "You had a sordid affair with a married man?"

"It wasn't sordid," she said quietly. "He loved me, and I loved him."

"But he was married to someone else," he said flatly.

She nodded without apology, her chin up, her eyes militant. "I never meant to hurt anyone. I gave up the love of my life and married your father, so you would never know how you were conceived."

"What about Dad? Did you mind lying to him?" Rye was doing his best to control his anger, but the blood was rushing in his veins, and his body was so hot, it felt like he was on fire.

"I didn't want anything to mar Paddy's love for

you. When I knew him better, I was sure I'd made the right decision. For both of you."

It grieved Rye to admit she was right. His see-things-in-black-and-white father might always have held Rye's birth against him. Or might never have married his mother in the first place. He clamped his jaw tight to keep from hurling accusations that wouldn't change anything.

"Dad's been dead for seven years," he pointed out. "You could have told me the truth any time since then."

"I could never find the right moment. And it just seemed . . . unnecessary."

Unnecessary? Rye couldn't help wondering what would have happened if she'd died before he'd found out the truth. "Who is he?" Rye demanded. "Is he still alive? I want to meet him."

"He's alive, but I don't think meeting him is a good idea."

"Why not? Is he still married?"

"His wife died in childbirth nearly thirty years ago. He has four sons, all grown. Your half brothers."

"You know an awful lot about a man who's supposedly a part of your past," Rye said, his voice filled with sarcasm. "Does he know about Cody?"

"He's seen pictures of the two of you together."

"And Lexie?"

She nodded.

Rye felt exposed. Naked before a stranger. "How much have you told him?"

"Whatever I've shared with him he'll keep to himself. He's promised me that."

"And you believe him?"

She gave a small shrug, glanced up at him, then back down at the hands clutched in her lap. "He loves me."

Rye's heart took an extra beat. It was clear now, if it hadn't been before, that his mother was much more involved with this man from her youth than he'd imagined. He had a million questions. What he asked was, "Do I look like him?"

"You get your green eyes from both of us—my hazel and his blue. The chestnut hair is from my side of the family."

"What else have I gotten from this father I never knew about until today?"

"A bad temper?" she said with the hint of a smile.

He pursed his lips.

"Stubbornness and pride," she said archly, "along with very broad shoulders, and an extra inch or so of height."

"Who is he?" Rye repeated.

"His name is Angus Ryan Flynn."

"You *named* me after him?"

Her chin lifted another notch and she added the missing part of her previous revelation. "I loved him. I still do."

"What about Dad?" he snarled. "Did you love him?"

"You know I did," she said softly. "More than life."

"Just not enough to tell him the truth."

"It would only have hurt him. As it's hurting you right now."

She was right about that. Rye's heart physically ached. "Did the sonofabitch who got you pregnant know about me before you married Dad?"

She nodded.

Rye winced. "He knew about me, and he just walked away?"

"I didn't give him any choice. He was married and had three sons. I didn't want to ruin so many lives. I told him how it was going to be. I was thinking about you when I married your father. I didn't want you labeled a bastard—awful word, and so unfair."

"And this Angus Flynn nobly kept his distance all these years?" Rye said scornfully.

She nodded. "It wasn't easy for either of us, but yes, he did the honorable thing and stayed away."

He had a sudden thought. "Have you been in touch with him recently?"

She lowered her eyes, which was all the answer he needed.

He muttered an obscenity. Through gritted teeth he said, "Where can I find him?"

"Angus has a ranch in Jackson Hole called the Lucky 7."

Chapter 23

MATT STOOD AT the back door of a one-story, wood-frame ranch house in the Hill Country, west of Austin, with Nathan by his side. His heart was pounding a mile a minute. He licked at the sweat that had beaded above his lip as he waited, hatless in the hot Texas sun, for Jennie to answer his knock.

His son gripped his hand a little tighter, peered up at him, and asked, "Are you sure Jennie wants to see us? She wouldn't let us come visit her in the hospital. Not once."

Matt realized Nathan must have overheard one of his frustrated phone conversations with Pippa. Reluctantly, his daughter had kept him informed about her mother's condition, including the fact that

Jennie had been moved home by ambulance this past week.

He met his son's worried gaze and said, "If Jennie wants us to leave, we will." But he was hoping she wouldn't be able to turn him away. Or at least, be unable to turn Nathan away. His own welcome was a great deal more in doubt.

Matt was willing to use every means at his disposal, including an adorable seven-year-old boy, to get his foot through Jennie's door. Once he was inside, he would find a way to stay and convince her to forgive his past transgressions. They'd already been cheated out of half a lifetime of loving each other. He didn't want to lose any more time together.

When his knock wasn't answered, Nathan said, "There's nobody home, Daddy."

Except, he knew Jennie had to be there. According to her ranch foreman, she was alone in the house and hadn't set foot outside since she'd arrived two days ago. The man knew Matt and Jennie had a daughter together and hadn't questioned Matt's concern about Jennie's well-being.

Matt turned the knob, and the kitchen door opened. Despite the West's vaunted "range hospitality," which offered respite and a cup of coffee to any stranger who showed up at the door, he was surprised to find it unlocked. Jennie was a public figure—she'd held her late husband's Senate seat until she'd given it up for health reasons—and sometimes crazy people did crazy things. He stepped inside, surprised at how hot and stuffy the house felt. He called out, "Jennie?"

He felt a chill of alarm when his call wasn't answered. It was eleven in the morning. She should be awake, and two weeks post-surgery, she should be up and around.

"Jennie?" he called again.

"I told you, Daddy. She's not home."

Matt didn't answer his son, simply headed through the kitchen to the living room, which was dusty and smelled stale, and then down the central hallway, checking each open doorway, looking for Jennie. He found her in the last room at the end.

Her bedroom was dark, the curtains closed. It smelled like a sickroom. Jennie was huddled under the covers with only her head showing. *Covers? In this stifling house?*

He turned to Nathan, who'd trotted down the hall behind him, and said, "Go back to the kitchen, and get Jennie a glass of water."

Nathan never questioned the order, merely turned and headed out of the room. Matt wanted privacy to discover what was wrong with Jennie. He gently touched her on the shoulder.

Instead of turning over, she moaned.

Matt's heart was in his throat. That couldn't be good. He'd read enough about double mastectomies to know Jennie was in pain, since she had tubes in her chest to drain fluid, which wouldn't come out for another week. The tightness in her chest, similar to an overinflated balloon, made it difficult to breathe or move her arms. *Why the hell hadn't she arranged to have a nurse come take care of her?*

Well, he was here now, and he'd be damned if she was going to get rid of him. He tenderly brushed his fingertips across her brow to test for fever. Her flesh was warm but not hot.

"Foolish girl," he whispered. "You can't do everything all by yourself. You need help once in a while, whether you want to admit it or not."

Jennie's independence was one of the things he'd admired most about her, but she was going to have to give up a little of it to let him into her life. She moved restlessly but didn't open her eyes. He debated whether to call a doctor but decided to wait and see how she felt when she woke up.

Meanwhile, he was going to let in some light and fresh air. He crossed to the window, shoved back the curtains, and raised the window. A breeze immediately flowed into the room. He headed down the hall in search of the control for the air conditioner. When he found it, he turned it down ten degrees. By then, Nathan was on his way back down the hall with a coffee cup filled almost to the brim with water. His limp was more pronounced, because he was being so careful.

"I found this cup on the counter," he said. "It was dirty, but I rinsed it out real good."

"Thanks, Nate," Matt said as he took the cup from his son. "Let's see if we can get Jennie to take a drink."

"Are you sure you want to wake her up?" Nathan asked, eyeing Jennie dubiously.

Matt grinned at his son. "Not really. But nothing ventured, nothing gained."

Nathan tilted his head like a quizzical bird.

Matt didn't wait for his son to figure out what he'd said, simply sat beside Jennie and gently lifted her into an upright position. She grunted with pain as her eyes fluttered open. "Matt?"

"Rise and shine," Matt said, smiling at her.

She looked confused as she glanced from him to Nathan and back again. "What's going on?"

Her voice sounded rough, and Matt used that as an excuse to offer her the cup of water. "You must be thirsty."

She looked at the cup he held out to her and admitted, "I am." She started to lift her arms to take it from him, but winced and hissed in a breath.

"I'll hold it for you," he said, bringing the cup to her lips.

She drank thirstily. When she was done, she said, "I needed that. Thanks."

Nathan puffed out his chest and said, "I got it for you. I rinsed out the cup all by myself."

"Thank you, Nate." She focused her gaze on Matt and asked, "What are you doing here?"

"Taking care of an idiot?"

Jennie pursed her lips and shook her head. "I suppose I must seem like one, coming here without arranging for a nurse. Now that I see I need one, I'll call—"

"Don't," Matt interrupted. "Let us help. Nate and I make a pretty good team. And we want to help, don't we, Nate?"

Nathan plopped his rump on the opposite side of the bed and said, "I can tell you stories. And Daddy can make you breakfast. Are you hungry?"

It took Jennie a moment to answer. "I believe I am."

"When was the last time you ate?" Matt asked.

"I'm not sure."

"What would you like me to cook?"

"You can cook?"

"Not as good as Pippa," Nathan interjected.

"Thanks a lot for the vote of confidence, pal," Matt said, pretending to be insulted.

"Daddy cooks pretty good eggs," Nathan conceded. "But sometimes he breaks the yolk."

Jennie laughed and then grabbed her ribs. "Oh, don't make me laugh. It hurts."

"Come on, little man," Matt said. "Let's go make Jennie some breakfast while she gets dressed."

He saw the surprise on Jennie's face at his suggestion she should get up and put on some clothes. He knew the sooner she was up and around after her surgery, the better. He wasn't sure how much of her retreat to a dark room was because of the physical pain she was in, and how much might be mourning the loss of her breasts, but he intended to minister to both ills with heavy doses of love.

Chapter 24

IF SHE'D FELT better, Jennie might have kicked Matt out the door that first day, but she was helpless to resist Nathan's boundless enthusiasm. She noticed Matt kept his distance over the next week while her body healed, letting Nathan win her heart, while he wore his own on his sleeve. She didn't want to forgive Matt. She'd lost a lifetime with her daughter. She'd also lost a lifetime with him. It was too late for them. Wasn't it?

She finished the bedtime story she was reading to Nathan and pulled the covers up under his arms. Then she did something she hadn't done before. She brushed the dark hair away from his forehead, leaned over, and kissed him there.

When she started to rise, Nathan caught her arm

and held her in place. "Sometimes Pippa kisses me, but she grabs my ears and plants one on my nose. I like the way you do it better."

"Thank you, Nate." She stood and shot a glance at Matt, who was leaning against the bedroom doorway with his hip cocked, looking more handsome—and less self-assured—than he had at sixteen. "What about the way your daddy does it?"

Matt crossed the room and sat beside his son. First, he ruffled Nathan's hair, which caused the boy to giggle. Then he kissed two fingers and placed them solemnly against Nathan's lips. In return, Nathan kissed two fingers of his own and placed them against his father's lips. Finally, they grinned at each other.

Nathan looked up at her and said, "It's the very best."

Matt rose, turned out the lamp beside the bed, and said, "See you in the morning, son."

"See you in the morning, Daddy."

Jennie felt a frisson of feeling scoot up her spine when Matt's hand touched the small of her back, ushering her from the room. As soon as Matt closed the bedroom door, she turned to him and said brusquely, "We need to talk."

She saw his shoulders tense, which told her how much he'd been fearing this conversation. She knew he'd been on tenterhooks since he'd arrived, wondering when she was going to send him away. He believed that moment had arrived.

The drainage tubes had been removed from her

chest today, and she was well on her way to recovery. She would be starting another round of chemo soon. There was no good reason for Matt to stay any longer. She didn't need to be waited on hand and foot and have her every desire fulfilled before she could even speak it aloud. She had to admit, she'd loved feeling like a princess in a fairy tale. But that wasn't reality. It was a fantasy a grown woman knew better than to believe in.

Jennie settled herself on the comfortable leather couch, expecting Matt to sit in the chair across from her. Instead, he lowered himself onto the other end of the couch like he was perching on a cactus.

"It was a dirty trick to show up here with Nate," she began.

"When you fight a war, you use the best ammunition you can find."

"He's quite a bombshell," she said with a smile.

"I love you."

Jennie was taken off-guard by the statement, which had come, once again, out of the blue. "I'm sure you *used to* love me," she replied in a quiet voice. "We were just kids, Matt. A lot of years have passed since then. You don't know the person I've become."

"I know enough," he argued. "I've never stopped loving you, Jennie. All these years, there's been a hole inside me that no other woman could fill."

"Which explains your two wives," she said sardonically.

"And two divorces," he reminded her. "Every time

I looked at our daughter, I regretted being forced to leave you behind."

"Forced?"

"You were only fifteen, Jennie. How could I have gotten you out of the country?"

He was right, of course. The blame she'd been heaping on him really belonged on her parents' shoulders. They were the ones who'd lied and told her Pippa had died at birth. They were the ones who'd kept her apart from Matt. She'd left them the instant she was old enough and come to live at this ranch with her grandmother. She'd never reconciled with her parents before they'd died, something she'd realized too late was yet another mistake.

It seemed like her life was full of them. Was this going to be one more? Should she let Matt stay? Or send him away? Which was liable to bring her the most happiness? Or the least pain?

"I've never forgotten how good we were together," Matt said. "I've never stopped wanting you."

Jennie sighed. "It wouldn't work, Matt."

"Why not?"

She shrugged, then winced, because she wasn't healed enough for any gesture that involved sudden moves with her upper body.

"Are you all right?" he asked, his eyes anxious.

"I'm fine." *Just hurting because I regret what we lost and don't believe we can ever have again.*

She hadn't realized her hands were curled white-knuckle tight until Matt scooted over and separated them, so he could hold them in his own. The earnest look in his blue eyes was enough to make her weep. Her throat ached. She felt the tears coming and blinked them back. She wasn't going to cry over him. She'd done enough of that as a young girl who'd lost both the boy she loved and the child she'd carried.

"Give us a chance, Jennie. That's all I'm asking. Let me love you. See if you can learn to love me again."

Silly man! That's what's wrong with me now. I hate you for leaving me behind. But I never stopped loving you.

Which meant he had the power to hurt her again. The power to disappoint her again. "If I let you stay—"

"I won't let you down."

"How do I know you won't change your mind and walk out, if things get tough?"

"You mean if the cancer comes back?"

She gritted her teeth and nodded, unable to speak.

"If you let me stay, if you let me love you, I promise—"

"Don't make promises you can't keep," she managed to say.

"Who says I can't keep them?"

She looked him in the eye. "I don't have breasts."

He lowered his gaze to her flattened chest, then raised it again and looked at her with solemn eyes. "I know. I'm sorry for your sake. To me, you're still as beautiful as you were the day I met you."

She felt a sharp pang in her chest that had nothing to do with her recent surgery. "There's a reason I no longer have breasts," she reminded him.

"You have cancer. I—"

She pulled one hand free and touched his lips to stop his speech. "The doctors believe this surgery, along with chemo, will keep the cancer in remission. But there are no guarantees. It could come back. I could die. You're dealing with a powder keg that could explode in your face."

He recaptured her free hand and held them both tightly to keep her from pulling away. "We couldn't control our lives when we were kids, Jennie. Our parents were making the decisions for us. We're adults now, able to chart our own course. I've lived long enough without you to know that, however long your life lasts, mine will be infinitely better—infinitely happier—if I spend it with you." He caressed her hands with his thumbs and met her gaze with a sparkle of mischief in his eyes. "And Nate needs a mother."

She rolled her eyes and gently tugged her hands free. "You don't fight fair."

"Why should I, when I'm fighting for my life?"

He had a point. A great deal was at stake. Happiness for the rest of their lives. Or misery, depending on how things turned out.

The senator's wife, Jennifer Hart, would never have taken the chance. She would have done the safe thing, the sure thing. But Jennie Fairchild, the girl who'd fallen head over heels in love with Matthew

Grayhawk when she was only fourteen, was willing to fight for their future.

"All right, Matt."

She saw the hope in his eyes. And the fear.

"All right what?"

"I'm willing to give this a shot."

Before she could take another breath, he'd picked her up, settled her on his lap, and planted his mouth on hers.

The jolt of pain in her chest was gone before she could protest. She pressed her hands against his chest, because she couldn't raise her arms to reach his hair, which was thick and silky and looked so very healthy. Unlike hers.

The doctors had tried chemo first, which had made her violently ill and caused her hair to fall out but hadn't stopped the cancer. They'd given her an ultimatum. Her life or her breasts. She'd chosen life.

Matt tipped the ball cap off her head and palmed her scalp, where bristly hair was trying hard to grow. When she groaned her dismay at what he must be seeing, what he must be feeling, he whispered, "I prefer ball caps to those turban things. Easier to get rid of, so I can touch."

What man wanted to caress a bald woman's head? Apparently he did.

His kiss was intrusive, involving lips and teeth and tongue, searing her to her very soul. He kept their bodies apart in deference to her healing flesh.

He made love to her with slow, delicious kisses, the kind where your breathing got sketchy because your heart was racing, and your skin felt hot, and your whole body thrummed with desire.

They kissed. And kissed some more. And kept on kissing. Heads twisting side to side, mouths melding, his hands clutched at her waist to keep them from roaming her body, from seeking to touch her warm flesh.

Because, of course, the most logical thing to touch would be her breasts. Which weren't there.

She fought a sob as the enormity of her situation finally sank in. She hadn't only lost her breasts. She still might lose her life.

"It's okay, sweetheart. We'll be okay. Everything will be okay." He said all the right things between kissing her throat and ears and eyes and cheeks, before his tongue teased its way inside her mouth, urging her to forget about everything except him and the pleasure he sought to give her.

Somehow, she did forget. For long moments, Jennie relished the taste of him, without being aware of anything else. Until she realized her hands had found their way under his shirt to his hair-whorled chest. She felt hard male muscle, and beneath that, his heart beating fast and strong.

She was so very glad he was here . . . until her doubts reared their ugly head again.

Sure, Matt could handle a bristly head, but how would he react when he saw her horrible scars? Would it really not ever matter to him that the symbols of her femininity that so many men valued were gone? Breasts were an erogenous zone for a woman.

Did she even want him to kiss her ravaged flesh, from which all pleasure had been stripped?

Jennie forced herself to focus on Matt's exhilarating kisses, on the way his tongue made forays into her mouth seeking honey, how his lips were soft and supple against her own. He showed his love as he had when they were teenagers, when kissing was all she would allow.

A long time later, he murmured, "You won't be sorry you let me stay, Jennie."

She didn't say it. But she thought it.

I hope not.

Chapter 25

THE *THUMP* OF something hitting the rag rug next to her bed woke Jennie. She jerked upright, afraid of an intruder. The sudden pain in her chest was excruciating and made her gasp. She gently laid a hand against the offended muscles, as though that could make them hurt less.

"I'm sorry," a small voice whispered from the gray dawn shadows. "I didn't mean to scare you."

Jennie reached up instinctively to rearrange the hair that was no longer there, having fallen out during previous rounds of chemotherapy, gasped again, and dropped her hand. She kept forgetting about her surgery. Forgetting she had limited range of motion. Forgetting she didn't have breasts.

She leaned her head back, huffed out a frustrated

breath of air, then focused her gaze on the boy kneeling beside the bed. He was replacing a coffee cup—filled with a handful of the blue morning glories that bloomed along the edge of her back porch—on the tray he was carrying. Whatever water had been in the cup had apparently spilled onto the rug.

"Good morning, Nate. What is this?"

He looked up at her from beneath shy, lowered lashes. "I brought you breakfast."

Jennie's heart squeezed with regret that she'd never experienced a moment like this with Pippa. And expanded with love for the little boy who was giving her such a gift. He carefully set a tray on her lap that held a plateful of scrambled eggs, toast, a knife and fork, a tiny glass of orange juice, a folded paper napkin, and the coffee cup full of flowers. "What's the special occasion?" she asked.

"Well, we might not be here for Mother's Day, so I decided I should do something nice for you now. I mean, you're not my mom, but you are Pippa's mom and she's my sister and she's not here, so . . ." He shrugged.

Tears burned Jennie's eyes and emotion knotted her throat. She didn't have a lot of experience with kids, but Nathan's thoughtfulness seemed out of the ordinary. Matt had done a good job raising him, and raising Pippa, she was forced to admit. She ruffled Nathan's dark hair as an excuse to touch him and said in a choked voice, "Thank you, Nate. This is lovely."

"I couldn't figure out how to work your coffee-maker, so I brought you flowers instead."

She picked up the bunch of morning glories and sniffed them before replacing them in the cup. "They're wonderful. Thank you. Why don't you join me while I eat?"

She didn't have to scoot over much to give him room to sit beside her, his legs outstretched on the bed. "I'm not sure where to start," she said, looking at the meal before her.

"Better start with the eggs. They're gonna be cold pretty quick. I didn't know what kind of jelly you like, so I just put butter on your toast."

"Just butter is fine." The eggs were indeed cold, and rubbery as well, and the toast was charred black, but she ate with gusto, because she would never do anything to hurt Nathan's feelings. "Where did you learn to cook like this?" she asked.

"Pippa taught me. We had to do for ourselves a lot in Australia since Daddy was out early working with the livestock. She gave me jobs so I could help."

"I'm surprised your dad lets you cook by yourself."

"He doesn't. But I remembered Pippa did this once for Irene. Irene was my mum. I guess she still is my mum, but she never came to see me after she got divorced from Daddy."

Jennie fought back a flash of jealous rage that her daughter had prepared breakfast in bed for a different mother and immediately squelched it.

Such feelings were futile and pointless. Better to focus on the present, on this little boy who was no longer sure what role his biological mother held in his life, and so obviously wanted a mother he could love.

I could be Nathan's mother. I could love him and give him the praise he deserves and let him know every day in every way what a wonderful person he is.

She carefully leaned sideways and kissed his temple. "You did a great job preparing all this food, Nate. I'm impressed."

"I kinda made a mess in the kitchen."

"No problem. We can clean that up in a jiffy."

Matt arrived in the doorway and said, "The kitchen looks like a tornado hit it. What's going on?"

Jennie shot Matt an admonishing look over Nathan's head and said, "Nate made my breakfast and served it to me in bed."

Matt looked both surprised and confused. "He did?"

"He even picked some flowers for me," she said, holding out a fistful of wilted morning glories.

"That was really nice of you, Nate," Matt said. "But Jennie's liable to throw up her hands in despair when she sees that kitchen. How about we clean it up for her?"

"Okay, Daddy."

"You can start by putting the eggs and orange

juice back in the fridge. I'll come help you with the dishes in a minute."

"I gotta go, Jennie." Nate leaned over to hug Jennie, and she held her breath to keep from crying out at the pressure on her wounded body. She welcomed that hug, however painful it was, because of what it represented.

Matt must have seen her wince because after Nate had limped from the room he said, "I'll remind him again to be gentle."

Jennie didn't want to talk about her mutilated chest. She had a more important question she wanted answered. "Why didn't Nate's mother ever come to visit him after your divorce? Did you keep her away from him the way you kept me away from Pippa?"

Matt's face bleached completely white. "If you believe me capable of that, it's no wonder you haven't forgiven me for what happened with Pippa."

"So Irene just waltzed out of Nate's life without looking back?"

"Irene barely spent time with Nate when we were married," Matt snarled. "She caused the accident that crippled him."

Jennie hissed in a breath.

"That wasn't the first time she'd put Nate in danger or the first time he was hurt because of it. I don't know if Irene was simply too flighty to pay attention to Nate, or whether she found responsibility for our son too much of a burden, but she wasn't a good mother. Part of the reason I left Australia was to get him away from her. I didn't trust her to spend time alone with him. He had too many 'accidents' when they were together."

"I'm sorry, Matt. I didn't know."

"I had an unbearable choice to make twenty years ago," he continued. "Leaving you behind when I headed to Australia was the hardest thing I've ever done in my life. Not telling you about Pippa's existence was a terrible mistake, but in the beginning I didn't know how to reach you, and when I finally did . . . The time just never seemed right."

He shoved a frustrated hand through his dark hair, leaving it askew. "The longer I waited, the more certain I was you would never forgive me."

He met her gaze and said, "I was right. You haven't been able to let go of the past. You haven't been able to look at what we might have now and in the future. It hurts to want you like I do and be excluded from your life, to be judged and condemned for something I did when I was a boy of seventeen. I'm a thirty-seven-year-old man, Jennie, willing to love you with every fiber of my being. I think I deserve better from you. I know I do."

"You're right."

His head jerked up, and he stared at her as though he didn't believe what he'd just heard. "I'm right?"

"I've focused on what you did wrong in the past instead of all the things you're doing now that make me want to be with you."

"You want to be with me?" He looked surprised and hopeful at the same time.

"I'm willing to consider a future with you and

Nate. I just need a little more time, Matt. To heal."

In body and soul.

He settled carefully onto the bed beside her and grasped her hands in his. He met her gaze with earnest blue eyes and said, "Time is precious, Jennie. Don't take too long making up your mind."

Chapter 26

"HOW THE HELL did you find me here?"

"Matt told me you'd been admitted." Leah swallowed past the painful knot in her throat and stepped inside King's hospital room at MD Anderson Cancer Center in Houston, where he'd previously been treated for leukemia.

"How did Matt find out?" her father snarled.

"He came to the hospital because the woman he loves was here having a double mastectomy. Since you're a bit of a celebrity patient—the wealthy former governor of Wyoming—and Matt has the same unusual last name, the receptionist asked if he'd come to see you. That told him you were here. Matt called me because he thought I might like to know you were lying in a Texas hospital bed instead of where you told me you'd be."

King had left her a note ten days ago saying he had business in Washington, D.C., and might be gone for a while. She should have known better. She should have guessed his true destination. Her stomach did a strange flip-flop as she met his gaze. He looked even more pale than usual in the fluorescent light. "I waited for you to call and tell me the truth yourself, but you never contacted me."

"Didn't want folks hovering over my bedside like a flock of vultures."

"I'm not 'folks.' I'm your favorite daughter."

He scowled. "I knew I shouldn't have told you that."

She crossed to the foot of his bed, swallowed over the painful lump in her throat, and said, "Is your leukemia back?"

King rubbed his nape. "Been feeling a little tired is all. Thought I'd come in for a checkup."

She knotted her fingers into fists while her heart raced inside her chest. "So? Is it back?"

He dropped his hand and met her gaze. "Yeah."

Leah's breath, which she hadn't realized she'd been holding, soughed out of her. Her knees wobbled, and she grabbed the foot rail to stay upright as she wailed, "Oh, Daddy."

She saw his shock at what she'd called him. Only rarely had she addressed him as "Father." All her life he'd simply been "King." Her cry of despair revealed the truth of what he'd become to her. It was the plea of a child for her beloved parent not to leave her.

It also made what she had to say next all the more important.

She lifted her chin and looked him in the eye. "I know what you've been hoping, but I've spoken to Matt, and he isn't coming back. Now you're sick in bed for God knows how long. What are you going to do about the ranch?"

"You're my daughter, all right. Forget soppy feelings about my illness." And then, more harshly, "Right to business."

She refused to be cowed by his lowered brows or his flattened lips. "You're the one who offered the ranch to someone who didn't want it."

He rubbed his chin, bristly with gray stubble. "I need a shave."

"Stop stalling."

"Guess Matt isn't leaving me any choice," he grumbled.

"You always have a choice. But I love the ranch." She hesitated, then added, "And I love you."

"Guess you think I should give it to you, since I'm on my deathbed."

Her heart took an extra, uneasy beat. "Who said you're dying? Did the doctors tell you that?"

He pursed his lips. "Didn't you hear me? The cancer's back."

"So? You do more chemo."

"The doctors told me the last time—"

Leah crossed to the head of the bed and took

King's shoulders in both hands, turning him to face her. "You can beat this," she said fiercely. "I don't intend to win the ranch by default."

"You mean because Matt walked away?"

"I mean because you're dead," she said flatly, letting her hands fall to her sides.

King smiled, and Leah heard the cackle that passed for his laugh. The sound was stunning because she couldn't remember the last time she'd heard it.

"What a woman," he muttered.

"I think so, too."

Leah felt a welling of joy when she heard the male voice behind her. When she turned, Aiden stood in the doorway to King's room. She'd told him where she was going and why. She hadn't asked him to come—she never would have admitted how much she needed him—but she was so very glad he was here. In light of her father's news, she desperately wanted a strong shoulder to lean on. Aiden crossed the room and slid an arm around her waist, pulling her close. She felt her body lean into his, as though it were the most natural thing in the world for her to lean on him for support.

"I came to see if there's anything I can do to help," he murmured in her ear.

"Your being here is enough." She rested her cheek against his chest just to hear the sound of his strong heartbeat.

King glared at Aiden and said, "You're not welcome here."

"If you send Aiden away, I go with him," Leah threatened.

"What's he doing here, Leah?" King demanded.

"Aiden is . . ." Leah hesitated. She almost said, "My husband," but the words got stuck in her throat. This wasn't the time to spring that news on King. "Someone I care about," she finished. "Flynn men have married two of my sisters. You should be used to having them around by now."

"Doesn't mean I have to like it," he shot back.

"Daddy." The warning in her voice must have gotten to him. Or maybe it was her use of *that word.* It shut him up. "Aiden and I are determined to end this awful feud between you and his father," she continued.

King crossed his arms. "Never gonna happen."

"Maybe the animosity between you two grizzlies won't end, but Aiden and I are going to pull your teeth and claws."

That image was apparently disturbing enough for King to ask, "How are you planning to manage that?"

Leah and Aiden exchanged a glance before she turned to King and said, "We want to merge the two ranches into one."

"The hell you say," King blustered. "I haven't given Kingdom Come to you yet, young lady, and if that's what you have in mind, you can forget about ever getting it!"

She heard Aiden hitch in a breath. Maybe telling King what they planned to do wasn't the wisest course. But the more Leah thought about it, the less she wanted to sneak behind King's back.

"Aiden and I want a future under one roof. We want to start a family. We can't do that so long as you and Angus are at each other's throats."

"Even if I were willing to bury the hatchet—and I'm not saying I am—Angus will never agree."

"Leave him to me," Aiden said.

"What sword are you going to dangle over his head?" King asked. "Nothing I've said or done has made a difference for forty years."

"My father wants more grandchildren," Aiden said with a sardonic smile.

Leah held her breath, waiting to see whether Aiden would admit the deal he'd made to name their first child after his father. King would have ten fits when he realized he'd be rocking a miniature "Angus" on his knee someday. Presuming she had a boy. Leah had no idea what Angus would demand if she and Aiden had only daughters.

King's brows arrowed down as he considered Aiden's statement. Finally, with a snort of disgust, he turned to Leah and said, "Get out and let me think about this."

Leah gasped. Was her dream one step closer to coming true? Or was this a delaying tactic, while King waited to see if Matt changed his mind about coming home?

"I don't think your damn fool idea will work," King said, "but I can't wait to hear what Angus has to say. Uniting our two ranches is going to take more than a little prestidigitation."

Leah was startled into laughter at King's use of a word that suggested she was going to need sleight of hand to unite one ranch with the other, as though her idea would only work if the deed were done by magic, before either of the two hoary bears could growl their disapproval.

She focused on the positive. At least King was willing to consider giving her the ranch. The chasm keeping her and Aiden apart was no less deep, but at least she had the first building blocks for a bridge across it.

Leah left the security of Aiden's embrace and crossed to King, slipping her arms around his neck and pressing her cheek next to his bristly hide. She lifted her head, smiled, and said, "You do need a shave."

He grunted and made a face.

"All I want is for you to get well and come home," she whispered in his ear, "so you can rock your next grandchild on your knee."

King frowned and leaned back to look her in the eye. "You said that like there's already one on the way."

Leah let go of King and rearranged his pajama top—no hospital gown for him. She gave a quick, sick laugh, glanced over her shoulder at Aiden, and said, "We're a long way from being married."

She wasn't a good liar, and she didn't want to hang around long enough for King to ask more awkward questions. She turned to Aiden, shoving him toward the door. "We have to go. We'll be back to visit tomorrow. Be good and do what the doctors tell you."

"Like hell I will," he retorted.

Once she had Aiden out the door, she hurried back to King's bed, stood over him, pointed a finger, and said, "You'll do everything you're told, Daddy, or I'll know the reason why."

King grinned and said, "That's my girl!"

She heard his cackle again as she kissed him on the cheek. She ran for the door, calling over her shoulder, "I mean it!"

She grasped Aiden's hand and hurried him down the hall, before he could ruin everything by telling her father they were already married. Or ask if she really was pregnant.

Chapter 27

AIDEN WAS HALFWAY down the hall before he realized he'd been hustled out of King's room before he could ask the question hovering on his tongue. His heart hammering, he caught Leah by the shoulders and turned her around. "Are you pregnant?"

Her eyes shifted sideways. "I . . ."

"Tell me the truth, Leah."

She met his gaze, her eyes glistening with tears.

His heart hitched, and his stomach dropped. He gently drew her into his arms and murmured, "Oh, baby." He realized what he'd said and waited for her to object to his use of the term. More than once she'd told him she was a grown-ass woman and didn't want to be treated like some helpless infant.

Only, he couldn't stop himself from wanting to protect her, never more so than now.

"We have to tell our parents we're married," he said.

"Not yet."

"How far along are you?"

"We should have been more careful, Aiden."

His chest felt so full of joy he thought it might burst. "I'm not sorry, Leah. I'm glad." He waited for her to express her own feelings, but she wasn't sharing.

Instead she said, "It must have happened on that beautiful day the first week of March. At least, that's the timing that works with what my doctor said."

He remembered the day well. She'd been feeling blue, because it looked like Matt was going to win his bet and force her to leave the ranch. He'd merely sought to comfort her by holding her close.

Because it was a warm day, they weren't wearing coats, and he'd tucked her softness into his hardness. She'd looked up at him, and he'd seen in her eyes that she needed him as much as he needed her. Clothes had gone flying. Boots had landed in the dirt. They'd made love on the cold hard ground, on a blanket he'd grabbed from the bed of his pickup.

He sighed. "I guess that was one of those times we forgot to use a condom."

She shot him an ironic smile. "Neither of us was thinking much at the time."

Aiden realized her pregnancy was going to force the issue. Leah would have to admit to their fathers that they were married, and the sooner the better, as far as he was concerned.

"What are you waiting for, Leah? We need to tell King and Angus we're married."

"King's health is too fragile—"

"Baloney. That man is a tank."

"He has leukemia."

"Which just means he needs to make a decision pretty soon about the ranch. He hasn't said no, Leah. And the truth is he doesn't have anyone else to give it to besides you."

"That may be true. But it doesn't do me any good to get Kingdom Come if you can't get Angus to give you the Lucky 7."

"I've been working on him, Leah. It can't be long now before he hands it over."

"It feels to me like we're stuck in a rut," she said. "We can't very well merge two ranches when we don't own either one of them."

"With a little more time I can convince Angus—"

"What do you think your father is going to say when he realizes we've been lying to him all this time?" she demanded. "That we've been married for more than a year?"

Aiden made a frustrated sound in his throat. "So we get married again."

"With my father in the hospital? Who's going to walk me down the aisle?"

"Details."

"Pretty big ones," she countered. "If we do this

again, I want a real wedding, Aiden, with my sisters as bridesmaids and your brothers as groomsmen."

"You're being difficult, Leah."

"*I'm* being difficult? I'm entitled, don't you think? You married me under false pretenses the first time, to win a bet with your brother. We stood in some brightly lit wedding chapel in Vegas, and you gave me a plastic ring. I'm carrying the baby of a man I hardly see, who's too scared to challenge his father for what he wants."

"Whoa, there! I'm not scared of that old man."

"Then why haven't you confronted him? What are you waiting for? If you want us living under the same roof, you need to get possession of the Lucky 7. The only way this marriage works is if we merge the two properties and build ourselves a house on land in the middle, where we can manage both ranches. Otherwise, I'm going to be stuck living and working at one ranch while you're stuck at the other. That means you won't be seeing a lot of me. Or this baby, either!"

She marched away but didn't get two steps before he caught her by the arm. "Wait a goddamn minute!"

"You keep God out of this," she spat.

"Look, baby—"

She yanked herself free. "I can't very well *be* a baby when I'm about to *have* one! Get that into your thick skull."

So now he was dumb? He started to reach for her,

and she put her hands up like a cop at a burned-out stoplight.

"Don't touch me!" she snapped.

"Can we talk about this?"

"I've done all the talking I intend to do. The person you need to speak with is your father."

"Angus isn't back from his trip."

"Where is he?"

"Montana."

"What's he doing there?"

"Hell if I know. He just said he had to go and left."

"You didn't ask?"

"He's my father," he said. "He doesn't have to tell me a thing."

"And didn't," she said in disgust. "How long is he supposed to be gone?"

"No idea."

She shook her head in disbelief and headed down the hall again.

He knew better than to grab her, but he strode along beside her. "You don't have possession of Kingdom Come yet, either."

"At least I asked for it."

"You're being totally unreasonable, Leah. Probably all those pregnancy hormones."

She shot him an acid look.

"When Angus gets home, I promise I'll speak to him. All right?"

She stopped in her tracks and turned to face him. "If it is hormones," she said irritably, "they're not going away anytime soon. So you'd better get used to me being 'unreasonable.' Just talk to your father!"

This time, when she marched off, Aiden let her go. He realized, now that Leah had pointed it out to him, how unusual it was for Angus to keep his travel plans a secret. After all, Aiden might need to consult him on ranch business. So where had he gone? And how long did he plan to stay away?

Aiden pulled out his cell and dialed his father's number. He let it ring until it went to voicemail and said, "Dad, give me a call when you get this."

It was the first of ten calls Aiden made that day without ever getting a reply.

Chapter 28

ANGUS FLYNN HAD done a lot of things he regretted in his life. Loving Darcie Covington—now Darcie Sullivan—wasn't one of them. Several years into his marriage to Fiona Townsend, his wife found out about Darcie and demanded he end the affair. He'd refused, arguing that he loved both women and couldn't bear to give up either one.

Hurt and humiliated, Fiona had pursued a devastating revenge.

Angus still grieved the loss of his wife, who'd died in childbirth, bearing a son she'd conceived in Angus's bed with another man. Around the same time, Darcie had married Patrick Sullivan, so the son she'd conceived with Angus would have a father. Angus had raised his fourth son, Devon, as though he were his own blood and obeyed Darcie's request and kept his distance, while the son they'd made together grew up loving a different father.

Sitting in the hospital cafeteria in Kalispell, waiting for Darcie to show up, Angus's heart was fluttering like some lovesick teenager. He hadn't seen her since she'd married Patrick Sullivan and moved to Montana. He still had all his hair, but it was more silver than black, and his face had been etched with harsh lines by wind and sun. When he felt for the six-pack he'd had when they were lovers, it was missing. Would she still find him attractive? Would she still want him in her bed?

Seven years ago, when he'd learned Paddy had died, he'd contacted Darcie, but she'd refused to see him.

"Rye doesn't know the truth," she'd said. "I don't want him hurt."

Angus had been shocked to learn that their son was named Ryan, after him, with the middle name Patrick, for the father who'd raised him.That sequence told him a great deal about Darcie's feelings for him and gave him hope. He'd been even more shocked when Darcie announced that his son had a child, and that his grandson's mother was Victoria Grayhawk. Angus was already busy figuring out how he might use that information against his nemesis, King Grayhawk, when Darcie made him promise not to breathe a word of what he knew to anyone.

It was a sign of how much he loved her that he'd forgone a perfect opportunity to pursue his vengeance against King. It was a secret he was still keeping, since Darcie hadn't given him permission to reveal it.

After all the years of separation, his love for Darcie still burned bright, and he'd made no effort to extinguish it. He was determined to do whatever was necessary to win her back, but it was hard to be patient. "We're not getting any younger," he'd argued a year ago. "I love you, Darcie. I want us to be together. How much longer do we have to wait? I don't want to live any more of my life without you."

"I can't see you, Angus," she'd told him. "Not now. Maybe never again." She'd been crying when she said it, which was how he knew she still loved him as well.

Over the past year, he'd often talked to her on the phone late into the night, each of them in their own beds, sharing the large and small moments of their lives while her family, and his, were sound asleep. But talking wasn't nearly enough.

He'd made a pretty good mess of his love life, but things were about to change, hopefully for the better. Rye had finally learned of Angus's existence and wanted to meet him. Darcie thought the meeting would go better if Angus came to Montana than if Rye went to him. So here he was, waiting with bated breath for a woman he'd loved for the better part of his life to make her appearance.

"Angus?"

He stood, his arthritic knees protesting, and turned to face her. Darcie's hazel eyes shimmered with tears, and her chin was trembling as she struggled to smile. Her face had suffered a similar fate to his, but her body was still slender. She was almost too thin, he thought. Likely she wasn't eating enough because of everything that was going on. He'd have to do something about that.

Although she'd tried to tame her hair in a bun at the top of her head, riotous curls had escaped her efforts to contain them, just as they had when she was a young woman. She was wearing what she'd always worn: Levi's and a belted-in plaid Western shirt with scuffed cowboy boots. She looked so very familiar. And so very dear.

He held out his arms, and she walked right into them.

Angus rocked Darcie in his embrace, feeling her soft curves against his body as he held her close. He was afraid this moment was a figment of his imagination, the dream that had haunted him for so many years, and if he let go, she would disappear. But he could feel her moist breath against his cheek, feel her body trembling as he held her close. Darcie was really here in his arms at last. Where she belonged.

He wanted to pick her up and whisk her away somewhere they could be alone. But he couldn't do that. Not yet. Darcie was a mother, with a mother's responsibilities. There was a young man, his son, with whom he needed to speak, another young man who required time to heal from his dreadful wounds, and a young lady who still had to finish college.

He was a father, but his four sons were all grown. Brian, Connor, and Devon were married and had started families, and Aiden had finally chosen his bride.

For the past year, Aiden had been pressuring him to hand over control of the Lucky 7. Angus's refusal had nothing to do with Aiden's qualifications to manage the ranch. His eldest son was a more than satisfactory boss. Angus had resisted because running the ranch was all he had left to fill his empty days. That was especially true since his feud with King Grayhawk, which had kept a fire in his belly for nearly forty years, had been put on hiatus so his son could court the eldest Grayhawk girl. Without hate for his lifelong enemy fueling every decision, Angus's life seemed to lack direction.

If Darcie came into his life, he wouldn't need the day-to-day demands of the Lucky 7—or his feud with King Grayhawk—to fill the hollow inside him. Loving her, making her happy, being parents and grandparents together, would be more than enough to give his life meaning.

All Angus needed from Darcie was one word of encouragement, and he would be happy to move to Montana, so they could be together. And once he and Darcie were married, giving Aiden the ranch might provide a much-needed spur to his eldest son's romance with Leah Grayhawk.

Angus met Darcie's gaze, wondering if she could

tell how scared he was that she would send him away once he'd met his son.

Darcie looked deep into his eyes and took his face between her hands. Her fingers were callused and surprisingly comforting. "I'm so glad you came."

He captured her hands with his, and said, "I would have come if I had to crawl on my knees. I love—"

She moved her fingertips to cover his mouth, forbidding him to say the words. His feelings were there for her to see in his eyes. Protestations of undying love had been off-limits during their long phone conversations. She'd been willing to share the minutiae of her life and hear the trials and tribulations of his, but she'd told him it was too painful to be called "darling" and "sweetheart." Not when he'd married another woman instead of her in a fit of pique. Not when he'd coaxed her into an affair that made her as responsible as he was for wounding his wife so badly.

Angus had known from the moment he met Darcie at the University of Montana that she was the girl for him. He was a couple of years older and wanted her to marry him when he graduated. She wanted to finish college first. He'd tried rushing her to the altar, but she wouldn't be pushed.

Darcie had liked him all right, but she told him to his face that she wasn't sure he'd make a good husband. He was far too arrogant, far too used to being able to buy anything he wanted with his money. She wasn't for sale.

Angus wasn't used to hearing a woman tell him no. He'd been stung by the harsh criticism from a woman he loved. Licking his wounds, he'd gone off and found someone who adored him just as he was, someone who didn't push back. When he got Fiona pregnant—something he couldn't regret without regretting the birth of his eldest son—he'd married her.

Angus bit back the excuses he hadn't been allowed to express for his choices all those years ago. They might make him feel better, but they wouldn't undo the damage he'd done to the two women he'd loved. He wouldn't make the same mistake twice. Now that Darcie had invited him into her life, he was never going to leave her again.

"I told Rye to meet me here," she said, her worried gaze darting toward the door to the cafeteria and back. "He doesn't know you'll be here, too."

He felt his heart skip a beat. He didn't like the idea of surprising the boy. The man. His son was almost thirty years old. "How soon will he be here?"

"Any minute."

Angus wondered why she hadn't tried to meet up with him sooner, so they would have had time alone before Rye showed up. One look in her fretful eyes told him the answer. She might want to be with him, but she was terrified of how Rye was going to react to finding him here, where her son wouldn't have any choice except to confront his biological father. Not to mention the decision she was about to make, now that their secret was out, to perhaps include this stranger in her children's lives.

"It's going to be all right, Darcie." He wondered if he should tell her his own pulse was racing, that his lungs were struggling to draw breath, that he was equally apprehensive about being judged by their son for what he'd done, and even more fearful of how Rye might resent, and therefore interfere with, his plans for Darcie.

"What the hell is this?"

Darcie jerked herself from Angus's embrace and turned to face the stiff-legged young man, hands fisted at his sides, whose suspicious gaze shifted from her to Angus and back.

"Is this him?" he snarled.

Darcie squared her shoulders as she faced Rye. She showed her son—their son—none of the anxiety and uneasiness she'd shared with Angus. Her voice was calm, although her chin quivered. "This is Angus Flynn. Your father."

"I had a father. This isn't him," Rye retorted.

"I'm your biological father," Angus said in a carefully modulated voice. "Your mother told me you wanted to meet me."

Rye shot a confused glance at his mother. "Why would you bring him here?"

"I wanted to be with you when you met Angus, and I'm not ready to leave Mike alone at the hospital. I thought if Angus and I were both here, we could answer all your questions at one time."

"In a hospital cafeteria?" Rye said with a sneer.

He yanked off his Stetson and rolled the brim in his hands. "I thought something had happened to Mike. My heart was in my throat all the way here, and it turns out it's only *him*. Why are we doing this here, Mom?"

"It's neutral ground. And I thought meeting at the hospital might keep you from making a scene. Which you seem, at the moment, determined to do," his mother replied in a steely voice.

Angus remembered that voice. She'd used it on him when she'd shoved him out of her life. He gestured toward a nearby table. "Why don't we all sit down?"

"I'd rather stand," Rye said belligerently. He focused his narrow-eyed gaze on his mother. "I don't like being manipulated."

"Especially when it's for your own good," she retorted. "Now sit down."

Angus held his breath, not at all sure Rye would stay. His son threw his Stetson onto the table before scraping back a chair and slumping into it. Angus watched Ryan's green eyes flare when his mother sat down across from him, next to her former lover.

"We've met," Ryan said sullenly, directing his gaze at Angus. "Now what?"

Darcie leaned across the table, reaching out with both hands to her son.

Rather than taking her hands, he folded his arms defensively—and defiantly—across his chest.

"Please, Ryan," she said in a faltering voice. "This isn't any easier for us than it is for you."

Ryan shifted his annoyed gaze from his mother to Angus. "I do have one question," he said at last.

"Ask me anything," Angus said.

"I saw you holding my mother in your arms. What, exactly, are your intentions?"

Chapter 29

"THAT DIDN'T GO as well as I'd hoped," Angus said after the few abrupt questions Rye had asked had been answered, mostly in ways that hadn't pleased him, and he'd stalked out.

"What did you expect?" Darcie asked, shoving her still-full cup of coffee away from her. Angus had gotten them each a cup after Rye left. "He loved Paddy. It's going to take him a while to adjust to having another father in his life."

Angus's heart gave an extra thump. "Am I going to be in his life?"

Darcie sighed, then reached out and covered his hand, which lay on the table next to his coffee cup. "It's bad enough wondering what Mike and Amy Beth will think when they find out you're Rye's father. I'm afraid to imagine what they might do if you and I become a couple."

"You've been a widow for seven years," Angus said. "Aren't you entitled to a little happiness?"

"Not at the expense of my children's well-being."

"If they love you, they'll be happy for you."

"I'm realistic enough to expect some pushback, but I also believe they'll be okay with our relationship in the long run. At least, I hope so," she said, her eyes brimming with tears. "Because I do love you, Angus. I've always loved you. And I suppose I have to admit I'm not getting any younger."

Angus was surprised by the sudden knot in his throat. She'd been stingy with words of love. He couldn't believe she'd spoken them now. "Will you marry me, Darcie?"

She looked adorably startled. "What?"

He took her right hand in both of his and turned in his chair to face her. "I was an idiot all those years ago. I don't want to make the same mistake twice. If I'm rushing you, tell me so. But I want you for my wife. I want the right to love you and cherish you for the rest of my life. I also want to make love to you till we're both too tired to wiggle a toe—or any other body part."

Darcie giggled. It was a surprisingly girlish sound. The giggle faded as her face sobered. "I'm sure your intentions are honest, but you'll understand if I don't believe you're willing to marry me just like that." She snapped her fingers. She blushed as she added,

"And this time around, a married relationship is the only one I'm willing to have with you."

"Try me," he said.

"What are you suggesting?"

"Do your children love you?"

"Of course they do."

"Do they want the best for you?"

"Of course they do."

"Then let's get married."

Her jaw dropped. "Isn't this a little sudden?"

"I've been sharing my thoughts and feelings with you on the phone for years, being patient, waiting for you, the way I was too foolish and proud to do all those years ago. But I've waited—we've waited—long enough for our happily ever after. Rye finally knows the truth. We can't predict or control his response to that knowledge. We can only help him learn to live with the new reality—that he's my son, and that I plan to spend the rest of my life loving his mother."

"This is all happening so fast," she said breathlessly.

"Do you trust me?"

"Of course I do."

"Then marry me. Today. As soon as I can get it arranged." He waited, his heart in his throat, for her to decide whether to leap off the proverbial cliff with him.

At last she said, "All right."

Angus left Darcie sitting there with hope in her eyes and her lower lip gripped anxiously in her teeth and headed off to locate a justice of the peace and find out what paperwork they needed to get married.

He got no farther than the exit to the parking lot before he literally ran into Rye, who was apparently on his way back into the hospital.

"Did you forget something?" Angus asked.

"I'm glad I caught you alone," he said brusquely. "I have a few more questions I want answered."

"Let's go outside, where we won't be interrupted," Angus said, heading out the door without waiting for Rye to agree.

The sky was cloudy, threatening rain or snow, depending on whether the temperature went up or down later in the day. Angus felt cold and buttoned his shearling coat, as though that could stem the chill of fear inside him.

Angus stopped far enough from the hospital doors that they wouldn't be disturbed by other visitors and turned to face Rye. He'd always believed attack was the best defense, and he used it now. "You hurt your mother when you jumped up and marched out of the cafeteria without saying goodbye."

Rye reared back as though he'd been slapped. "I'll apologize to her later. Right now, I have a few things I need to know from you."

"I'm listening."

"Did you continue your affair with my mother after she was married?"

Angus let his disgust show on his face. "You

should know your mother would never have allowed it."

"How do I know that? She was your lover when you were a married man."

"And it tore her up inside," he replied. "I was the selfish one. I was the one who refused to let her walk away. When she got pregnant, there was no question of her priorities. She chose your future happiness, your well-being, over any considerations of mine—or her own."

"She loved my father!"

"I believe she came to love him very much." Angus let that comment sit there, with all its ramifications. That perhaps she hadn't loved Paddy when she'd married him. That she'd sacrificed her relationship with Angus for the benefit of their unborn child. That she'd cared more for her son than for her own happiness.

Angus saw the troubled look on Rye's face. "I regret the pain I caused your mother, but I don't regret loving her. I've never stopped."

"Have you been in contact with her over the years?"

Angus shook his head. "She wouldn't take my calls. Not until after Paddy died. Since then, we've spoken often."

Rye looked appalled. "You've been talking to her?"

"Almost every night."

"For seven years?"

Angus nodded. "She wouldn't let me see her because she was afraid you would find out the truth about your birth. She didn't want you hurt. She still doesn't want you hurt."

"It's a little late for that," Rye muttered.

"Explain that to me," Angus said. "What is it that bothers you most? The fact that you have a different biological father or—"

Rye cut him off. "The fact that she lied! To me. To my father." He bit off a curse and said, "To the man who raised me. Paddy's the only father I ever had, or ever will have, as far as I'm concerned."

"I hope you're wrong," Angus said quietly. "I hope you'll give me a chance to get to know you."

"Why would I do that?" Rye snarled.

"Because your mother's going to be my wife."

"The hell she is!"

"She loves me, and I love her. Are you going to deny her a second chance at happiness? Because you have that ability. If she believes you hate me, that you're determined never to have anything to do with me, she'll give me up again for your sake. You'll win. I'll be miserable and unhappy. But I guarantee you, so will she. You have a grown-up choice to make here, Rye.

"Are you going to be the bigger man, and forgive her—and me—for loving each other enough to create you? Or are you going to be the bastard you might have been if she hadn't married Paddy, and keep the two of us apart?"

Two red blotches appeared on Rye's cheeks. "You can't put this on me. I'm not the bad guy here."

"Not yet, anyway," Angus said in a hard voice. "You certainly have the power to ruin the rest of my life, and I believe hers as well. Think about it. Then decide if you can swallow your gorge and tolerate me enough to let your mom be happy again."

Angus found himself standing alone. Rye had stumbled away without a backward glance.

Chapter 30

"THE SONOFABITCH WANTS to marry her!" Rye raged to Lexie as he stalked back and forth in front of the fireplace. He stopped abruptly, turned to face her, and said, "Over my dead body. That's how he's going to marry her."

"Does your mother love him?" Lexie asked in an irritatingly calm voice from her seat in the rocker.

"What does that have to do with anything?"

"Everything. If they love each other, why shouldn't they be together?"

"She lied to my father. She never told him about her sordid affair—"

"How do you know it was sordid?" Lexie interjected. "From what you've said, Darcie and Angus have waited a lot of years to be together because your mother was worried about how you might be affected when you learned the truth about your birth."

No matter when his mom had revealed that Paddy wasn't his biological father it would have hurt, Rye thought. But worse than the lie he'd been told was the fact that she'd concealed it for so long. And it seemed a betrayal of his dad that she'd harbored this secret love for some other man, even if she hadn't acted on it. Rye saw the reasons why his mom had behaved the way she had, but he felt angry and confused by it all.

"I'm still in shock that Angus Flynn is your father," Lexie said. "I mean, what are the chances? They must be infinitesimal. I've known Angus practically all my life. He and my father are mortal enemies. Omigod! What if he tells my father about Cody? Or tells my family before I have a chance to do it myself?"

"That isn't going to happen."

"Why not?"

"Because Angus made a promise to my mother that he wouldn't. And since he's known about me and you and Cody for a while and hasn't said anything, it seems he's keeping his word."

Lexie let out a relieved sigh. "Thank goodness. I still can't believe the 'awful Flynn boys' I mentioned in the stories I told you and Pete when we had dinner at Casey's are your brothers." She shook her head and laughed. "I probably know all the men you're related to better than I know you, since every one of them is either married to or dating someone in my family. It's surreal."

"'Surreal' describes the situation perfectly," Rye muttered.

"What did you think of Angus when you met him?" Lexie asked.

Rye didn't want to admit that when he'd first spied Flynn he'd had an impression of power. His father had stood ramrod straight, shoulders squared, and met Rye's gaze unabashed and unashamed. And he'd been brutally honest about his intentions toward Rye's mother.

Rye had glanced at his mother, whose face had blanched—in fear of his reaction, he'd realized—before she twined her fingers with Angus's, showing her willingness to go along with his plans. Rye had been too shocked by the turn of events to say much of anything. After a few brief questions, he'd grabbed his hat and fled.

He'd gotten no farther than the hospital parking lot before he'd returned to confront them both and had that second, gut-wrenching conversation with Angus.

Rye wasn't a dog in the manger. He wanted his mother to be happy. He just wasn't sure he could handle having this stranger thrust into their family circle.

"I don't like the sonofabitch," Rye said.

"Why not?"

"Probably because I was raised by Paddy Sullivan to believe there's right and there's wrong, and what

Angus did with my mother—having an affair with her when he was married to another woman—was wrong. His actions caused a lot of pain for my mom. I can't forgive that."

"Is it her pain or yours that's making you so angry?"

"My mom has certainly been miserable. What pain are you suggesting I'm suffering?"

"Finding out you aren't who you thought you were."

"I'm not going to change who I am because of this," he said.

"But everything *is* changed," Lexie pointed out. "You have four new brothers. And now you know Mike and Amy Beth are not related to you in the way you thought. Have you spoken to them about any of this?"

"I'm leaving that to Mom."

"Are you sure you want to do that?"

"Why not?"

"Because the two of them may be angry with your mother as well. The news might be easier on her coming from you."

Rye conceded she had a point. He dropped into the overstuffed leather chair next to her and said, "Sorry to dump all this on you. I needed somewhere to vent."

"Should we tell Cody he has another grandfather?"

"Not yet. Maybe not ever, depending on how

things turn out between my mom and my . . . Angus," he finished.

"Are you going to get in touch with 'those awful Flynn boys'?"

Rye snorted. "I'm sure they're not any more ready to meet me than I am to meet them." He rubbed a hand across the day's growth of dark beard on his chin. "Hell. I'm not even sure they know yet that I exist."

Lexie laughed suddenly. "It just occurred to me that your relationship with Angus means I'm involved with one of 'those awful Flynn boys'—biologically speaking—too!"

"So now we're involved? The last I heard, you wanted me to keep my distance."

Lexie blushed and lowered her eyes. "I just meant . . ."

She nervously brushed her hands against her thighs but didn't finish her sentence.

"I was raised by Patrick Sullivan," Rye said. "He was my father. He taught me to be the man I am. There's nothing 'Flynn' about me."

She eyed him sideways. "You might not think so, but I see a surprising amount of 'Flynn' in you."

He frowned and leaned back in his chair. "What do you mean?"

"It's an attitude. A certainty that nothing and no one can get in the way of what you want. You might have gotten it from your mother. She possesses that same 'I will not be denied' belief in herself. It might be what attracted Angus to her in the first place. I noticed it about you right away. I just didn't associate it with Angus. Was Patrick Sullivan like that?"

Rye was perturbed to realize that the man who'd raised him wasn't anything like that. Paddy had expected disaster at every turn. He planned for it, so he was never defeated by it. But he never believed he would thrive and survive no matter what. He was always waiting for the other shoe to drop, for adversity to destroy him.

Rye had never understood that sort of thinking. He'd always been willing to try something new, to take a chance, firmly believing that everything would turn out all right in the end. Could something like that, a belief in oneself, be inherited? Wasn't it something he'd learned, most likely from his mother?

He shook his head in denial. "Belief in myself isn't something I inherited from Angus Flynn."

She arched a questioning brow. "Isn't it?"

"What else have you got?" he countered. "How else am I like Angus?"

"The way you stand."

He wrinkled his brow. "Explain that."

"Straight. Tall. Unbowed." She made a speculative sound in her throat before she said, "Proud, but not cocky."

Rye thought back to Angus's appearance at the hospital. How he'd seemed so formidable, completely undaunted at the prospect of meeting a son he'd sired but never seen.

He didn't want to be that man's son. He wished his father—Paddy Sullivan—were still alive. He missed him. Missed his honest goodness. From everything he'd learned about Angus Flynn, that was *not* something Rye would have inherited from him.

"Angus and I don't really look alike. If you stood the two of us next to each other, no one would suspect we're related," he pointed out to her.

"I suppose not. There's a great deal of your mother in you. All of Angus's sons—except the last, who isn't related to him by blood—have black hair and blue eyes."

"He's got a son who isn't related?" Rye asked, astonished.

"Apparently, his wife found out about your mother. She retaliated by having an affair, and Devon Flynn was the result. Tragically, Angus's wife died in childbirth. Devon only recently found out that his biological father is a Texas rancher named Shiloh Kidd."

"More lying. More deceit," Rye said bitterly.

"What purpose would have been served, in either case, by telling you boys the truth? What would have been different in your lives?"

"We would have known."

"So what?" she argued.

Before he could pursue the subject, he heard his son cry out, "Mommy! Mommy! Help!"

Then Cody screamed, a sound so chilling it made all the hair on Rye's body stand on end.

Lexie was gone in an instant, sprinting toward Cody's bedroom. Rye was half a step behind her.

She banged open the door and raced to Cody's

side, dropping onto the edge of his bed and drawing their son into her arms.

"A bear was going to eat me!" Cody said between heart-wrenching sobs, huddling as close to her as he could get.

A trembling Rye sat next to Lexie and captured both mother and son in his sheltering arms. Cody had sloughed off his fall into the river, likely because he'd been rescued so quickly and because Rusty had been the hero in the story. But the bear attack on Mike persisted in causing Cody to have nightmares.

"Shh," Lexie said. "You're all right, Cody. It was only a dream."

"Mike's bear came back to the ranch," Cody said, his eyes wide with terror. "He was eating my head!"

Rye felt Lexie's body quiver and realized the image Cody had painted was frightening her as well.

"That grizzly is long gone," Rye said.

"No, he's not!" Cody cried. "I heard Mommy talking on the phone. He killed a girl who was hiking in the park."

Rye exchanged a questioning look with Lexie, who nodded.

He started to say, "It's probably not the same grizzly." But a wounded grizzly, like the one that had attacked Mike, was far more likely to be the culprit.

"Mommy's going to hunt for that mean bear tomorrow with some rangers and sheriffs. Don't go, Mommy," he pleaded, gripping her more tightly. "That grizzly will eat you, too!"

Rye's jaws were tight when he spoke. "I guess a

lot happened while I was at the hospital. When were you going to tell me?"

"I'll talk to you about this later," she said, "after I get Cody back to sleep."

His son—their son—was still grasping her as though she would disappear if he let her go. It suddenly dawned on him that when Cody had needed solace and safety, he hadn't called out to Rye. He'd called to his mother, and he was clinging to her now like some grizzly cub afraid to venture out on its own. He should be jealous. Instead, he felt glad, for his son's sake, that he had a mother he trusted and loved so much.

"You don't have to worry about that grizzly," she murmured to Cody. "He can't hurt me."

"Promise?" Cody said.

"I promise," Lexie said, as she met Rye's gaze with troubled eyes. "That grizzly will never hurt anyone again."

Chapter 31

IT TOOK A long time to calm Cody down, but when Vick finally turned out the light and left Cody's room, she was startled to find Rye waiting for her in the hall.

"Want to fill me in?" he said, his jaws tight.

"Not really. I need to get some sleep. Cody might wake up again, and I have a long day tomorrow."

"Hunting grizzly?"

"Shh. You'll wake Cody."

Rye snagged her arm and hustled her through the closest doorway, which happened to be his bedroom. Once inside, he closed the door and leaned his back against it, preventing any attempt she might make to escape.

"I didn't realize Cody was listening to my phone

conversation," she said, "or I never would have discussed the injuries to that poor girl." She put a hand up to stop him from speaking and added, "Yes, I'm going on a hunt tomorrow in Glacier National Park with a few members of the Wildlife Human Attack Response Team. That grizzly has to be caught. And killed."

"I'll bet you're sorry about that," he said in a mocking voice.

"I am," she replied. "That bear didn't ask to be wounded by some poacher. But the sooner that grizzly's caught and killed, the less panic and talk there will be about the 'danger of grizzlies in the park,' and the less chance they'll end up as targets during the next hunting season."

"I'm coming, too."

"I was going to ask you to take care of Cody while I'm gone."

"My mother can do that."

"But she's—"

"If she can leave Mike long enough to meet with her lover, she can leave him long enough to watch Cody while we're both gone," Rye said.

"You're not part of the team."

"I'm making myself part of it. That bear attacked my brother on my land. I'm going."

"You won't be allowed to shoot a gun in the park. You can't go, Rye."

"Try and stop me."

"This is getting us nowhere," she said, shoving a few stray hairs from her brow. "I'm tired, Rye."

He opened the door and said, "Fine. Get some sleep. I'll see you in the morning."

But when she came abreast of him, he palmed the door shut, caught her by the waist, and pulled her close, tucking her head under his chin and folding his arms around her. She didn't fight him, but she didn't lean into him, either.

Vick could feel Rye trembling and wondered whether it was Cody's nightmare or his confrontation with Angus Flynn that had made him seek comfort from her. Both, she figured. Although, from his next words, it appeared he was only going to acknowledge one of the two.

"When Cody screamed like that, my heart nearly stopped," he admitted.

"I should have been more careful on the phone."

"He'll get over it."

She leaned back and searched his features, finding the distress she'd expected to see as a result of his meeting with Angus. "Will he?" *Will you?*

Rye shrugged. "Grizzlies and wolves and mountain lions are a part of life in Montana. You accept it, or you move somewhere more civilized."

"So you don't want to kill the grizzly?" she asked.

Rye's lips tilted in a rueful smile. "I didn't say that."

Vick leaned her cheek against his chest. Would Rye ever be able to accept the new father who'd suddenly appeared in his life? Or would he move on without him? She knew Rye was hurting, but she had no idea how to ease his pain. Vick didn't want to feel so much. She wanted space from him. "Is there any way I can convince you to stay home tomorrow, and let me go on my own?"

"No, Lexie, there isn't."

Her arm slid up around his neck and played with the hair at his nape, sending tremors through his body. "Why do you call me that? My name is Vick."

"Lexie is the girl who stole my heart and then vanished like a wisp of smoke. I miss her."

Her body tensed before she met his gaze and said, "Lexie was a fantasy. Someone I made up. She's not me. I'd rather you call me Vick."

"And let go of the fantasy?" he said quietly.

She grasped his hair and used it to angle his head downward. "Yes. Vick is the real me, the flawed woman, who makes mistakes and can't be painted in black and white. My mixed-up life is a rainbow of pink and purple and yellow and green and a thousand colors in between."

"I'll settle for the woman in my arms. Are you going to kiss me, Vick, or just stand there and think about it for a while?"

With their mouths a breath apart, Vick didn't have the strength to turn Rye away. She wanted his kiss. She wanted him. And he apparently wanted her, humanly imperfect though she was.

Could a kiss be both gentle and carnal? Vick stood on tiptoes to fit their bodies more closely together and leaned into the strength of the man who held her in his arms. She felt Rye's hand urging her belly against his erection, and knew that if she let this go on even a moment longer, she would be in bed with him. Perhaps, with his willingness to call her "Vick," he no longer viewed her as the fantasy woman he'd created in his mind. But she wasn't sure he perceived her as the person she really was, either.

Better to give him time to sort all that out in his head. Better not to add sex to the equation quite yet. Better to back off and walk away.

Except, Rye's kisses were awfully persuasive. His hands found their way to her breasts, and his mouth slid to her throat, creating havoc. She indulged her need to touch and found the hard ridge beneath his jeans. She heard him make a sound in his throat that might have been a plea. Or a prayer.

She wanted to touch warm flesh. Craved the touch of warm flesh. She settled for shoving Rye's shirt up out of his jeans and sliding her hands along his muscular chest to male nipples that had become hard buds. He gasped as her fingernails scraped across them.

His mouth latched on to her nipple through her shirt, and he bit down hard enough to make her gasp with pain and with pleasure. Before she realized what he was doing, he had her belt unbuckled and her jeans unzipped and his fingers were down inside her panties and then inside her.

A knock on Rye's door interrupted them. "Hey, Rye," his sister called quietly through the door. "Are you in there? I don't want to wake up Cody. Can I come in?"

Rye's hand was out of her body—and his mouth left her breast so fast—Vick almost laughed. He was acting like a teenager caught in the act by his parents. Although, she supposed having your sister on the other side of a door when you had your hands all over—and inside—a woman wasn't much better.

"I'll be out in a minute." He swore when he realized Vick had undone his belt buckle and unbuttoned his Levi's and had her hand down inside his shorts. He gently eased her encircling fingers free and said, "My sister has rotten timing."

Vick thought so, too, but she wasn't going to agree with him. If not for Amy Beth, she'd be having sex with Rye right about now. She was on the pill but that didn't mean she was a hundred percent protected. She could vouch for the fact that accidents happened. It was beyond stupid to take the chance of getting pregnant when things were so unsettled between them. But apparently, they both tended to be foolish when they got anywhere near each other.

Even though they were quiet as they put themselves back together, Vick was sure they weren't fooling Amy Beth. The proof of that was the smirk on her face when Rye finally opened the door.

"What the hell are you doing here?" he asked, his sexual frustration making his voice harsh.

"I decided I'm old enough to make up my own mind where I belong." Before he could protest she added, "I got my professors to give me an extension on my work so I can be here to help." She eyed Vick's flushed face and mussed hair and said, "Looks like I got here just in time."

"Actually, you did," Rye said as he ushered her

back down the hall toward the living room. "I'm going grizzly hunting tomorrow with Vick. We need someone to stay with Cody. How about it?"

"I guess I can do that," Amy Beth said, eyeing the two of them over her shoulder. "Grizzly hunting? With Vick? For the bear that attacked Mike?"

Rye nodded. "He attacked and killed a woman today in the park."

"Oh, no!" Amy Beth turned and said, "Is there any chance that bear will come back here? I mean, should I keep Cody inside?"

Vick hadn't considered the possibility that the grizzly would return to the place where it had been shot, but it had found an easy meal with one of Rye's Angus calves. Why not come back for another helping? And it was obviously out of hibernation now. "Staying close to the house is probably a good idea," she said at last.

"Now that I'm back, where is Vick going to sleep?" Amy Beth asked her brother with a sly smile. "We need to keep Mom's room available since she said she might come home for an evening, and you've seen Mike's room. I wouldn't put a raccoon in there."

Vick flushed.

Rye said, "She can have my room."

"Where are you going to sleep?" Amy Beth asked, eyeing the two of them with a smirk.

Rye glared at his sister and said, "On the goddamn couch."

Chapter 32

AFTER A NIGHT spent sleeping on the couch, Vick had expected Rye to be grumpy. He was gruff and blunt and sullen with her at breakfast and spoke not a word on their ride to the west entrance to Glacier National Park. To her surprise, the members of the Wildlife Human Attack Response Team who met them there, Flathead County Deputy Sheriff Pete Harrison and Glacier National Park Ranger Johnny Lightfoot, were happy to have Rye come along.

Vick watched for signs of resentment or jealousy from Pete when he and Rye greeted each other, but Pete acted as though they'd never been rivals for the same woman—in a competition he'd lost. Their respectful behavior toward each other made her like both men better.

Pete and Johnny had only brought three snowmobiles, so Rye would have to ride double with her. She'd brought her rifle, a short-barreled Marlin 1895, but she'd reminded Rye he should leave his Remington M700 in his truck, since firing his weapon in a national park was illegal, and he was just along for the ride.

"Why do you get to shoot at the bear that attacked Mike and I don't?" he demanded.

"I'm only planning to shoot if we get attacked by a grizzly and bear spray doesn't stop it," Vick replied.

"I thought that was the point of this trip—to find that grizzly and kill it."

"It is, but I would rather someone else did the killing besides me." Which was why she'd brought a gun that was no good for long distances. She was willing to help track the bear, but she didn't want to be the one to put it down. If she spotted the grizzly, she would contact the other team members and let one of them take the shot.

"I brought my rifle with me," Rye said to the ranger. "Do I have permission to shoot if I see that bear?"

To her amazement, Lightfoot said, "You bet. We can use all the help we can get on this hunt."

Rye shot her a smug look and shouldered his rifle using its sling.

The ranger went on to explain, "After what happened to Mike, we set a string of steel leg-hold traps in likely places. This bad boy was either hibernating or too clever to get caught."

"Don't take any chances, and don't wait on us," Pete said. "If you see that grizzly, take the shot."

"How will I know it's the right bear?" Rye asked.

"The young woman who got mauled was Terry Smith," Lightfoot said. "Another hiker, Robin Coffman, was with her during the attack. They didn't have bear spray with them, so Robin had no way to help her friend. She got herself up a tree and waited the bear out. Needless to say, Robin got a good look at the grizzly. The bear has a streak of gold across its hump, and Robin saw an ear tag, Number 437, which turned out to be a bear called Goldilocks."

"Park bears have names?" Rye said incredulously.

Vick explained, "Most of the bears in the park are tagged, and a lot of them have radio collars so scientists can monitor their habits, for purposes of research. The person who first tags a bear and tattoos its inner lip gives it a nickname."

"Goldilocks doesn't have a radio collar," Lightfoot said.

"Goldilocks doesn't sound like the best name for a renegade bear," Rye pointed out.

"She wasn't a renegade until she got shot," Vick said.

"Killing cattle doesn't make her a renegade?" Rye asked.

"Until we find the remains of the calf you lost, we have no way of knowing whether it was actually killed by a mountain lion or wolves." Vick saw the disgusted look on Rye's face at her defense of the grizzly. But her version of events could very well be the truth, and a grizzly feasting on carrion left by other predators wasn't a menace to ranchers like Rye.

Unfortunately for this bear, it had been shot by a poacher and had subsequently attacked Mike and killed a young woman. It had to be put down.

Vick shuddered at the thought of what the surviving girl must have witnessed. The screams of her friend. Her agonizing cries for help as the grizzly mauled her body. The growls and chuffing of the bear. The copper smell of blood. Robin would have to live with that memory the rest of her life.

At least, Vick thought, the girl would have the satisfaction of knowing she'd helped to identify the bear that had killed her friend. The gold streak across the hump on its back, distinctive to grizzlies, would help them recognize Goldilocks from a distance. Of course, the ear tag would clinch it.

"This grizzly also limps on its right forepaw," Lightfoot said.

Pete turned to Rye and said, "Sound familiar?"

Rye nodded. That information coincided with what he and Pete had discovered about the bear that had attacked Mike.

"Not much of Going-to-the-Sun Road is plowed," the ranger said. "We'll take the snowmobiles as close as we can get on the road and hike the rest of the way to the site of the attack." He looked at each one of them intently and asked, "Everybody got bear spray?"

"I thought we were going to shoot this bear," Rye said.

"Goldilocks isn't the only bear in these woods," Lightfoot replied. "I walk with my gun over my shoulder and a can of bear spray in my hand—with the safety off. And I carry a second can of spray on my belt."

"Are you kidding?" Rye said.

"You only have to get attacked once to know you don't have much chance with a rifle if a grizzly surprises you," Lightfoot replied. "They're faster than you can imagine."

"I suppose you speak from experience," Rye said.

Lightfoot pulled his coat collar down, where the sort of scars Mike was going to have once he healed angled down the ranger's scalp and neck. He turned to Pete and said, "Ready to go?"

Pete nodded, put on his helmet, and started up his snowmobile.

"I'll drive," Vick said to Rye as she handed him an extra helmet. "I know the park better than you."

"Don't be so sure of that. I've done a lot of hiking in Glacier."

"I've done more."

At his inquisitive look she explained, "I've spent days on end in the park with donors who wanted to see a grizzly in the flesh."

"And have they?" he asked.

"Ninety-nine percent of the time."

"I hope you can deliver today."

"Me, too." Vick was aware of Rye's arms snug around her waist and his muscular thighs surrounding hers as they bumped over the snowy road. They had to shout to be heard over the loud engine.

"I thought more snow would be melted," Vick said.

"It should help us tracking that bear," Rye shouted back.

It was a serious hike through the muddy grass and snow from the spot where they left their snowmobiles to the site of the attack, on Reynolds Creek near Deadwood Falls. The air was fresh and clear and cold. The vast Montana sky and the crystal clear water in the creek seemed to be fighting with each other to see which could be a brighter blue. Cow parsnip and monkey flower, both grizzly forage, were pushing up through the snow.

Vick listened to the chatter of a red squirrel that had claimed a fallen log and trekked through a stand of hemlock filled with raucous jays that seemed to resent their intrusion. The fact that the hikers were so far off the main trail went a long way toward explaining why this tragedy had occurred.

"Looks like they were bushwhacking," Vick said.

"They were from Chicago. They wanted to be sure to see a grizzly," Lightfoot said with a grim smile.

Vick saw where the grizzly had scratched out a

bed beneath a ponderosa pine. There was evidence Goldilocks had eaten sedge and skunk cabbage and stolen most of a squirrel's stash of pine nuts. It appeared the grizzly had been awakened from sleep and charged the two girls when they surprised it.

According to the surviving girl's account, her friend had made the fatal mistake of fighting back, which was likely why she'd ended up dead. Vick knew from her research on grizzlies that they attacked other bears only until they surrendered, and they exhibited the same behavior when charging humans. When people did what seemed natural—fighting back—grizzlies continued their attack. When humans surrendered, the bear bit and clawed, but usually left within minutes. The difficulty, of course, was to stifle your screams and lie unmoving, preferably on your stomach with your hands protecting your head, while your flesh was being viciously clawed and your bones were being crunched by a five-hundred-pound grizzly.

"I did some scouting," Lightfoot said, "and Goldilocks left this location headed east, in the direction of St. Mary Lake."

Vick bit her lip at the thought of the sort of trek they might be facing if the bear headed up into any one of the three rugged mountains, each between eight and nine thousand feet, that towered over the lake. The dense forests at the base of the mountains were filled not only with bears but with other dangerous predators.

Goldilocks could easily move fifty square miles within the park looking for food, and they'd brought supplies in case an emergency arose that forced them to spend the night. Each of them carried a heavy backpack, with Vick hauling her fair share of the load. She'd been on other hunts in the past, when bears were being tracked to be collared and tattooed, and she knew the terrain could be grueling.

Vick wore binoculars on a strap around her neck, and her rifle was slung sideways across her chest by cords around both stock and barrel that were connected to her backpack across each shoulder, supporting the weight of the weapon. That kept her rifle easily accessible and left her hands free to carry pepper spray.

"The trail peters out about a quarter mile from here, so my suggestion is we follow the trail as far as we can, then split into two teams until one of us picks up the trail again," Lightfoot said. He turned to Pete and added, "You come with me. Vick can partner Rye."

Vick saw the surprise on Rye's face when the ranger suggested he team up with her. It was a vote of confidence, an acknowledgment that she knew as much about tracking in the park terrain as Lightfoot did.

"You've got your sat phone?" Lightfoot asked her.

Vick nodded. A satellite phone could be a lifesaver in an emergency, and it was the best way for them to communicate if they got more than shouting distance apart.

"Give me a call if you find Goldilocks's trail, and we'll do the same." Lightfoot turned to Rye and said, "Keep your eyes and ears open." Then, to both of them, "Good hunting."

Chapter 33

ONCE THE TWO teams separated, Rye found himself consumed by a primitive dread. He and Vick were noisily shoving their way through dense brush along Reynolds Creek that might very well be concealing the grizzly that had gravely injured one person and killed another. He found Vick's serenely undisturbed demeanor irritating.

"You're not going to carry that pepper spray in your hand like that all day, are you?" Rye was having trouble accepting the fact that pepper spray would be a better deterrent to a grizzly charge than a bullet.

"I am. With the safety off," Vick replied.

"That sounds dangerous."

"If we spook a bear, I might not have time to get

my pepper spray out before I end up flat on my back with a grizzly standing on top of me. Better safe than sorry. Where's your pepper spray?"

"In my pack."

Rye walked three more steps before he realized Vick wasn't with him. He turned and asked, "What's the matter?"

"Get it out."

"What?"

"Your pepper spray. Get it out right now and attach it to your belt."

"You're being ridiculous," Rye said. "You've got spray right there in your hand. Why do I need it, too?"

"Because if a bear puts me down and comes after you, my pepper spray isn't going to do you much good."

"I've got my rifle."

"Were you listening to Lightfoot?" she said. "Did you hear a word he said? If I have to point it out to you, Mike had a shotgun with him that turned out to be useless. Guns are great from a distance. I hope we're able to take out this bear without putting anyone in danger. But there are eight hundred grizzlies in Montana—three hundred of them in this park—and bushwhacking like this, our chances of running into one of them, not necessarily the one we're hunting, are pretty good."

Rye dropped his pack in the snow with a grunt of disgust and rummaged through it for his pepper spray. It was near the bottom, so maybe she had a point about it not being readily available. He pulled it out and snapped a holster containing a metal can the size of the Yeti he used for his morning coffee onto his belt, then slung his backpack back on before reshouldering his rifle. "Satisfied?"

"Thank you. Frankly, I thought you were going to be stubborn about this."

He grinned. "Did you have a Plan B?"

"I was going to let the next five-hundred-pound grizzly we encounter take a bite out of you."

Rye laughed. It dawned on him that he was thinking of Victoria Grayhawk as "Vick," not "Lexie," and interacting with the woman she was today, not the fantasy he'd held in his head for so many years. His change in attitude toward her was something he likely would have shared with Mike while they were doing dishes together. He missed his brother. It hadn't taken him long to realize that it didn't matter one bit that they had different fathers.

Vick veered closer to the creek and stopped to examine a spot where dirt was splattered across the snow. "A bear dug up a bunch of glacier lilies for breakfast this morning, but it used its right paw, and I don't see any blood, so maybe not our bear."

"Our bear might be healed if the wound was slight," Rye said.

"That's possible." She started walking again, glanced at him, and asked, "What shall we discuss?"

In order not to surprise any bears, it was necessary to make noise, which meant they had to keep talking. That was something Rye hadn't considered when he'd decided to come along. For however many hours they spent hunting Goldilocks, he and Vick would need to talk about . . . something.

He grimaced and said, "I've been thinking a lot about what happens if Angus marries my mother."

"Oh?"

He made a face at her. She was leaving the entire conversational ball in his court. He sighed and said, "I don't think I can live in the same house with him."

"Why not?"

"It would feel too strange to have another man sleeping in Dad's bed or sitting at Dad's place at the table or slouching in Dad's chair in front of the fireplace."

"Does your mother want Angus to come live in her home? Or is she planning to go to Jackson Hole to live with him?"

Rye's brow furrowed as he considered the second option Vick had suggested. "I don't think she'd leave Montana before Amy Beth gets her degree."

"Why not? Amy Beth is away most of the year at school. Your sister could either stay with you and Mike in the summer or spend her summers with your mom and Angus in Wyoming."

"My mom has been doing the lion's share of taking care of Cody while Mike and I work the ranch. I don't think she'd want to leave me without help."

An uncomfortable, and quite literally dangerous, silence grew before Vick said, "I could help with Cody's care."

Rye knew Vick wanted more time with Cody, and

that she was willing to go to court to get it. But the reason she'd first given for relinquishing custody of her child remained an issue. "What about your work?"

She lifted her chin militantly. "There are lots of spaces between travel and events when I could be with Cody. You—we—could hire someone to fill in when I'm gone."

Rye noticed Vick was no longer adding the qualifiers, the "If it's all right with you," or the "If you think it's a good idea," when she made suggestions about spending more time with their son. He realized how much his attitude had changed, when it dawned on him that her change in attitude was okay with him. That long-ago promise he'd made to a seemingly irresponsible girl named Lexie didn't apply to the woman he'd come to know as Vick. "Sounds like a plan," he said.

"One problem solved. What else have you got?" Vick said with a cheeky grin.

"How about sending Angus back to Wyoming with his tail between his legs?"

"How about giving your mother a chance to be happy?" she shot back.

"I don't like the guy. I don't expect I ever will. But you have a point. Mom obviously loves him. I guess my having to give blood was a blessing in disguise, since now she'll be able to reunite with her long-lost love."

"You sound bitter," Vick said.

"She should have told me the truth sooner."

"People make mistakes," Vick said. "It's hard to judge the choice she made, since we have no way of knowing whether things would have been better or worse for you if she'd told your dad the truth. Haven't you ever done anything you regretted?"

"Yeah." He met her gaze and said, "Keeping my distance from you for way too long."

The surprise on her face was comic. "When did you decide that was a mistake?"

"I've known for a long time. It's only since you moved to Montana last year that I admitted to myself what an ass I've been. I could've been loving you all this time. Instead of despising you."

"Can you shut it off like that? Loathing me, hating me, spurning me? Can you banish it with the snap of your fingers?" She snapped her fingers, but with her gloves on, there was no sound.

He shrugged. "It felt like you rejected me when you rejected our son. And it wasn't easy to accept the fact that you thought so little of our night together that you could walk away without looking back."

She met his gaze, her eyes filled with distress. "The night we met, I told you a little about my situation. That my mom ran off and left me behind. That my dad was pretty much absent from my life. What I didn't say was that I didn't trust you—or any man—to hang around once you'd gotten what you wanted."

His face flushed as a wave of anger washed over him. He couldn't believe she'd held such a low opinion of him. But what else was she supposed to think? After all, they'd hooked up in a bar and ended up in bed. If it looks like a duck and quacks like a duck . . . But damn it, she was wrong. "That night wasn't only about sex."

"Wasn't it? I don't remember us doing a lot of talking once we got to your hotel room," she reminded him. "It was all about touching and kissing and very gritty, down-and-dirty, pretty amazing . . ." She hesitated, met his gaze and said, "Sex."

"I thought I'd found my soul mate!" he blurted. Rye was immediately sorry he'd spoken. Why reveal how stupid he'd been, pinning his hopes and dreams on a total stranger? Why make himself vulnerable to a second rejection by admitting how important he'd believed she was to his future happiness?

Vick stopped in her tracks and turned to face him, setting a gloved hand against his cheek. She looked deep into his eyes and said in a quiet voice, "I had no idea you felt like that, Rye. I'm sorry if I hurt you."

Her apology poured balm on a wound he hadn't previously acknowledged. Her eyes slid closed as he lowered his head to place the barest kiss on her lips. Except, that touch wasn't nearly enough. He slid his arm around her waist and tried to pull her close but was hindered by their bulky coats and equipment. He shoved her binoculars out of his way as his mouth captured hers, and he was soon lost in the taste of her, caught up in her urgent response. Apparently, she understood what he'd been saying, maybe even wanted the same thing. He'd have to ask her to be sure, but he was too busy now for words.

Suddenly, he heard a *woofing* sound and branches crackling. He jerked his head around and locked eyes with a grizzly bear cub as shocked to see him as he was to see it. Every hair on his body stood on end as the cub made a screeching sound, like a newborn calf in distress. It whirled and ran directly into a second cub, tumbling them both into a heap, creating a cacophony of fearful shrieking noise meant to attract their mother.

Their mother.

Rye realized two things at once. First, he didn't want to shoot a mother bear. That would be dooming the cubs. And second, he wasn't going to be able to get his rifle off his shoulder and into his hands in time to shoot anything. While he was still frozen in place, the cubs disappeared into the undergrowth.

He waited for the mother bear to show her face, to charge him, but he heard nothing. Not a sound.

"Where is she?" Rye croaked. "The mother bear."

"I don't see her," Vick said in a quiet voice.

He couldn't believe she was so calm. One look at her face and he knew she wasn't as unruffled as she'd sounded. Her eyes were wide as saucers, and the hand that held a can of bear spray was shaking badly. "What do we do now?" he asked.

"Let's stand here a minute and talk quietly without moving. If the cubs are back with her, maybe the mother grizzly won't think we're a threat, and she'll take them and leave."

What seemed like the longest two minutes of his life later, he heard Vick release a long, loud sigh of relief. "There they are," she said, pointing with the bear spray in her hand at the mother and her two cubs, halfway up a nearby slope and heading even higher, weaving in and out of the pines. "I think we're okay."

Rye heard a long, loud *psssss,* like a locomotive letting off steam. Confused by the sound, he turned to his left, and was stunned by what he saw, because it seemed so impossible.

A second grizzly emerged from the tangled brush and took several giant leaps toward him. The first thing he noticed was the gold streak across the bear's hump.

Goldilocks!

His body still hadn't stopped trembling from his encounter with the cubs, and the sudden appearance of this known man-killer seemed supernatural. There was no question in his mind that the grizzly was going to attack. Rye noticed what seemed like odd facets of the bear in the moment. Her little round ears sticking out from her big skull. The muscles rippling in her gold-streaked fur. Her dark underbelly as she lifted herself onto her back feet for just a second before coming down on all fours again, favoring her right forepaw.

He stood his ground, knowing he didn't stand a chance if he ran. He couldn't remember where he'd heard a grizzly could travel fifty yards in three seconds, but he was sure Goldilocks had moved at least that fast when she appeared out of nowhere. His body wasn't responding to the commands of his brain, and he couldn't seem to move. He had trouble getting his rifle off his shoulder, because it kept getting hooked on the knife he held in a sheath at his waist. He couldn't catch his breath, and his heart felt like it might rocket out of his chest.

The grizzly's mouth was open as she *woofed* a warning. He saw long, sharp teeth and drooling slobber. He wondered if he was imagining her fetid breath, or whether he was only remembering what Mike had said.

Then she charged.

Rye's rifle never made it off his shoulder. When the enormous grizzly was less than ten yards away, he heard a whooshing *pfffft* that stopped Goldilocks in her tracks. It took him a second to realize her terrifying visage was enveloped in a cloud of orange-yellow mist. *Bear spray*. The grizzly was getting a heavy dose of capsaicin, derived from the hottest of hot chili peppers, blinding her eyes and burning her nose and swelling her throat and lungs, making it hard to breathe.

Rye grabbed for the bear spray at his waist, fighting with the Velcro cover that held it in the holster.

He was fumbling to get the safety off when he heard a deafening *craaack!* That was followed by a second *craaack!* Both sounds echoed off the surrounding mountains.

When he looked up again, bear spray finally at the ready, Goldilocks took one step, teetered, and fell onto her side. If the grizzly had continued its charge, he would have been far too late to save himself.

His whole body was trembling, and his heart was thundering in his chest from the burst of adrenaline it had gotten. He turned to Vick and saw that her face had blanched as white as chalk. His tongue was dry of spit, but he managed to say, "You shot her."

Vick's mouth was opened wide, gasping for air. "She had to be put down." She'd dropped the empty can of bear spray at her feet and let go of her rifle, which hung across her chest on the cords attached to her backpack, to grab the second can of bear spray from her belt with shaking hands. "Not sure why Goldilocks was here, so close to the mother bear and her cubs, but with our luck there's a third bear out there somewhere."

He held his palms up as he approached her, afraid she would reflexively spray him. He tried to speak, but nothing came out. He cleared his throat and croaked, "We're okay, Vick. The grizzly's dead. You killed it."

Her shoulders slumped and tears of relief sprang to her eyes, as she heaved a single, desperate sob.

He held on to his bear spray as he opened his arms wide, and she stumbled into his embrace, shivering and shaking. His arms folded around her, and he murmured words of comfort.

"We're all right. You saved us. We're okay." He added, "I'll be carrying my bear spray in my hand with the safety off from now on."

That made her laugh. And cry.

When she looked up at him with tear-filled eyes, a smile on her face, he gave her a quick, hard kiss. Short and sweet. He wouldn't make the mistake of getting distracted again in grizzly country.

Vick's satellite phone rang and she answered it. "Yes," she said. "I got two bullets into Goldilocks, and she's down." She pulled the phone from her ear and said to Rye, "Can you check to make sure she's dead?"

"Sure," Rye said, unslinging his rifle with surprising ease, now that the emergency was past. He approached the grizzly carefully, made a quick examination, and said, "Two wounds. One to the chest, one to the head. This grizzly has gone to bear heaven."

Vick made a face at his levity, then gave the other members of the team confirmation that the grizzly was dead and coordinates for where they were. Finally, she said, "If you'll take care of removing the carcass, we'll head home. Sure. We'll leave the snowmobile where we found it."

When she ended the call, she said, "We're done here."

"I'm sorry."

"For what?"

"That you had to be the one to kill Goldilocks."

Her eyes looked bleak. "Fine savior of the grizzly I am. I hope I never have to do anything like that again."

"You made sure that bear won't harm anyone else," Rye said.

"I want to catch the poacher who wounded Goldilocks and made her a killer," Vick said, her eyes narrowed and her mouth thinned. "And string him up by his thumbs."

"I'm with you there," Rye said.

"Pete will retrieve any evidence he can from Goldilocks, so we can prosecute if we ever catch the guy."

"I learned a very important lesson today," Rye said.

"What's that?"

"How to stay alive during a bear attack."

She shot him a quizzical look.

He explained, "You were right. I never got my gun off my shoulder in time to use it for defense. If you hadn't stopped that bear in her tracks with pepper spray, I would have been down for the count."

Rye shuddered as he recalled Mike's gruesome wounds and realized that he'd barely escaped being similarly injured. He finally understood why Vick had brought two cans of bear spray. If you were ever attacked and used one can on a bear, you'd have a second for protection from other bears—attracted by the smell of blood, if you were injured—on the way out.

"I'm just glad we managed to come out of not just one, but two bear encounters unscathed, and that we didn't have to hurt the mother of those cubs," Rye said. "In the millisecond I had to get a look at them, they were kind of cute."

"Are you sure you're okay?" Vick asked. "Because you mentioned something about grizzly cubs being *cute.*"

"You look like you're about to faint," Rye said.

Vick snorted a sound that could have been a laugh. "Look who's talking. You're trembling like a leaf in a windstorm."

"Yeah, well, I saw my whole life flash before my eyes when I realized I had no chance to get my rifle off my shoulder before that grizzly got to me. And by then, it was too late to get to the bear spray on my belt."

"We were lucky we had the wind at our backs when I used that spray," she said. "Or we might have gotten a snootful of that stuff ourselves."

Rye released Vick as she pulled away and took a step back, then watched as she bent to retrieve the empty can of spray.

"Can you open my backpack and drop this in for me? I don't want to litter in the park."

"Litter? We were almost toast, and you're worried about litter?" Rye laughed until he was bent over double. With relief that they'd survived unharmed. And joy that he had a whole life ahead of him with this woman . . . if he could just convince her that he was a man worth loving.

Chapter 34

VICK FELT TOTALLY wiped out. She'd never killed any animal, much less a grizzly, and shooting Goldilocks had been a horrible experience. Her heart still felt unsteady, fluttering and juddering and a little out of whack. But it wasn't just the two grizzly encounters that had her off-kilter. It was the stunning revelations Rye had made when he'd been forced into talking as they tracked Goldilocks.

It was a mistake keeping my distance from you for so long.

I could have been—should have been—loving you, instead of despising you.

I thought I'd found my soul mate.

Each extraordinary revelation suggested that Rye had been thinking of her in different terms than she'd ever imagined. Nevertheless, she questioned his statements.

Could you really shut off feelings like you fixed a leaky faucet? Was it possible to simply forget the past and move forward as though it had never happened? Was there really such a thing as a "soul mate," or was that the sort of romantic fantasy grown-ups put aside as they got older and wiser?

She and Rye had at least an hour of talking to do before they got back to where they'd left the county's snowmobile, but a knot of fear in her gut, as debilitating in its own way as what she'd felt facing the grizzly, kept her from asking about Rye's romantic intentions. It was easier to address other issues.

"Does the ranch belong to your mom?" she asked as they began walking. "Or to you and Mike and Amy Beth?"

"It passed to Mom on Dad's death," Rye said. "Why do you ask?"

"It occurred to me that it might be difficult for you to keep Angus out of the house if your mom wants him there, since the ranch belongs to her."

Rye was holding his bear spray in one hand, but he swiped the other across his chin. "This relationship of hers with Angus is a real ball of worms. I don't see Flynn sitting on his thumbs if he moves in, which means he's going to want a say in running the ranch. That's been my job since Dad died. To be honest, there's nothing else I'd rather do, and nowhere else I'd rather be. So where does that leave me?"

"Have you asked your mother what she wants? Maybe she isn't so anxious to run off with Angus Flynn as you think."

"I saw them together at the hospital. When she looked at him her eyes . . . glowed. It was like she was lit up from the inside. I know that sounds stupid—"

"No, it doesn't. You're saying she comes alive when she's with him." Vick knew the feeling. She'd experienced it with Rye.

"I never thought of it quite that way, but maybe you're right. I know she hasn't been happy, but I thought she was just missing Dad." His voice had an edge as he added, "While she's really been missing Flynn."

"Her relationship with Angus doesn't diminish what she had with your father," Vick argued. "Darcie didn't die with your dad. She's allowed to love—and be loved—again. Don't you want that for her?"

"Yeah, but—"

"No ifs, ands, or buts. Do you want her to have a full life? Or not?"

"I want her to be happy!"

"Then you have to find a way to get her together with Angus Flynn. I'm not saying you have to let him move in," she said, when he opened his mouth to object. "There may be other alternatives you haven't considered."

"Like what?"

"Angus is incredibly wealthy. He can afford to buy a home here in Montana with a few acres of land where he and your mother can live, close enough so she can easily stay in touch, but with enough distance so Flynn isn't trying to run your life."

One of those dangerous silences ensued, while Rye absorbed what she'd said.

At last he said, "I don't want to talk about Angus and my mom anymore. I want to talk about us."

Vick was startled enough to trip over a ridiculously tiny stone in her path and lose her balance. Rye caught her arm to keep her upright, but she reflexively jerked free. He shot her a questioning look, and Vick realized she was reacting as she would have in the past, when touching was off-limits. It wasn't as easy to shrug off all the years Rye had kept her at arm's length as he seemed to think.

"I'm not sure talking will solve anything," she said.

"I've told you my feelings. I haven't heard yours."

The knot tightened in her belly. She glanced at him, then put her eyes back on the rugged terrain in front of her. "What is it you want me to say, Rye? That I have feelings for you? I do, but they're pretty confused right now. It wouldn't have made much sense to let myself fall in love with you, would it? I mean, you've wanted nothing to do with me for years. Suddenly, you say your feelings have done a one-eighty. How do I know they won't change back again?

"I want to believe in happily ever after," she said,

swallowing over the painful knot of emotion in her throat. "I'm just not sure I do."

"So do we pursue this 'thing' between us and see where it leads? Or not?" he asked.

Vick felt like she was standing on the edge of a precipice, unsure whether the fall would kill her if she leapt, or whether she would end up flying. But if she didn't take the risk and jump, she would never know for sure.

She met Rye's gaze with guarded eyes and said, "I'm willing, if you are."

She heard him release a breath of air she hadn't realized he'd been holding. All he said was "Good."

Chapter 35

RYE FELT SICK to his stomach, and his head was pounding. He'd slept intermittently, waking twice in a panic, once with a grizzly's teeth crunching his skull and once with his face being ripped off by a grizzly's claws. At 4:13 a.m., he'd finally given up on sleep. He sat slumped at the kitchen table with a cold cup of coffee in front of him, conceding in disgust that his life was in shambles.

However badly he'd acted in the past, he intended to spend the rest of his life loving Vick. All he had to do was convince her—he wasn't quite sure how—that he would be there for her through thick and thin, that no matter what calamities they faced, he would never abandon her the way her mother and father apparently had.

First, he had to get his mom's situation with Angus worked out. He'd decided the best way to start was to take Vick's suggestion and simply ask his mom what she wanted to do. He told everybody at the breakfast table, which included a suspicious Amy Beth, a surprisingly shy Vick, and a rambunctious Cody, that he had some work to do on the range. Then he got into his pickup and headed straight for Kalispell.

Rye had expected to find his mom at Mike's bedside, but when he stepped into the room, Mike was wide awake and all alone. "Where's Mom?"

"Not even a hello? Or a how are you? I'm fine by the way. Itchy as hell from all the stitches healing, but well on the road to recovery, thank you."

Rye laughed and said, "My bad. How are you?"

"Never better."

Rye pursed his lips at Mike's sarcasm and perched his hip on the edge of his bed. Because of his own recent experience, he had a new awareness of what Mike might be dealing with besides his physical injuries. "Do you have nightmares about the attack?"

"Who told you?" Mike said, running a tentative finger across the wounds on his neck.

"I had a couple myself last night."

"Whoa! What did I miss?"

"Vick and I ran into a mother grizzly and her two cubs yesterday in Glacier. They weren't even out of sight when I got charged by the bear that attacked you. I saw my life flash before my eyes—twice."

"You're here in one piece, so I guess things turned out all right."

"That grizzly couldn't have been more than ten yards from me when Vick gave it a nose full of pepper spray. It stopped as though it had hit a wall. Then she shot it dead."

"Victoria Grayhawk, lover of all things grizzly, *that* Vick shot the bear that attacked me?"

Rye nodded. "I couldn't get my rifle off my shoulder fast enough to use it. When that grizzly charged, I thought my life was over. I didn't get a scratch, but imagining what *could* have happened—recalling the damage that bear had done to you—woke me up a couple of times last night in a cold sweat."

Mike nodded. "I wake up hyperventilating, smelling that bear's foul breath."

"By the way, that bear's name was Goldilocks."

"That's just wrong!" Mike gestured at his mutilated head and face. "How am I going to have any cred in the local bars if I have to admit Goldilocks did this to me?"

Rye smiled. "I think your scars will do the talking for you."

"Mom's with Angus Flynn," Mike said.

Rye froze at the sudden change of subject. He stared at his brother, his heart beating against his ribs. "What do you know about him?"

"I know he's your biological father."

"Shit."

"Not that it makes any difference to me," Mike said, rearranging the sheet at his waist and tucking it under his arms. Then he looked Rye in the eye and asked, "Are you going to be staying around here? Or leaving?"

"Why the hell would I leave?"

"I heard Flynn's filthy rich. He's acknowledged you as his son, so he'd probably give you anything you want. You wouldn't be stuck with a piddly four-hundred-acre ranch like ours. Except, the Rafter S is really only a hundred acres, since the other three hundred are leased."

"Don't be an idiot," Rye said, angry that his brother believed he could be tempted away from his home with the offer of something bigger and better. "I don't need more land than we have. I don't need more cattle or horses. I don't need anything more than I already have except a woman to love. And I'm working on that."

Mike lifted a brow and winced when it apparently hurt. "So who's the lucky lady? Do I know her?"

"It's Vick, of course."

"There's no 'of course' about it," Mike said. "When did this happen?"

"While you've been stuck here in the hospital, Vick has been living in the house, taking care of Cody."

Mike smirked. "I always knew you were in love with her."

"How the hell did you know that, when I didn't know it myself?"

"Since you started running into her in town this

past year, you've made a point of *not* looking at her. I kind of figured you didn't want to get drawn in by those pretty blue eyes, which followed you whenever you weren't looking."

Rye found that observation both intriguing and encouraging. "Why didn't you say something?"

"It was too much fun watching the two of you dance around each other. How's the big romance coming? Taken her back to bed yet?"

"That's none of your business," Rye flared.

"You have!" Mike said with a grin. "I gotta get out of this place. I'm missing too much of what's going on."

"You seem to know more than I do about what's happening with Mom and Angus."

Mike shrugged and winced again. "She asked last night if I would mind if she didn't stay with me. I told her I was okay on my own."

"That's all she said?"

"Well, Angus was standing at her shoulder when she asked, and her face was so rosy, I had a pretty good idea where she was planning to spend the night instead."

Rye's lips flattened. "If he hurts her, I'll make him sorry he ever set foot in Montana."

"I wouldn't be in too much of a hurry to wipe him out. I think Mom's in love with him."

"Why would you say that?"

"She *named* you after him, Rye. Angus *Ryan* Flynn. I Googled him," he said before Rye could ask how he knew. "She must have cared a lot about the guy to do that. The instant he reappears in her life, she's all gooey-eyed over him. And she kept the truth about you a secret, even from Dad, all these years."

Rye tensed. "How do you know she kept Dad in the dark?"

"If Dad had known, he would have told you, because telling you would have been the right thing to do. Dad was pretty definite about right and wrong. With him, there was black and there was white and there was nothing in between."

Rye nodded. "Mom was afraid he wouldn't have loved me the same if he'd known the truth."

"She might have been right," Mike conceded. "So why did you come to see Mom? What is it you need?"

Rye was caught off-guard by Mike's directness, but he realized his brother might be able to help him figure out the best approach to take with their mother. "Have you followed Mom's relationship with Angus to its logical conclusion?"

"You mean marriage?"

Rye nodded. "Assuming they marry, where do you suppose they'll decide to live?"

"Aaah," Mike said. "I see where you're going with this. Our ranch house is too small and simple for someone like Angus, who's used to something a lot bigger and fancier."

"I imagine the Coldspot would be gone the day after he showed up," Rye muttered.

Mike laughed. "That refrigerator should have

been gone ten years ago. I don't understand your attachment to it."

"The humming sound it makes provided the background for our whole lives growing up."

"So keep the damn thing. That's not the real problem, though, is it?"

Rye shook his head. "I haven't had a boss for seven years, and I'm not looking for another one."

"Me, neither."

"Vick said maybe we can talk Angus into buying a spread somewhere near us where he and Mom could live."

"I already have one," a booming voice said from the doorway. "Your mother and I have been talking about that exact subject ourselves."

Rye leapt to his feet and turned to face the couple, who'd slipped inside without him hearing them come in. Each had an arm around the other's waist. Rye saw the same rosy flush of embarrassment on his mother's cheeks that Mike must have observed, leaving no doubt with whom she'd spent the previous night or what they'd been doing in the dark.

"I own a ranch northwest of Whitefish," Angus said. "I bought it so I'd have a place to stay while I was up here hunting elk. The house is small, maybe four thousand square feet, only eighty or so acres, but I think your mother and I could manage there just fine."

Four thousand square feet is small? Rye thought. Angus Flynn really did live in a whole other world.

"What about your ranch in Wyoming? You don't need to be there to manage that?"

"I guess the time has arrived to pass it along to my eldest son, now that he's about to marry and start a family of his own. Any other questions?" Angus said.

Mike grinned at Rye, then turned to the couple and said, "When's the wedding?"

"We were married yesterday by a justice of the peace," Angus replied. "Your mother wouldn't have me any other way."

"Good for you, Mom," Mike said, wincing as his grin became broad enough to affect his stitches.

Rye's mother met his gaze, her heart in her eyes, as she waited for his judgment of what she'd done. A lot of feelings rioted inside him, and a painful lump grew in his throat. Mostly, he was glad for her. He crossed the room and shook Angus's hand. "Congratulations, sir. Take good care of her."

"I will," Angus promised.

Then Rye turned to his mother, wondering if she could even see him through the tears blurring her eyes. He pulled her into his arms, hugged her tight, and whispered in her ear, "I love you, Mom. Be happy."

Chapter 36

"I HAVE THE ranch. It's mine!" Aiden said as he caught Leah under her arms and lifted her high.

"Put me down," she said with a laugh.

He slid her body down the front of him until she was standing on her feet, but he kept his arms around her. The April weather was surprisingly warm for Wyoming, leaving the ground muddy from melting snow. They'd met in the same clandestine spot between their two ranches where they'd carried on their romance when it had been a secret from their families.

"How did this miracle happen?" Leah asked, her heart beating like a captured bird inside her ribs. It was a toss-up whether she was more happy or scared. At least now they had a place they could call their own if King never gave her Kingdom Come. And it was a huge step toward their goal of merging the two ranches.

"Believe it or not," Aiden said, his blue eyes sparkling with excitement, "my dad got married yesterday in Montana. He's planning to live there from now on and has his lawyer busy transferring the ranch into my name, so I can manage it on my own."

"Who did Angus know in Montana well enough to marry?"

Aiden pursed his lips. "His lover when he was married to my mom. Her name is Darcie Sullivan, and she has a ranch near Whitefish."

"Have they been in touch all these years?" Leah asked incredulously.

"I don't think so, but he told me they have a grown son together. Darcie never told her son that Angus was his father. His name is Ryan Patrick Sullivan."

Leah gasped when she realized Aiden's half brother bore Angus's middle name.

"Ryan gave blood when his younger brother was attacked by a grizzly, which is how the secret came out. Once Ryan knew the truth, Darcie got in touch with Angus so father and son could meet. The rest is history."

"What happens now?" Leah asked.

"We move in together at the Lucky 7. We live happily ever after."

Could it possibly be that easy? Leah had no doubts about her own feelings of commitment, only fear about Aiden's. What if, after they moved in together, he betrayed or abandoned her? What if he didn't love her as much as he said he did?

Leah knew her feelings were foolish, that they had no basis in fact. Yes, her mother had walked away without looking back, but Aiden had been faithful to her for an entire year while she'd held him at arm's length. He showed her every day how much he missed her, how much he cared for her. Her fear that he would abandon her was irrational, but she couldn't seem to shake it, even when she knew it was keeping her from being happy.

That feeling of worthlessness, of not being good enough to be loved, had been woven into her psyche at a very young age. She'd tried shrugging it off. She'd tried reasoning it away. She'd tried believing that, because she was capable of love, she was a person worthy of being loved. She'd done the best she could to believe Aiden when he said she came first in his life, before anything or anyone else. But the doubt, the fear of being abandoned, had never gone away.

Leah had a perfectly good excuse to delay moving in with Aiden. Did she want to use it?

"King's life is still hanging in the balance," she blurted. "Telling him we're already married and moving in together is going to be a shock."

"Seeing you pregnant and believing you're *not* married is going to be a bigger shock," Aiden retorted. He let her go and took a step back, his face a picture of disappointment. "I know you wanted a second wedding, with all our family and friends there to see King walk you down the aisle, but there's no telling how long he might be in the hospital," he said in exasperation. "Or whether he'll recover at all," he added in a more somber voice.

She crossed her arms defensively over her chest. "I'm not ready to give up on our dream of merging the two ranches. I don't want to give King an excuse to deny me Kingdom Come."

Aiden pulled his Stetson low on his forehead. "We've been married for more than a year, Leah, living separately all that time. I've done what you wanted. I have possession of the Lucky 7. You have the hope of getting Kingdom Come, even if it isn't yours quite yet. We can build ourselves a house someplace in the middle—on my land—and manage both ranches. Do you want to be my wife? Or not?"

"Of course I do!" she cried. "I just—"

"You just don't want to give up your dream of owning Kingdom Come. Or is it that you don't love me enough? Or trust me enough?"

Of course, it was a little of all three, Leah realized. Admitting to any one of them would hurt Aiden. But he was already unhappy, and she wasn't sure what to say to take the discouraged look off his face.

"I need a little more time," she pleaded.

"For what? To wriggle out of our marriage? You don't need time for that," he snarled. "I can let you go right now. I'll have my lawyer file the papers this afternoon."

She grabbed his arm as he whirled to leave. “Aiden, no!”

He turned his head, his jaws tight, his eyes snapping with anger, but he kept his body angled away from her. “I’m tired of being jerked around, Leah. I’ve been more patient than any man should have to be. I want to be there every day to watch our baby grow inside you. Or is that one more thing I’m supposed to experience from afar?”

“Please, Aiden—”

“I’ve had it, Leah,” he said in disgust. “I’m done waiting. Either be my wife, or let me put us both out of our misery.” He turned and headed for his pickup.

Leah let Aiden take two steps before she ran after him, her heart in her throat. She was quaking with fear, but she knew if she let him walk away now, she would regret it the rest of her life. “Aiden, stop. Don’t leave!”

He ignored her cries and kept moving.

“I love you.”

She’d expected those three powerful words to hold him in place. He not only didn’t stop, he walked faster, reaching his pickup and climbing inside and gunning the engine, his tires slinging mud as he swerved dangerously and sped away.

Leah stared after him, her eyes filling with tears of frustration and anger. She was learning something she hadn’t known about the man she’d married. His patience had limits. Did his current behavior justify her fears that he would abandon her someday? Or had Aiden proved his love by refusing to live separately from his wife for one more moment than necessary?

Either be my wife, or let me put us both out of our misery.

Leah hated ultimatums. The thought of coming to her husband as a supplicant, begging him to take her back, made the hairs on her neck bristle. Swallowing a little pride might be good for her character, but it went against everything she'd learned growing up as King Grayhawk's daughter. Unfortunately, she was going to have to choose between maintaining her stiff-necked posture or bending a knee for the sake of love.

Leah had a sudden thought. She sniffed back her tears and swiped at her eyes. Maybe there was another choice somewhere in between.

Chapter 37

JENNIE WAS IN the stable alone, relishing the familiar smells of leather and hay and manure, which she'd missed during her confinement in the house for the past three weeks. Warm sun shone through cracks between the boards of the old barn, and she could see dust motes in the air. She hummed an upbeat rock tune as she brushed her favorite mare in its stall.

She'd asked Nathan if he wanted to join her, but he'd decided to stay inside and play a video game. She waved at a fly that landed on her forehead and hissed at the stab of pain caused by lifting her arm so high. She was pretty much healed from her surgery, but she kept forgetting she didn't have complete range of motion and wouldn't for a while yet.

Jennie smoothed her hand down the mare's neck and said, "You'll just have to settle for being half groomed, Lady, since I can't reach your back."

The mare turned to look at her, stomped a hoof as though in complaint, then went back to munching hay Jennie had put in the feed trough.

Jennie laughed and patted Lady's neck in apology. She immediately thought about sharing the mare's comical response with Matt, which surprised her. He'd left early that morning, planning to drive to Austin, about a half hour away, then take the family jet to Houston—a three-hour-long drive, but a very short flight.

Matt had explained he wanted to visit King at MD Anderson and asked if she would mind taking care of Nathan, who hated hospitals. She'd agreed without hesitation. It was only after Matt had left that Jennie realized she would have enjoyed going along, if he'd asked. She could easily have kept Nathan busy somewhere else while he visited King, and they could have had lunch at one of Houston's great restaurants before flying back.

How the mighty had fallen.

Jennie not only didn't want Matt gone from her ranch, she treasured the time she spent with him and didn't want it to end. She'd been so determined, when he'd shown up on her doorstep, not to forgive him for the terrible wrong he'd done her. But during the time they'd spent together while she recovered from her surgery, he'd figured out ways to remind her why she'd been attracted to him in the first place.

Jennie was very much afraid she was in love with Matt all over again. Head over heels. Smitten like only a teenager could be. The funny thing was Matt made her feel young and silly and free, like the girl she'd been all those years ago. He'd done everything in his power to show her how wonderful their life together could be.

She'd fought her feelings, but he'd been so thoughtful, so gentle, so understanding, so romantic, so considerate in every way that she'd finally stopped resisting and let all those powerful, first-love-type emotions roll over her.

Jennie chuckled. No man was as perfect as Matt had been acting. They'd had arguments enough when they were teens for her to know that he had moods where he snapped at her with every word out of his mouth, or where he simply took off to be by himself. He could be bullheaded when he didn't get his way and blind to her side of an argument. He'd come to her sweaty from a pickup ball game, a little drunk from beer, and stinky from punching cows. He'd let his black hair get shaggy enough to fall in his eyes and his dark beard get prickly enough to scrape her delicate skin.

Not one of those flawed human behaviors had shown up over the past three weeks. Which made her love Matt all the more for working so hard to hide them from her.

In days past, Jennie had turned herself inside out to be the political wife her late husband had needed by his side. She'd forgone having children because he didn't want them. She'd repressed her natural enthusiasm, and every word out of her mouth had been carefully chosen.

It wasn't until she was widowed that Jennie realized everything she'd given up for love. It wasn't until she was widowed that she realized a man who'd truly loved her would never have asked her to turn herself inside out and become someone other than her real self.

Jennie conceded she was equally responsible for allowing what had happened, but with life so precious, and maybe not as protracted as she might have hoped, she intended to do exactly, and only, what would make her happy in the future.

Spending her life as Matt's wife and Nathan's mother might be just the ticket.

Jennie had considered how unfair it would be to Matt, letting him into her life when it might be cut short. But whenever she expressed her worry that the cancer might not stay in remission, he reminded her that no one was promised more than the moment they were living. It was up to her to make the most of every single day.

"Can I help?" Nathan asked.

Jennie was startled enough to drop her arms suddenly and cried out at the jarring pain.

"Hey! Are you okay?" Nathan climbed up the railed stall door lickety-split and dropped onto the bedding of hay inside.

"Are you?" Jennie asked, wondering how he'd managed to climb with such nimbleness.

He saw her looking at his shortened leg and said, "It doesn't hurt when I walk, and I can run okay, but it aches sometimes when it rains." He took an awkward, limping step closer, put a hand on her arm, looked up at her with concerned blue eyes very like his father's, and said, "You made a noise like you were hurt. Are you all right?"

She was amazed at the empathy of a child so young, and realized that, as someone who'd had his share of operations, he must understand a great deal about pain. "I moved a little too fast," she said. "I can't lift my arms very well yet."

"Daddy told me about that. He said I shouldn't ask you to lift anything heavy." He grinned and said, "Like me." The concerned look was back as he asked, "Are you sure you're okay?"

"I'm fine," she reassured him. "I'm surprised to see you in this stall with me and Lady. Your dad told me you're afraid of horses."

He lowered his gaze. "I can pet them and brush them." He proved his point by running his hand across Lady's velvety nose. Then he looked up and admitted, "I'm just scared to ride."

"That's too bad. Lady's been stuck in the barn for quite a while, and I was going to take her out for a long walk, but I don't want to go too far from the house by myself."

"If you're just going to lead her—"

"I was going to ride bareback," she interrupted. "Do you think you could come up behind me? You know, with your arms around my waist to keep me steady?"

"How will I get up there without a saddle?" he asked.

"I've got a mounting block. You know, a kind of stair-step we can use to get on. I'll need help from you to put the bridle on, too, because I can't lift my arms all the way to Lady's head."

"She'll probably lower it for you," Nathan said. "But I can help with that if she won't."

"Good. Shall we give it a try?"

It hurt to lift her arms high enough to get the bridle down from its peg, but once Jennie had the idea to take a ride, she knew it was something she wanted to do. She could have called on one of the men working around the ranch to help, but she was afraid they might spook Nathan, who looked like he would rather be anywhere else, except maybe a hospital. Besides, no pain, no gain. Jennie had to exercise her arms to get better.

Matt had explained the accident that caused Nathan's injury, along with his hope that someday Nathan might be willing to ride again. Maybe riding with her, being skin to skin with the horse, wouldn't be as intimidating as riding by himself, where he needed to control the animal.

Lady did lower her head for the bridle, but it was Nathan who ended up sliding the bit into her mouth, while Jennie eased the crownpiece over her head and around her ears. Jennie buckled the chin strap and said, "Would you mind unlatching the stall door so we can get out?"

Nathan held the door while Jennie led Lady along the central aisle and outside through the open barn door, where a freestanding three-step wooden stair sat near the corral. When Jennie got there, she slid the reins over Lady's head, then used the mounting block to get high enough to slide a leg over and ease herself onto Lady's bare back.

She reached a hand down to Nathan and said, "Come on up."

Nathan had a lot more trouble climbing the three stairs than he'd had getting over the stall door. Jennie wondered if fear was holding him up. When he shot a glance at her, and she got a good look at his eyes, she saw his uncertainty and his fear. She kept her hand out, and he finally took it, using it gently as a lever to help him pull himself up onto the horse and slide his shortened leg over Lady's rump. Jennie didn't let go until he had one hand around her waist, at which point he quickly slid his other hand around her and threaded his fingers together in front of her.

His cheek was pressed hard against the back of her Western shirt, and she could hear his erratic breathing. It might be her imagination, but she thought she could actually feel his heart thumping against her back. "Where shall we go?"

"To the windmill," he said.

A windmill stood at the top of a hill about a quarter mile away, with a huge live oak near it. "Perfect. There's a low limb on that live oak we can use as a mounting block, if we decide to get off and take a nap."

"I'm too big to take a nap."

Jennie laughed. "I'm not. Ready?"

"I guess so."

"Then let's do this." Jennie gently nudged Lady's flanks and laid the reins against her neck, and the mare began walking in the direction of the windmill.

"I'm a little scared," Nathan said in a small voice.

"Lady's gentle as a lamb."

"But a lot bigger than one."

Jennie laughed. "Yes, a lot bigger. But she'll go as slow as we want. Is this okay?"

Nathan gripped her more tightly. "I guess so."

"Then this is as fast as we'll go."

"I've been wanting to see that windmill up close, but Daddy didn't want to leave you alone to take me there."

"I'm glad I can show it to you. I've had a lot of picnics under that tree with your sister."

"I miss Pippa."

"Me, too. Maybe we can all go visit her together."

"I thought you wanted us to live here with you."

"Wherever you and your daddy are is where I want to be."

Jennie realized as soon as she spoke the words that they were true. There was no reason to put off telling Matt how she felt. She'd given up her seat in the U.S. Senate when she'd gotten ill. Nothing was holding her here in Texas. She would be happy to go with Matt to Wyoming, if that was where he wanted to live, especially since Pippa lived there. To add icing to the cake, if they ended up anywhere near Jackson, she would have grandchildren close enough to spoil.

She hoped Matt would finish up whatever business it was he had to do and come home soon. She didn't want to wait one more minute to start the rest of her life.

Chapter 38

"WHY ALL THE need for secrecy?" Matt demanded as he sat down at a table in one of the luxury lounges at William P. Hobby Airport in Houston where Leah perched on the edge of her chair waiting for him.

"I needed to speak with you, and I didn't want to do it over the phone, or with anyone hanging over either of our shoulders making comments or offering suggestions," she replied tartly.

"You've got me here. Talk."

"I want you to come back to Kingdom Come."

Matt was stunned. "You just spent the past year doing everything in your power to throw me out on my ass. What's going on, Leah?"

"I'm pregnant."

"Who's the father?" Matt said through tight jaws. "That sonofabitch—"

"Aiden Flynn," she interrupted. "I've been married to him for the past year."

Matt was glad he was sitting down, because otherwise he would have fallen down. He put a fist against his heart, which had been working overtime ever since he'd gotten Leah's call. He'd been afraid she was going to tell him that their father was dying, that the leukemia had won. Her pregnancy was a surprise, but a good one. He grinned at her and said, "I presume both good wishes and congratulations are in order."

"You can save that for my wedding day."

"I'm confused again."

"Aiden and I got married in Vegas, but I intend to have a second wedding with everyone in the family present, including you and Jennie."

Matt scowled. "Jennie hasn't forgiven me yet. She may never forgive me. I've been the nicest human on the planet for weeks on end, and if I have to smile one more time when I feel like yelling bloody murder, I'm going to go off the deep end."

"Jennie doesn't need you to be perfect, Matt. She just needs you to love her."

"I do love her. It isn't working."

"Give it time."

"That's the one thing I don't have. You know Jennie has cancer."

"I thought it was in remission."

"It is. That doesn't mean it can't come back. I

want us to be a family now. I don't want to wait another day longer."

"Then you're going to have to buck up your courage and propose."

It struck Matt suddenly that he'd told Jennie he loved her, but he hadn't offered her a ring. He slapped his forehead. "How stupid can I be?"

"Pretty stupid."

"Watch it."

Leah smirked.

"I get that you're married and pregnant," Matt said. "What does that have to do with me coming back to Kingdom Come?"

"You may have wanted all of us Brats gone from the moment you arrived, but I only wanted you off the ranch so I could get King to give it to me. Unfortunately, King's sitting on the fence, waiting for you to change your mind and come home."

"I'm not going back."

"I know. But his illness and your absence leaves me with more work than I can handle. I want you back at the ranch. Bring Jennie. You can occupy the same wing of the house you were living in when you arrived last March."

Matt lifted a dark brow in disbelief. "What am I missing? What, exactly, will I be doing if I show up?"

"Running the quarter horse operation you started."

"What about the cattle?"

"I can manage the cow/calf operation. The point is Aiden and I are going to have a lot on our plates with two ranches to manage and a baby on the way. If you could handle the quarter horse operation at Kingdom Come that would be a big help."

"What do I get out of this?"

"I thought I made that clear. A home at Kingdom Come for the rest of your life. And, of course, the quarter horse operation."

"You're *giving* it to me?"

She grinned again. "The first thing I did when you left was have King transfer the quarter horse operation to me. It's mine, so I can offer it to you free and clear. I'm happy to have family making use of the ranch house, so it can remain available for holidays and special occasions."

"Where are you going to be?"

"As soon as we can get a house built, Aiden and I are going to be living on the boundary between the two properties. Kingdom Come will be a place the whole family can gather." She looked down at her hands and said, "And it'll be a place where any of us girls can go if things don't work out with our husbands."

It didn't take a genius to figure out that she thought she might end up back there herself. In a quiet voice he asked, "It sounds like you don't trust Aiden to stick by you."

She shot him a quick, guilty look from beneath lowered lashes. "I don't have much experience with trust. I've already been blindsided once."

"You mean when Aiden took that stupid bet with Brian to make you fall in love with him?"

"You know about that?"

He nodded.

"Is there anybody who doesn't know?" she said, shaking her head in disgust.

"Probably not. I should point out to you, if you haven't already figured it out for yourself, that it would have been a simple matter for Aiden to have your marriage annulled anytime over the past year. The fact that he hasn't—and that you haven't—suggests to me that you two just might love each other."

"How can I know if Aiden's love will last?" she cried plaintively. "I'm scared it won't. Not forever. The more time I spend with him, the more I love him, and the worse it'll be when he leaves me."

"Who says Aiden's going to leave you? Does anything he's done suggest that he isn't committed to you?"

"My mother acted like she loved me, too, until she took off and never came back," she said bitterly.

Matt took her shaking hands in his and held them tight. "That was a long time ago, Leah. Have you talked to Aiden about your fears?"

"He knows how I feel. I asked him for more time before we move in together, but he won't give it to me."

"The man's a saint as far as I'm concerned. If I were married to Jennie, I don't think I could handle living apart for an entire year. And all because you don't trust him not to leave you . . . someday?"

"It makes me sound pretty selfish the way you say it."

"What other way is there to put it? Despite Aiden's having hung around, when it might have been a whole lot easier to walk away, you still distrust him enough to keep Kingdom Come as a bolt-hole in case you have to run?"

"That makes me sound awful."

"If the shoe fits . . ."

"What am I supposed to do?" she demanded.

"Love him. Cherish him. And believe he'll love and cherish you in return. There are no guarantees, Leah," he said earnestly. "If there's one thing Jennie's cancer has taught me, it's how short life can be. You have to reach out and grab for happiness. Forget about a second wedding. We can have a big party when the baby's born. Maybe King will be well by then, and he can join us."

"Maybe he won't," she said in a small voice.

"Maybe he won't," Matt agreed. "But we keep on living. We keep on loving."

After a long silence, while his words of advice hung in the air, she asked, "Are you going to take me up on my offer?"

"I'm not sure Jennie will want to leave Texas."

"You might be surprised."

"Why is that?"

"I've learned a few things over the years, too. A house isn't a home, Matt. If Jennie loves you, she'll go wherever she has to go for you to be happy. I think that's Kingdom Come."

"Did you bring something for me to sign?" he asked with a cheeky grin.

She held out her hand. "A handshake should do it for now."

Matt shook her hand.

"I'll have the paperwork ready when you show up at the ranch."

He stayed where he was for a few minutes after Leah took off to arrange her flight home, mulling his change in fortune. He'd been willing to give up Kingdom Come and all the wealth it promised to be with Jennie. Now it seemed he could live and work at the ranch where he'd grown up and have Jennie, too. There was just one little hitch.

He had to convince the woman he loved to marry him . . . and move to Wyoming.

Matt realized he needed to take some of the very good advice his stepsister had given him. And there was no time like the present. He stopped in Houston long enough to buy a ring, then flew back to Austin, finally arriving at Jennie's ranch late in the afternoon.

As he approached the house, Matt was both nervous and excited. He wanted to believe Jennie would accept his proposal, but a man never knew for sure until the woman said yes. He stepped inside the kitchen door and immediately felt the emptiness of the house. A quick search revealed Jennie wasn't there. Neither was Nathan.

He hurried back outside and saw Jennie's SUV, which meant she hadn't left the ranch. His heart hammered in his chest as he searched the horizon, where the sun was heading down. It would be dark in another half hour. Where were they?

He saw a single horse walking slowly down the hill from the direction of the windmill. The rider was wearing a ball cap.

"Jennie?" he whispered. "What on earth?"

Then he saw two small hands wrapped around her midriff.

Tears sprang to his eyes. "Oh, my God. Nate's riding with Jennie."

When she saw him, Jennie smiled and waved. She said something over her shoulder, and Nate stuck his face out from behind her back. His son grinned at him, but he didn't let go of his tight hold on Jennie to wave as she had.

Matt headed toward them walking fast but not running. He didn't want to do anything to spook the horse. They reached the corral nearest the barn about the same time he did.

He stood by the horse's head and stared up at the two of them with a painful lump of joy and pride in his throat. Nathan was wearing a smile so big it hurt to look at it.

"I'm riding," his son announced.

"I see that."

"Bareback," Nathan added.

"Pretty impressive," Matt said.

"Jennie's steering the horse," Nathan said. "I'm just holding on."

"I see that, too," Matt said, feeling the tears sting his eyes and nose. "Are you ready to get down?"

Nathan let go of Jennie and reached for Matt, who opened his arms wide as his son threw himself into them. Nathan's arms tightened around his neck as he whispered, "I'm not scared anymore, Daddy. Wait till Grandpa King sees me. He's going to be so happy!"

"We'll have to sneak you into the hospital again, so you can tell him yourself," Matt said.

Nathan leaned back and said, "I guess I could stand to go back there just this once."

Matt laughed and set his son on his feet. He turned to Jennie and asked, "Do you need some help getting down, too?"

"There's a mounting block—"

When Matt held out his arms, Jennie lifted her leg over the horse and slid into his embrace. He was careful to hold her in a way that would cause the least pain, but he didn't let her go right away. "I have something to ask you."

She leaned back and searched his face. "What is it?"

Matt swallowed over the awful knot in his throat and said, "Will you marry me?" He let her go and dropped to one knee, looking up at her with all the love he felt in his eyes. "I love you, Jennie. I don't want to spend another day of my life without you."

Nathan took a step closer to Matt's shoulder, looked up at Jennie, and said, "Me, neither."

Matt pulled a box from his pocket and opened it to reveal a diamond and sapphire engagement ring. His heart in his throat, he held it up to Jennie.

She hadn't moved since he'd let go of her, just stood there with her hands clasped before her.

"Are you going to marry us, Jennie?" Nathan asked.

She smiled at Nathan and said, "Yes, I am."

Matt rose and took her hand in his. He struggled a little getting the ring out of the box, but once he did, he tossed the box to Nathan, and quickly slid the ring onto her finger.

She admired the setting for a moment, then put one hand on Nathan's shoulder and the other on Matt's chest. "I love you both very much. I can't wait for us to start our life together."

Matt's stomach was still tied in knots. There was one more detail he hadn't mentioned. He cleared his throat and said, "Leah invited me to live at Kingdom Come and gave me the quarter horse operation. How would you feel about moving to Wyoming?" He wondered if his face looked as frightened as he felt.

She searched his features and said, "Are you thinking I won't want to go?"

"Will you?"

She laughed. "Will I move to Wyoming, where my daughter and son-in-law and twin granddaughters make their home? That's a dream come true!"

"Are we gonna live near Pippa?" Nathan asked. "And Grandpa King? And Leah?"

Matt picked up his son in one arm and drew his fiancée close with the other. "You bet we are! We'll be on our way as soon as we get our bags packed."

Chapter 39

RYE FELT THE persistent knot in his gut finally ease the day his brother was well enough to come home from the hospital. Unfortunately, Mike's return meant Rye would have to put his plan to court Vick on hold while he focused on making sure his brother had everything he needed to get well.

Rye chafed at the delay.

Yes, he'd waited a lot of years to make his move, but now that the prize was within his reach, he was afraid Vick's work would send her sprinting off to Washington, D.C., or her family would draw her back to Wyoming or some cowboy in town would catch her eye. He remained calm because he was sure it would only be a few days until Mike was settled, and nothing and no one was liable to cut Rye out of the picture in that amount of time.

"Boy, am I glad to be home," Mike said as he eased onto the couch in the living room with a sigh that seemed to come from deep in his soul.

"What can I get for you?" Amy Beth asked, leaning over his shoulder. "Coffee? Coke?"

"Black Jack neat," Mike said.

"You can't have alcohol, not with the antibiotics and pain meds you're taking," Amy Beth chided. "Iced tea? Water?"

"Nothing right now," Mike said.

"How about a blanket? Are you cold?" Amy Beth asked, despite the unseasonably warm late-April day.

"I'm fine," Mike said, rolling his eyes at Rye.

"Are you sure there isn't something I can do for you?" she asked anxiously.

"Don't fuss over me, Amy Beth," he said irritably. "I'll tell you if I need something."

Rye took one look at his sister's crestfallen face, shot a reproachful glance at Mike, and said, "One of those scabs on Mike's cheek where the stitches came out is bleeding. How about getting him a Band-Aid?"

Mike put a finger to his cheek, which came away bloody. "Amy Beth, I need—"

"I'm on it," Amy Beth said, scampering away like a jackrabbit chased by hounds.

"God help me!" Mike said when she was gone

from the room. "She's chattering at me worse than a magpie in the woods."

"When women love you, they want to do for you," Rye said.

Mike laughed. "Now you're an expert on women?"

"I'm learning."

By then, Amy Beth was back with a box of Band-Aids. She knelt in front of Mike, tracing the many half-healed wounds with her eyes, her expression revealing how much it hurt her to see his face so torn up. It took several winces from Mike before the offending spot was covered to Amy Beth's satisfaction. "Now what can I do?" she asked.

"I'm going to lie down and take a nap," Mike said, easing himself onto his back and lifting his legs onto the couch. Amy Beth's mouth was already open to speak when he said, "I would love to have some meat loaf and mashed potatoes for dinner, if you could manage that."

"Vick's out grocery shopping right now for some ground pork since we were out of it and I thought you might want meat loaf since it's your favorite and it tastes better when you mix the beef with pork," Amy Beth said, all in a single breath. "I could get started peeling potatoes."

"Thanks, sis. You're the best," Mike said, patting her shoulder with a hand that trembled a bit and looked a lot skinnier to Rye than it had before the attack. Just how weak was Mike? Rye noticed his brother's body looked emaciated. Apparently, he hadn't been enjoying the hospital food. Well, home cooking would fix that.

It was obvious to Rye that his sister wanted to hug Mike but was afraid of hurting him. "Go ahead and give him a hug, Amy Beth," Rye said. "He won't break."

When Amy Beth was too close to see Mike's face, Rye's brother scowled at him. A moment later, his face contorted with pain, despite Amy Beth's care as she gently laid her hands on his shoulders and bent over to kiss his cheek where stitched spots had barely healed.

Rye was startled by Mike's reaction. Why had they let him out of the hospital if such a light touch could cause him so much discomfort?

Because nobody likes being in a hospital bed day after day. Mike probably lied and told them he was fine, when he's far from it.

Rye was going to make it his business to be sure Mike got the rest he needed to get well. Which probably meant he was going to be running interference with all the women who would want to minister to his brother.

"I am *sooooo* glad you aren't dead," Amy Beth said.

"Me, too," Mike quipped. "Now scoot, and let me sleep."

Amy Beth reluctantly headed toward the kitchen, glancing at Mike over her shoulder the whole way.

"Have I mentioned I'm also glad you're alive?" Rye said when she was gone.

"I survived that bear attack, but if you don't do something," Mike said, "all this attention is going to kill me for sure."

Rye heard a commotion in the kitchen, and a moment later his mother fluttered in like a butterfly seeking a flower upon which to land. Angus followed, hovering like a blackbird eyeing the butterfly as potential lunch.

"You're awake," she said, tears brimming in her eyes when she spied Mike. "I was afraid you would be asleep, and I'd miss seeing you. We stopped by to find out how you're doing."

Mike was obviously settled comfortably, but their mother made him sit up so she could put a couch pillow behind his head. She grabbed the blanket she'd always kept folded over the arm of her rocker and spread that over him as well. "Are you okay?"

"I'm good, Mom. Don't—" He bit his lip and shot a look at Rye, who realized Mike had been about to give her the same admonishment he'd given Amy Beth. *Don't fuss over me.*

"Really, I'm fine," Mike said instead.

"Is there anything I can do for you?"

Rye heard voices in the kitchen and realized Vick was back from doing the grocery shopping with Cody in tow.

Cody raced into the living room and took a flying leap over the back of the couch, yelling, "Uncle Mike! You're home!"

He landed with both knees on Mike's stomach, took one look at Mike's face, and screamed in terror.

Rye could see that Cody's frantic efforts to escape the monster he'd discovered lying on the couch, instead of the doting uncle he'd expected to find, were hurting Mike. He caught his son under the arms and lifted him away as Mike grunted in pain.

Cody grabbed Rye around the neck and hid his face against Rye's throat, gasping and sobbing, "Uncle Mike is— Uncle Mike is—" He never finished the sentence, but Rye knew what he was trying to say.

Apparently, so did Mike.

Rye's insides twisted when he saw the horrified look in his brother's eyes. Rye could easily read Mike's thoughts.

Why didn't you tell me I'm a monster? How could you let me pretend that what I see in the mirror isn't as bad as it looks?

When Rye had first observed the stitched-up nightmare that was Mike's face, his brother had been in a coma and unable to comprehend Rye's revulsion. Over time, as the swelling had gone down and the bruises had changed color and he'd gotten used to the stitches that reminded him of Frankenstein's monster, Rye had seen only the improvement in his brother's condition, not the terrible damage that had been left behind by the bear's attack.

His son was seeing Mike for the first time, and seeing him as he looked after a grizzly had mauled him.

"The bear bit and scratched Uncle Mike's face so

bad the doctors had to sew him back together," Rye said as he patted his son's back.

Cody stopped sobbing, lifted his head, and glanced over his shoulder at his uncle. Rye felt his child shudder before Cody pressed his nose back against Rye's throat, tightened his hold on Rye's neck, and said, "He looks too scary."

Rye noticed Mike's eyes were closed, and his jaw was working where his teeth were gritted. He couldn't bear his brother's pain or his son's fear.

He settled on one knee so Cody's feet hit the floor and took his son's shoulders in his hands to separate them, so he could look him in the eye. "I want you to think about how Uncle Mike is feeling right now. He was looking forward to seeing you as much as you were looking forward to seeing him."

Cody peered at Rye from beneath eyelashes spiked with tears. "But—"

"Mike's face is like a jigsaw puzzle the doctors had to stitch back together after that old bear bit him. When you fit all those scabs and scars back together, you'll see it's just Uncle Mike." He slowly turned Cody so he was facing Mike, holding his position as his trembling son backed up against him. "And you told me just this morning how excited you were that Uncle Mike was coming home."

Rye met Mike's agonized gaze, hoping his brother would do his part in this little drama.

"I'm sorry I frightened you, Cody." Mike traced a few of the raised pink and purple scars on his face with a finger and said, "The bear scratched me pretty bad, but it won't be long before I'm as good as new."

Rye wondered if Mike believed what he was saying and realized he must know better. His wounds were too awful. His face would never be the same again.

Rye could feel Cody trembling, but he'd never been so proud of his son as he was when Cody said, "I'm sorry I screamed like that, Uncle Mike. I was just . . ."

"Startled by this face of mine," Mike filled in for him. "I am a little scary looking right now. But the doctor told me the scars will fade and pretty soon I won't look so bad."

"That's good." Cody took a hesitant step toward Mike and said, "Did I hurt you where the bear bit you, Uncle Mike? I'm sorry if I did."

Mike reached out and circled Cody's waist and drew him close until the little boy was leaning against him. "I'm good, little man. Give me another week, and we can play like we used to."

Vick called from the kitchen, "Cody! We need your help in here."

"I gotta go, Uncle Mike." Then Cody ran for the kitchen.

"That sounds like my cue," their mother said.

Rye had completely forgotten that she and Angus were there.

On her way out of the room, his mom paused to lay a hand on Rye's face and gently touched Mike on the cheek. "You are two amazing men, and I'm proud to be your mother." A moment later she was gone.

Where the butterfly fluttered, the blackbird followed.

When they were alone in the living room, Mike said, "Thank you, Rye."

"I should have prepared Cody. I'm sorry."

"I'd better get used to it," Mike said, his voice bitter.

"The doctor promised the scars will fade."

"Doctors lie all the time to their patients," Mike retorted.

"I'm afraid you're going to have to put up with a lot more sighs and sympathy before you're through."

"Not if I can help it. No joke, Rye. I need some time on my own."

Rye was alarmed at the desperate look in Mike's eyes and the broken sound of his voice. "I'll do what I can, Mike. Go ahead and take that nap. I'll make sure everyone leaves you alone."

At supper that night, their mother announced, "If you don't mind, Rye, Angus and I will stay a few days to help take care of Mike. We can sleep in my room."

Rye couldn't send his mother away. It was her home.

Over the next few days, Cody was delighted to have a grandpa to read to him and a grandma to bake him cookies. Amy Beth loved having her mother back home and Vick seemed delighted to be treated as one of the family at dinners that turned out to be a great deal of fun, although he was usually seated at the opposite end of the table from her. The three women were always involved in some project that kept Vick occupied, and getting a moment alone with her was impossible.

Rye bit the inside of his cheek raw to keep from saying anything as a few days became a week, and a week turned into two weeks.

Mike retreated to his room and shut the door. Vick took over Rye's room, at his mother's insistence, since both Amy Beth and Darcie were using theirs. He was sleeping on the goddamn couch.

It was not a situation conducive to romance.

Two weeks and two days in, Rye tried tiptoeing from the living room to his own room after everyone was asleep, to see if Vick could be talked into letting him share his comfortable bed and whatever other bedtime activities she might allow. Unfortunately, Mike had been awakened by a nightmare and caught him sneaking down the hall. Mike's voice woke their mother, which got Angus out of bed.

Rye gave up. At least for the night.

He tried again a few days later, waiting until the wee hours to make his foray down the hall. He was surprised—and delighted—to see a light under the door, but when he eased it open, he found Amy Beth being held by Vick while tears streamed down his sister's face. From the look on Vick's face when she spotted him, he was as welcome as an ax murderer.

"What are you doing here?" she asked in a sharp voice.

"I wanted—"

"Can't you see your sister's upset?"

"Yes, I can. What's wrong?"

"That's none of your business," Vick said as Amy Beth quietly sobbed. "Go away."

He backed his way out in a big hurry. *Boy trouble,* he thought. What else could it be? He knew how that could upset a person. He was having a bit of *girl trouble* himself. How was a man supposed to woo the woman he loved when his whole family was in the way?

His third foray down the hall was interrupted when he heard Cody whimpering. He slipped into his son's darkened room and eased himself onto the bed, taking Cody in his arms.

"What's wrong?" he whispered.

"Mike's bear was going to eat me," his son said.

"That bear can never hurt anyone again," Rye said. "Your mom shot it dead."

"She did?"

"She sure did."

He heard a relieved sigh before Cody said, "That's good." In a few minutes, he fell back into a sound sleep. So did Rye.

When Rye had given up all hope of finding time alone with Vick, a miracle happened. Her fraternal twin, Taylor, went into labor.

"I need to be there," Vick told him when she hung up the call, her heart in her eyes.

"Of course you do," he replied.

"I want to take Cody with me."

"That's a great idea. Why don't I come along, too?"

"You don't trust me with him," she said, her mouth drooping.

"I absolutely trust you. I thought you might want someone along to take care of Cody while you spend time catching up with your twin."

"You'd do that for me?"

"Of course." He would do anything to get the two of them out of this house, where they would have some time together all by themselves. Their son would be with them, but Vick had a large family with lots of sisters to help take care of a little boy, while his parents worked on their relationship.

At least, that was the way Rye imagined things happening when they got to Jackson Hole. The reality was somewhat different.

Chapter 40

"MOMMY TOLD ME she grew up here," Cody said, as Rye drove them through Jackson Hole toward his first meeting with his Flynn brothers. "There it is!" Cody exclaimed, pointing as they passed the town square. "A bazillion elk antlers are stacked up in arches so high you can walk under them."

Rye was only half paying attention to his son and simply replied, "Uh-huh." He felt edgy and tense, because he wasn't sure what to expect from the four men he was about to meet. Then he realized what Cody had said. He met his son's gaze in the rearview mirror of the SUV and said, "A *bazillion* antlers?"

"So many you can't count them all," his son explained.

Rye had left Vick at Taylor and Brian's home in

Jackson, where her female relatives had gathered to admire the couple's twin daughters. Rye's destination was a restaurant near the fire station where Brian worked. Ryc wasn't sure how he felt about being forced to meet his new relatives in a public setting, but maybe it would keep everyone civil. Not that he expected violence to erupt, but if his half brothers felt anything like he did at the moment, emotions were sure to run high.

Rye would much rather have been spending the day with Vick. He was frustrated because he wasn't getting the time alone with her that he'd hoped for when he'd decided to join her on this trip. When they'd arrived in town three nights ago, he'd dropped her off at the hospital, where Taylor was in labor, and used Cody's sleepiness as an excuse to avoid meeting the various Grayhawks and Flynns waiting there for the babies to arrive. He'd fled to the closest hotel.

He hadn't seen Vick over the past three days except in fits and spurts. He played digital games and watched G-rated movies with Cody while she visited Taylor at the hospital. As far as he knew, Taylor was still the only one who was aware of Cody's existence, which was why he and Cody were staying out of sight.

At breakfast this morning at the hotel, Vick had hardly been able to sit still, fidgeting with the salt and pepper, then picking up her coffee cup and setting it down and picking it up again, then playing with her spoon until it clattered on the table.

She met his gaze with worried eyes and said, "Everything is arranged. You and Cody are going to have lunch today at the Snake River Grill with the Flynn brothers, while my sisters and my niece and I visit Taylor and the twins at Brian and Taylor's home, where I plan to tell everyone about Cody."

Vick took a deep breath and continued, "Then you and Cody will come pick me up and meet my family, except for my father."

No wonder she was nervous, Rye thought. "Where will your father be?"

"King's in the hospital in Houston. His leukemia is back."

"I'm sorry, Vick. I had no idea."

"He beat it the last time. Hopefully, he will again."

So here he was on his way to a lunch he would have avoided like the plague, if he'd had any choice in the matter, with another meeting filled with potential pitfalls on the menu for later.

"The place where you first saw Mommy has saddles you can sit on, instead of chairs," Cody said.

Rye wondered how the subject of his first meeting with Vick had come up. He eyed Cody again in the rearview mirror, where he was constrained in his car seat, and said, "If you want to see them, I'll hold you up, so you can look in the window. You have to be a grown-up to go inside."

"Mommy said you were really, really handsome, and she liked you right away," Cody continued.

That was nice to hear. "I liked her, too. A whole lot."

"And because you liked each other so much, you made me."

Rye was a little shocked at that last sentence, but it was a good way of explaining something to a child in terms he could understand. "Yes, we did." He was impressed at Vick's use of that first indelible meeting between them to explain to Cody how he'd been conceived.

Rye wished there were some way to re-create the magic of that moment, but he didn't see how. He took a deep breath and slowly, quietly let it out. It felt like his whole life was hanging in the balance. Maybe the thing to do was take Vick back to where it had all started and speak his heart.

Rye wanted to believe that Vick would hear what he had to say and fall into his arms, and they'd live happily ever after. Life didn't always turn out that way. Otherwise, Vick would have stayed in bed, they would have had breakfast at the Wort Hotel in the morning, and maybe he would have found a way to turn their one-night stand into something more substantial. But at this point, he was willing to try anything.

He put his plans for a drink with Vick at the Million Dollar Cowboy Bar on hold as he entered the Snake River Grill holding Cody by the hand.

He recognized his brothers at once. They shoved their chairs back and rose as one. He saw three tall, black-haired, blue-eyed, broad-shouldered, narrow-hipped men, and one chestnut-haired man who was a little shorter and a little leaner than his brothers. That would be Devon.

Rye felt Cody sidle closer to him and picked up his son to reassure him. He held him close as he extended his hand to the closest Flynn. "Ryan Sullivan," he said.

"Aiden Flynn," his brother said as he shook Rye's hand. He gestured to the man next to him. "This is the proud papa."

"Brian," he said with a grin as he extended his hand for Rye to shake.

"I'm Connor," the third brother said. He pointed with his thumb at the last man and said, "This little guy is Devon."

"Not so small where it really matters," Devon said, grinning at his brother. He shook hands with Rye and gestured to one of the two empty chairs at the table for six. "Have a seat."

All four men stared at the child in his arms and Rye suddenly realized that while Vick was planning to tell her family about Cody, she'd left it to him to introduce their son to his Flynn relatives. Except, he noted with surprise, the second empty chair already contained a booster seat intended for a child.

He stared at Brian and said, "I thought only Taylor knew about Cody."

"She's my wife. We don't have secrets from each other."

"I wondered why you had the waitress bring that kid's seat," Aiden said. "Who is this young man?" he said, his gaze directed at Cody.

"I'm Cody Sullivan."

"Victoria Grayhawk is his mother," Rye said, meeting their gazes one by one and daring them to make a snide remark.

Rye noticed the widened eyes, the indrawn breaths, and the speculative looks on three of the four brothers' faces, but no one said a pejorative word.

"We should sit down," Aiden said, suiting word to deed, "and order some food. I'm hungry. How about you, Cody?"

To Rye's surprise, as he settled Cody in the booster chair his son said, "I want a cheeseburger."

"A cheeseburger it is," Aiden replied. "In fact," he said as the waitress arrived, "how about cheeseburgers and fries all around?" Everyone nodded or spoke an assent. The Flynns already had beverages, so Rye ordered drinks for himself and Cody, and the waitress disappeared.

Rye sat on the edge of his chair for the first fifteen minutes, while they made small talk and waited for their food to arrive. It quickly became apparent that the Flynns had accepted him as one of them almost without a blink of an eye.

"I thought this would be more awkward," Rye admitted as he stuck a salty French fry in his mouth.

Aiden smiled wryly. "It might very well have been if Angus weren't Angus."

"Are you suggesting he had a lot of lovers?" Rye said, his neck hairs hackling at the suggestion his mother might be merely one of many women in Angus's life.

"Not at all," Aiden said. "But Angus does what he wants without regard to the rules that keep the rest of us on the straight and narrow. We've gotten used to expecting the unexpected."

"I know a little of what you're going through," Devon said. "I had a similar adjustment to make when I discovered last summer that Angus wasn't my biological father."

"It never made any difference to the rest us," Connor said. "We still love the little guy."

"Cut out that 'little guy' stuff, or I'll show you who's really the bigger man," Devon said, punching Connor in the arm.

"You *are* the youngest," Connor pointed out.

"Am I?" Devon said, lifting a brow in Rye's direction.

"I'm twenty-nine," Rye said.

"Damn!" Devon said. "Twenty-eight."

"Guess that settles that," Connor said with a grin. "Still the baby of the family."

"Cut it out, asshole!" Devon said.

"Stop it, both of you," Aiden said. "There are impressionable ears sitting at this table."

Cody apparently didn't know he was the "impressionable ears" at the table, because he was still completely focused on getting the right amount of catsup on one of his fries.

Rye wished Mike were here. They could show the

Flynns what a knockdown, drag-out fight between brothers was really like.

"I suppose you realize we're all involved with Grayhawk women ourselves," Brian said.

"Vick and I aren't exactly 'involved,' " Rye admitted.

Brian shot a glance at Cody and back at Rye. "Really? Having a son together doesn't qualify?"

"Romantically involved," Rye said.

"But I thought—" Brian cut himself off. "Oops."

"Spill, Brian," Connor said. "What is it you thought?"

Brian met Rye's gaze and said, "I thought you two might have feelings for each other."

Rye realized the only way Brian could have made a supposition like that was if Taylor had discussed it with him. Which meant Vick would have had to discuss it with Taylor. Had Vick told her sister she cared for him? "I have feelings for Vick," he admitted. "I'm not so sure the reverse is true."

"Good luck," Brian said with a cheeky grin. "Those Grayhawk women are worth all the effort it takes to win them."

"If that's really the way you feel, how would one of you like to babysit for Cody tonight so I could spend an evening out with Vick?"

"We can take him," Connor volunteered. "My two older kids, Brooke and Sawyer, will enjoy playing with him. We're having dinner in town before we head back to the ranch. You can drop Cody off at the restaurant, and he can join us for supper. I'll give you directions how to get there."

The rest of the meal was taken up with harrowing stories of how each of the brothers had wooed, and all but Aiden had won, the Grayhawk women they loved. Rye was feeling a little sick to his stomach when they were done, aware that he was a long way from winning the Grayhawk woman he'd chosen for himself.

"How would you like to ride in a fire engine?" Brian asked Cody.

Cody's mouth dropped open in surprise. "Really?"

"Really," Brian said.

Cody turned to Rye and said, "Can I, Daddy? Please?"

"Sure," Ryan said. "That's really nice of you, Brian."

"Anything for family." He winked at Rye and said, "And maybe future in-laws?"

The knot in Rye's gut loosened a little after his lunch with the Flynns and his visit to the fire station with Cody, but it tightened back up again as he and Cody headed to Taylor and Brian's home to meet with Vick and the rest of the Grayhawk women. He hoped she'd experienced as easy a time of it explaining she had a son, as he'd had meeting his Flynn brothers.

When Vick answered his knock on Taylor's door, and he saw the anguished look in her eyes, he knew she had not.

Chapter 41

VICK EXPECTED THE three members of her family gathered in Taylor's living room who had no idea Cody existed, to be upset when she revealed she had a five-year-old son they knew nothing about. So she waited until the five of them—she and her three sisters and her niece—had *oohed* and *aahed* over Taylor's daughters, Ashley and Annie, for a good hour before she met her twin's gaze and announced, "I have some news of my own to share."

"You're getting married," Eve guessed as she set down a baby bottle on an end table beside the couch and settled Ashley over her shoulder to burp her.

"To Ryan Sullivan," Leah said with a grin as she handed Annie back to Taylor, who was relaxing in a rocker near the fireplace with a blanket over her lap.

Vick blushed to the roots of her hair. She shot a look at Taylor, who shook her head, indicating that she hadn't revealed Vick's feelings about Sullivan to her two sisters. Instead of saying something like, "Where did you get a crazy idea like that?" and denying the whole thing, Vick settled back in the overstuffed chair next to the rocker and asked, "How do you know about Ryan Sullivan?"

Leah's lips quirked as she crossed to the fireplace and used a poker to stir up the fire so it crackled and sparks flew. "A little birdie told me."

"Aiden," Vick said flatly. "Where did he hear about Sullivan?" Had Angus spilled the beans despite his promise to Darcie?

"I think Brian told him," Leah said, replacing the poker and perching on the wide stone bench that bordered the front of the fireplace with her long legs outstretched. "I'm afraid there are no secrets between siblings in this family, Vick. The only confidences that get kept are between husbands and wives who swear each other to silence."

If Angus wasn't the culprit, she knew who probably was. Vick confronted Taylor and said, "Did you tell Brian what I told you at Christmas about my feelings for Sullivan?"

Taylor looked abashed. "I'm afraid I did."

"I suppose Connor told you about Sullivan," Vick said, turning to Eve.

She nodded but looked guilty.

"And Devon told you," Vick said, staring down her niece.

Pippa tucked her stocking feet under her on the couch and said, "I didn't ask to be told your secret. Devon volunteered it."

Vick searched the female faces in the room, wondering how much of a fool she'd been to believe that she'd kept Cody's existence a secret, her skin so flushed she literally felt hot under the collar, and finally blurted, "So every one of you already knows about Cody?"

"Who's Cody?" Leah asked.

Vick focused her gaze on Taylor. "You didn't tell Brian about Cody?"

"I did, but I swore him to secrecy, because I knew he wouldn't be able to resist telling his brothers."

"Who's Cody?" Leah repeated.

"My son," Vick said almost viciously. "My five-year-old son. He lives on a ranch in Montana with his father, Ryan Sullivan, who has sole custody."

Leah was on her feet in an instant. "How could you keep something so important a secret from me? I'm your—"

Vick realized Leah had almost said "mother" but cut herself off. The truth was Leah had stood in that role all Vick's life, so she could understand why her eldest sister would feel hurt at being kept in the dark.

"I didn't tell anyone but Taylor," Vick said, as though that could ease Leah's wounded feelings.

Leah rounded on Taylor. "And you didn't tell me? How could you keep this from me? I'm ashamed of both of you!"

Leah's rebuke struck Vick like the lash of a whip. "I couldn't tell you, Leah," she protested. "You would have made me keep the baby."

"You're damn straight I would!" Leah shot back. "How could you give up your own flesh and blood? The sister I raised would never do something like that."

"There were reasons—"

"There is *no reason on earth* that justifies abandoning your child," Leah cried. "My mother did that to me. It's the worst thing I can imagine one human being doing to another. I can't believe you walked away from your helpless newborn baby."

"Leah, you have to understand—"

"I don't understand!" Leah blinked and two tears slid down her cheeks. "Any of this. Where's your son now?"

"Sullivan and Cody flew to Jackson with me. Sullivan's been keeping Cody at a hotel in town. He's bringing him here this afternoon to meet all of you."

"Cody's been in Jackson for the past three days, and we're just now meeting him?" Leah said. "Why wasn't Sullivan with you at the hospital? What kind of man drops you off and doesn't stick around to meet your family?"

"Sullivan was right," Vick muttered.

"About what?" Leah snapped.

"He suspected there was going to be a scene—when one or two or all of you found out about Cody—where you condemned me for the choice I made." Vick swiped her sleeve across the tears streaming from her eyes and the snot dripping from her nose. "I'm not like our mother, Leah."

"Tell me how what you did is different," Leah challenged.

"I came back."

Leah sank onto the floor beside Vick, put her hands over her face, and sobbed.

Vick dropped from the chair to her knees beside Leah and said, "Six months after I gave Cody up, I realized what a terrible mistake I'd made. I gave up custody when Cody was born, but I still have visitation rights. Once each month for the past five years, I've spent Friday through Sunday with my son at my cabin in Montana."

Leah moaned. "I thought you were going to Montana once a month on business. I thought you moved there so you wouldn't have to travel so much."

"I moved there so I could spend more time with my son," Vick said. "This past year, I've attended school and church events where Cody was participating. Since March, I've been living at the Sullivan ranch taking care of Cody every day. I like and respect my son's father. I may even love him. We've been getting to know each other better, and there's hope we might end up as a couple.

"But even if we don't, I would never, ever, ever abandon my son, like our mother did to us. I've lived every day of my life wondering what happened to her and blessing whatever God gave you to me as a sister. You've taught me what a mother should be, Leah, by filling that role in my life. You've shown me what love means. And I'll always love and respect and be grateful to you for that."

Leah dropped her hands from her face with a pained cry and opened her arms to Vick, who threw herself against her sister's body as though she were still a child and was quickly enveloped in her sister's familiar, comforting embrace.

"Well," Eve said, sniffling. "I can't wait to meet your son. And Sullivan, too, of course."

Vick heard Leah take a shuddering breath and let it out before she eased Vick upright and began to stand. "Oh, God. I can't do this anymore."

Vick put one hand on her sister's shoulder to keep her from rising and said, "What's wrong, Leah?"

Leah met her gaze, then looked at each of Vick's sisters and her niece in turn. "I've been lying to all of you."

"About what?"

Leah shoved a nervous hand through her hair. "I've been married to Aiden Flynn for a year. And I'm pregnant with his child."

Vick stumbled to her feet and towered over her sister, her fisted hands on her hips. "And you had the *nerve* to read me the riot act for keeping Cody a secret? How could you, Leah? Why would you keep your marriage a secret from us?"

"It's a long story," Leah said.

"So why are you telling us now?" Vick asked.

"When I considered how hurt I was that you've been hiding important parts of your life from me, I realized that keeping my secret isn't fair to any of you, either."

"Not to mention the fact that you were going to have a lot of explaining to do when you started to show," Eve pointed out.

Leah managed to smile. "Not to mention that."

"Why did Aiden agree to keep your marriage secret?" Taylor asked. "I would think he'd want you to be living together."

"Aiden and I have been diligently working to end the feud between his father and ours, between his family and ours. The possibility that we *might* get married was part of that negotiation. Hence the need to keep our status as husband and wife a secret."

Eve snorted. "I think 'those awful Flynn boys' have pretty much shut down the feud between our families by marrying all of us."

Pippa giggled.

Taylor chuckled.

Leah just shook her head.

Vick exchanged a look with her twin, laughing at the undeniable truth of Eve's comment.

"Eve is right, of course," Leah conceded. "I suppose Aiden and I holding out for peace between Angus and King was an exercise in futility. We should have been living together a long time ago. Feel free to tell your respective husbands—or boyfriends," she added, glancing at Vick, "that we're husband and wife."

When the doorbell rang, Vick's head shot around

and she stared at the door. "That must be Rye and Cody."

"Before you open the door, let me dry my tears," Leah said.

"That goes for me, too," Taylor said.

"And me," Eve parroted.

"And me," Pippa said.

"What a bunch of crybabies you are," Vick said, swiping at her own tears again with her sleeve. She found a box of tissues on an end table and ran around the room offering them to her sisters and her niece. When they'd all wiped their eyes and blown their noses she said, "Are we ready?"

"Ready," Leah said, retaking her seat on the bench near the fire. "Bring 'em on."

Vick blinked her reddened eyes and patted her flushed cheeks to make sure they were dry, but one look at Rye's face, and she knew she hadn't fooled him. "Come in," she said. "Everyone wants to meet you and Cody."

"Are you sure about that?" he murmured so only she could hear.

She laid a hand on his arm and said, "It's all right, Rye. The worst is over."

Cody ran past Rye toward Vick, pulling to a sharp halt an instant before he would have rammed into her. He seemed barely able to contain his excitement as he recounted his day. "I have four uncles! And I rode on a fire engine and saw some really long hoses for putting out fires and really sharp axes for breaking down doors and I got to meet a lot of firefighters. Some of them are girls!"

Vick laughed and said, "Have you decided to become a firefighter?"

"Maybe." He added uncertainly, "Some of the stuff they have to carry is really heavy."

"Someday you'll be so strong those things won't seem heavy at all," she said, brushing a stray curl off Cody's brow.

Vick watched her son stand up a little straighter at the thought of being tough enough to become a firefighter someday.

"Don't forget the dog," Rye said.

"Oh, yeah," Cody said. "They have a dog that's white with black spots and they call him Spot and he's really friendly and he licked my hands. But I still like Rusty best, 'cause he can do more than just catch a ball. He can catch squirrels and gophers and snakes and turtles . . . and rats!"

Vick heard her sisters laugh.

Vick met Rye's gaze and saw his eyes were also crinkled with laughter. He whispered the word, "Rats!" then scrunched up his mouth to expose "rat" teeth and held his hands up curled like tiny rat paws.

Vick laughed and realized he'd done something so silly because she'd looked so sad. She brushed a hand through Cody's hair to straighten it, then said, "There are some people here I'd like you to meet."

Cody looked curiously at the four women in various positions around the room. She led him first to

Leah and said, "This is your aunt Leah. She's my eldest sister."

Cody ducked his head shyly and said, "Hello."

She led him to the rocker and said, "This is your aunt Taylor. She's holding your newborn cousin Annie."

Cody peered over the top of the blanket shielding the baby's head and said, "She's really small."

"Yes, she is," Taylor said. "She was only born three days ago. It's nice to meet you, Cody."

Vick took Cody's hand and led him over to Eve. "This is your aunt Eve. She's holding Annie's twin sister, Ashley."

"Twins means they look alike," Cody announced to Eve.

"Yes, it does," Eve said. "I'm pleased to meet you, Cody."

Cody leaned over to inspect the baby and exclaimed, "They both have blue eyes!"

"Yes, they do," Vick said with a laugh. "Come meet your cousin, Pippa."

Pippa was rising to her feet as she said, "Hello, Cody. I'm glad to meet you, but I'm afraid I can't stay. I have to be getting home."

"Before you go," Vick said, "I want you to meet Cody's father, Ryan Sullivan."

"I think I can remember your names from the introductions Vick made to Cody," Rye said as he went around the room shaking hands. "It's nice to finally meet you."

When he got to Leah, she was on her feet. He

took her hand and held it in both of his. "Vick has told me how much you did for her when she was growing up. Now that we've met, I'm hoping we'll be seeing more of each other."

"Does that mean you'll be coming to the family picnic on the Fourth of July?" Leah asked.

Rye seemed to be caught off-guard by the invitation, but he quickly recovered. He shot a look at Vick before he said, "I'm sure we can work that out."

"Good," Leah said. "I'm sorry to take off so soon after we've met, but I've got to get back to the ranch."

"I need to get home to my kids," Pippa said.

"Me, too," Eve said, rising and laying Ashley in Vick's arms.

"Annie's finally asleep," Taylor said as she stood, grabbing the blanket that had been on her lap to keep it from dropping to the floor and laying it across the arm of the rocker. "I'm going to put her in her crib and then take myself off to bed for a nap. Stay as long as you like, Vick. Just leave the baby when you go," she said with a grin.

Within moments, the living room was empty except for Rye, Vick, Cody, and the baby in Vick's arms.

"I'm going to lay Ashley down in her bed," Vick said, "and we can leave." She hesitated, turned to Rye, and said, "Unless you'd like to hold her first." Vick had only offered out of courtesy. She was surprised when Rye said, "Why not?"

She carefully lowered Ashley into his waiting hands, where the newborn fit perfectly.

Rye held the baby snug against his chest, touching her fingers and counting her toes. "I forgot how tiny newborns are," he said, his voice filled with reverence and awe. He smiled at the baby, who watched him intently with wide blue eyes. "You're a beauty, Miss Flynn," he said. "Yes, you are."

"She just looks like a baby," Cody protested.

Vick wondered if Cody might be a little jealous.

"All babies are beautiful," Rye said as he sat on the couch, presumably so Cody could see the baby more easily.

Cody edged his rump onto the couch beside Rye, frowning as he surveyed Ashley's features. "Was I this little when I was born?"

"Not quite," Rye said. "But pretty close."

Within a pound or two, Vick thought. But who was counting?

"Why aren't you and Mommy married, like Ashley and Annie's mommy and daddy, and Brooke and Sawyer's mommy and daddy?" Cody asked. "Did you get a divorce?"

The question came out of the blue, but Vick had been anticipating it, dreading it, for some time. Although Cody had been exposed to a lot of different parental combinations at both church and school, he'd never asked about Rye and Vick's relationship. Likely, he'd presumed they were divorced, since they didn't live together.

Except, now they did.

Vick exchanged a glance with Rye, unsure how best to answer Cody's question. She crossed to sit beside Cody, so he was flanked by his parents and said, "Your father and I aren't divorced because we were never married."

He looked perplexed by her answer. "Don't you have to be married to have babies?"

Vick shook her head. "It's a good idea, but it's not a requirement."

"So . . ." Brow furrowed, Cody looked at her and asked, "Am I a bastard?"

Vick's face drained of blood so quickly she almost keeled over. Her mouth opened, but no sound came out.

"No," Rye said, balancing the baby on his lap so his hands would be free to place them on his son's shoulders. "That's not a word I'd ever use to describe you."

"I heard—"

"Your mom and I weren't married when you were born, but from the moment we saw you, we both loved you very much."

Vick's head jerked in Rye's direction at his rewrite of history. Tears brimmed in her eyes, and her hands came up to cover her mouth.

"Why did you live in two different houses?" Cody asked.

Rye made a face. "It's complicated. But you should know that your mom and I have always done everything we could to make sure you knew how much you're loved." He brushed the same wayward curl away from Cody's forehead as Vick had, then dropped his hands to cradle the baby in his lap.

Vick waited with bated breath to hear what Cody might say next.

Cody shifted his gaze from one parent's distraught face to the other's and said to Rye, "If I'm not a bastard, why is Mommy crying?"

Vick suddenly understood why Darcie might have decided to keep the true details of Rye's birth secret. Her guilt for having put her own child in the same position was palpable, and her gut was twisted in a hard knot. "Bastard" was an ugly word and ought to be stricken from the dictionary. Certainly, Vick never, ever wanted to hear her son refer to himself using that term again.

Vick pulled Cody into her lap with his back against her chest, then leaned forward so they were cheek to cheek. "I don't know where you heard that word, but it's a mean way of saying your parents weren't married when you were born. You should ignore anyone unkind enough to use it. You're a wonderful little boy, the apple of my eye, and your father's favorite son."

"I'm his *only* son."

Vick smiled and met Rye's gaze. "You're his most perfect, nobody-can-compare-to-you favorite son."

Cody looked at Rye to see if she was kidding.

Rye nodded solemnly.

Cody grinned and said, "Can I have an ice cream cone every night before bed?"

Vick and Rye exchanged a rueful smile before Vick said, “No, you may not.”

Rye tousled Cody’s hair. “But because you’re my most perfect, nobody-can-compare-to-you favorite son, you can have an ice cream cone at Moo’s this afternoon.”

Seeing how they’d managed this difficult conversation with their son together—leaving Cody not only feeling loved, but also cheeky enough to see what he could get away with—Vick was more certain than ever that she wanted to make a home for her son that included a mother and father.

Now all she needed to do was convince Rye she would make a good wife.

Chapter 42

HAVING HER SON called a bastard had been one of Vick's worst fears. Her teeth were clamped so tight at the thought of someone saying that to Cody's face, a muscle in her jaw jerked. During the drive back to the hotel in town where they were staying, it dawned on her that she hadn't asked Cody who'd used the term. She couldn't imagine anyone in her family saying such a thing. On the other hand, it was easy to imagine Angus Flynn making some snide comment while he was staying at the Rafter S that Cody had overheard.

Angus had always been a villain in her life story, and despite his marriage to Darcie, it was hard to think of him in any other terms. It was also possible that Cody had overheard one of "those awful Flynn boys" using the word "bastard" in conjunction with his name sometime today.

But if Angus's sons weren't guilty, that sort of accusation would cause a lot of hard feelings. Besides, she couldn't imagine the women in their lives, who were her sisters and niece, allowing Cody to be spoken of that way. And since Cody seemed content with her explanation, she didn't want to bring the subject up again to ask him just who the shameful party was.

Vick unclenched her jaw. She was willing to give the younger Flynns a pass, but she would be damn sure to confront Angus when she got home.

Home.

Although she'd been living at the Rafter S for more than two months, it wasn't home. She'd occupied Rye's bedroom once his family moved back in, and he'd been forced to sleep on the couch. As a result, he'd had the temper of a grizzly most mornings, because he wasn't getting enough rest. She didn't belong there. She had to leave and let Rye's life and her own and Cody's get back to normal.

The one thing she knew for sure was that she could never go back to the way things had been in the past. She'd been with Cody constantly since Mike got home, but she hadn't forgotten the deadline she'd given Rye. If he didn't freely offer her more time with Cody when she moved back into her cabin, she would go to court and fight him for it.

Vick dreaded the thought.

Rye had made that awful promise in the lawyer's

office at a time when he'd been angry and hurting. Being Paddy Sullivan's son, he'd never gone back on it. But just as she'd changed over the years she'd been a mother, Rye had been changing over the years he'd been a father. He was no longer the same man who'd denied her the right to spend any more time with her child than the law allowed.

Tears sprang to her eyes when she remembered how Rye, always honest to a fault, had told a lie to their son to keep Cody's love for her from suffering a terrible blow.

From the moment we saw you, we both loved you very much.

She looked out the window of the SUV they'd rented as she blinked back tears, so Rye wouldn't see them. Her stomach churned as she thought back to the achingly lonely day her son had been born.

Vick hadn't allowed herself to love Cody from the moment she saw him, because she'd known she was giving him up. It would have hurt too much to allow herself to feel the emotions churning inside her. It was only after she'd handed her son to his father to raise that Vick realized she would always love Cody, no matter where he was in the world or who nurtured him.

The ugly truth was it had taken six full months for her to get the courage to show up at Rye's back door.

Rye could have told a very different story to Cody at Taylor's house. Vick wondered if he'd merely been protecting Cody from a brutal fact about his mother, or whether he'd lied for her sake.

Probably, it was a little of both.

Vick would always be thankful to him for it. She glanced at Rye and realized he was scowling. What was wrong now? Was he still upset that someone had called Cody a bastard in their son's hearing? Or was he worrying about Mike and his mother and Amy Beth at home needing him, while he was here with her?

She glanced over her shoulder at Cody and saw he was playing a handheld digital game. She kept her voice low so Cody wouldn't hear as she asked, "Is everything all right?"

"Why do you ask?"

"You were frowning."

"I was going to invite you out tonight, but I don't know if we should leave Cody, after the conversation we just had with him."

"Cody's fine. Where did you have in mind to go?"

"It's a surprise."

"I don't like surprises."

"Why not?"

"Most of the surprises in my life haven't turned out so well."

He smiled and said, "Maybe we can break that string tonight."

"Can't you just tell me what you have in mind?" Too late, Vick realized how irritated she sounded. "I would love to go out with you. I'd just like to know where we're headed."

He was quiet for so long she realized he was reluctant to reveal what he had planned.

"Just tell me."

"Never mind," he said curtly. "We can stay at the hotel."

"For heaven's sake! It can't be that big of a deal."

"It was to me," he muttered, his eyes pinned on the road.

Vick heaved a long-suffering sigh and threw up her hands. "All right. Fine. Surprise me."

He shot a questioning look at her, as though making up his mind, then focused his gaze back on the road. "I'm going to drop Cody off with Connor and Eve. They're having dinner in town with their kids before they head back to their ranch. Then I'll come back for you."

Her eyebrows rose. If Cody was spending the night with one of Rye's Flynn brothers, he must be intending for the two of them to be out late. Or not come home at all.

It suddenly dawned on her where Rye might want to go. She'd just have to wait and see whether they ended up at the Million Dollar Cowboy Bar.

Chapter 43

RYE STOOD IN the hallway outside his hotel room and sniffed under his arms. Thank God the deodorant was doing its job. He'd splashed on too much piney cologne, and he was suffocating from the smell of it. He pulled a hanky from the back pocket of his jeans and swiped the nervous sweat from his brow and upper lip, then tucked the hanky back out of sight. He'd wanted everything to be perfect tonight.

So far, everything was royally fucked up.

Despite getting an ice cream cone from Moo's earlier in the day, and expressing a willingness to stay overnight with his cousins, when Cody got to the restaurant where Connor and Eve were having dinner with their kids, he'd balked at the idea of spending the night with them. It had taken some fancy talking on Rye's part, and an offer from Sawyer to play a video game Cody liked when they got home, to get him to stay. Rye had promised Connor and Eve that, if necessary, he'd come and pick Cody up tonight.

He would. If necessary. Rye had an awful feeling he was going to get a call to come get his son at the worst possible moment. Was it any wonder he was on edge?

Rye glanced at the closed door to Vick's hotel room. He'd been in and out of the shower in five minutes, shaved and dressed in Levi's, a Western shirt, and boots in another five, and had been waiting for her for forty-five. The last time he'd called her room, she still wasn't ready. He paced the hall, jumpy as spit on a hot skillet. At least there was no one around to see him behaving like a teenage boy on his first date.

He ought to forget about reminding Vick what they'd had in the past and focus on convincing her that what they had right now was worth keeping. That actually sounded like a better plan than reminding her of something that had been so amazing it couldn't be duplicated.

All he needed was a way to do that. Which wasn't coming to mind. Better to stick with his first plan, even if it was filled with hitches. At least it *was* a plan.

As Vick's door opened, he ran a finger around the inside of his too-tight shirt collar, which was buttoned all the way up, with a bolo tie cinched at his throat. He swallowed over the aching lump in his throat, shoved his sweaty hands down the thighs of his jeans, and waited for her to step into the hall.

His heart tripped when he saw what she was wearing.

"You aren't—" He had to stop and clear his throat. "You aren't dressed."

"I thought we might stay in."

Her voice was husky, and her eyes looked sultry. She was wearing a full-length, filmy black nightgown with skinny straps that barely held the thing up, giving him a shadowy view of nipples and knees and all the titillating things in between. Blood surged to his neck, to his ears, to his groin. In an instant, he was hot and hard. She was holding on to the half-open door with both hands, as though she hadn't yet decided whether to invite him in or shut him out.

Rye was afraid to move, afraid he'd do something wrong, and she'd rescind the obvious invitation to take her to bed. He stood there, waiting for Vick to make the first move.

It took him only a moment to realize his mistake. She'd already made the first move by opening the door wearing a see-through nightgown. As he stood there frozen, neither accepting nor rejecting her offer, he saw her confidence begin to falter.

Her chin trembled, and her lashes lowered to hide her eyes.

She gasped in surprise as he swept her up in his arms, shoved the door open far enough to get inside with her, and slammed it shut with the heel of his boot.

She'd already folded down the bed, soft music was playing from her phone, and several candles flickered on surfaces around the room. She must have planned this in advance, since their hotel rooms hadn't come stocked with candles.

He grinned at her and said, "Am I being seduced?"

She slid her hand around his nape, raising chill bumps, and met his gaze with a shy smile. "I thought I might give it a try."

He eased her bare feet onto the carpet beside the bed and settled his hands around her hips to keep their bodies aligned. "I think you just didn't want to end up on one of those saddles at the Million Dollar Cowboy Bar."

"That, too," she said with a chuffing laugh.

Rye was pleased to find her so willing to share her bed. And, he admitted, a little suspicious.

Why this sudden change of mind? Vick had confessed that she not only had reservations about her feelings for him, but also concerns that he couldn't turn his feelings for her around on a dime. She'd been reluctant even to go on a date with him tonight. He'd had to talk her into it. So what was going on here?

What's wrong with you, Rye? No man in his right mind turns down a night of sex with a woman he desires. Stop thinking and start enjoying what's being freely offered.

Except, he wasn't only interested in having sex with Vick. He wanted a lifelong relationship.

Her fingernails gently scratched the skin at his nape, raising goosebumps. Rye decided now wasn't the time to try and figure out what was going on in Vick's head. He would show her how much he cared by cherishing her body, by loving her with every part of his being, and sharing all of himself with her.

They would have plenty of time to talk after they'd made love.

He lowered his head and kissed Vick's fathomless blue eyes closed, then kissed the tip of her nose and caressed each cheek. He finally found his way to her mouth and ran his tongue along the seam of her lips until she opened to him.

Her nightgown came off with two flicks of his wrists, and cascaded to her feet. Vick flushed, but she didn't lower her gaze or try to hide herself.

Rye looked his fill. "You're beautiful."

"I would return the compliment, but I can't admire what I can't see," she said with a teasing smile.

Rye yanked the bolo tie down and over his head, then attacked the too-small buttons on his shirt.

Vick was laughing at his frenzy, and at the same time unbuckling his belt, unzipping his jeans, and shoving both jeans and underwear down. He yanked the half-unbuttoned shirt off over his head, then sat his naked ass on the bed while he pulled off his boots and socks and shoved his jeans the rest of the way down and off. When he rose again to stand across from her, he was as naked as she.

His desire for her was evident, but when she reached out to touch, he felt himself harden even more. A small drop of liquid appeared at the head of his shaft, and she slowly dipped to one knee, surrounded him with her hand, and licked it off.

Rye thought he might explode. This was going to be over before it started if she kept that up. He raised Vick onto her feet and pressed her naked skin against his, rocking her in his arms.

"Whoa, sweetheart," he murmured. "We have all night."

"I want to do all the things we didn't do the first time. I want this night to be different."

He wasn't sure what it was he heard in her voice. Nervousness? Hope? He wished she would look at him, so he could get an inkling of what she was thinking, but her eyes were focused on his belly, where she was sifting her fingertips through the soft hair that trailed down to the thicker bush surrounding his sex.

He'd wanted this night to be the same, only better, although that seemed a difficult, maybe even impossible goal to reach. So maybe she had the right idea.

"All right," he said. "All the things we didn't do."

She met his gaze suddenly, her eyes filled with mischief. "Well, some of the things we did would be okay, too."

She obviously hadn't forgotten their night together, but she wanted new memories. So did he.

Rye took his time touching, playing with her, searching for the places he might not have touched before, seeking the ones that pleased her most. He marveled at how the flickering candlelight made her body a constant mystery. He watched her nipples peak into hard buds as he focused his gaze on them and took a nipple in his mouth to suckle as her body writhed with pleasure.

Vick touched him in return, her tongue tasting, her hands teasing, her fingernails gently scratching in places he hadn't known could bring so much pleasure.

Rye's knees threatened to buckle, which was when he realized they were still standing. His heart was pounding, his shaft was pulsing, and his throat was raw with emotion. It would have been simple to lift her and impale her and satisfy his desperate need for her where he stood.

Instead, he took a step back and said, "Maybe we should lie down."

Vick moved in and out of the shadows like some mystical creature as she eased herself onto the bed to lie naked and exposed before him, allowing him to look his fill, to drink in her loveliness. He covered her body with his, inhaling the unique scent of her wafting from her heated body and feeling the human warmth of her from breast to hips. Rye slid his leg between her thighs to open them, to give him room to slide two fingers inside, and heard her gasp. He felt her hands clutching his hair, felt her teeth rake his shoulder.

He released her and slid down far enough to slip her legs over his shoulders so he could taste her and tease her and bring her to the heights of pleasure. He loved her mewing cries, her moans, her guttural, animal groans of satisfaction.

She returned the favor, causing him to gasp and moan until he stopped her, unwilling to spill himself until he was inside her. He heard her tremulous sigh of pleasure as he glided into her, slow and deep. Her hips lifted to urge him even deeper.

Thrust and parry. Need and satisfaction. Desire and fulfillment.

It had been good the first time. This was better. Far better. Vick surged against him, transporting them higher, taking them to peaks he'd never imagined. Rye felt himself coming apart and threw his head back, gritting his teeth against a pleasure so great it was almost pain, until, at last, a primeval cry of triumph was wrenched from deep within him.

He lowered himself to Vick's side, pulling her close, feeling her lungs sucking air along with his own. Surely, this night was a turning point. Surely, from now on, Vick would understand they belonged together. Surely, she could tell how much he cared.

That was the last thought Rye had as sleep claimed him.

When he woke up, she was gone.

Chapter 44

VICK'S HEART HAD finally stopped galloping in her chest after the hair-raising drive she'd just made along a winding road through an ominous forest on a pitch-black night.

After Rye had fallen asleep, she'd heard his phone buzz and had a terrible premonition of disaster. She'd searched until she found his cell in the pocket of his jeans. When Vick saw who it was, she'd gone into the bathroom to take the call, so she wouldn't wake him.

Eve told her that Cody had woken up frightened by a nightmare and was tearfully pleading to go home. Vick had felt frantic to get to her son, to ease his distress, to hold him close and comfort him. She'd grabbed jeans and a sweatshirt out of her suitcase, pulled on her Uggs, and snatched her coat from the chair as she left.

It never occurred to her, not once, to wake Rye. She could handle the problem on her own and would. It was what she'd done her whole life, taking care of herself, solving her own crises, doing what had to be done.

With any luck, she would be back to her room—and back in bed—before Rye woke up. The last thing she wanted was for him to think she was flying the coop again. She was done running away. Tonight had proved that.

When Vick arrived at Connor and Eve's ranch, Cody was sitting calmly at the bar in the kitchen drinking a cup of hot chocolate loaded with marshmallows. Eve and Connor hovered on either side of him in their pajamas, slippers, and robes, eyes bleary, hair askew. She thanked them, lifted Cody into her arms, strapped him in his car seat, and headed back the way she'd come.

Vick wondered why Cody had been so insistent about leaving. He hadn't stayed awake in the SUV more than a few moments, and once she laid him down in his bed, in the room he shared with Rye, he'd turned on his side and hadn't moved again. Had he really had a nightmare? Or had he simply woken up and missed his parents?

Cody had done pretty well, considering this was the first time he'd spent the night away from both of his parents. It had been a risky move on Rye's part, but it had been worth it.

When Vick had opened her hotel room door to Rye's knock tonight, her heart had been stuck in her throat. What if he refused her offer? What if he told her to stop playing games and get dressed? She'd envisioned a thousand ways he could reject her.

But he hadn't.

Rye had eaten her with his eyes. And tasted her with his lips. And made love to her with his nimble fingers and agile tongue and pulsing shaft until she'd come and come and come. What had happened between them, the things they'd never done before, and the things they'd done again, had brought them closer than she'd ever imagined two human beings could be.

Dawn was still a ways off when Vick crept down the hall and eased open the door to her hotel room. She'd blown out all but the largest candle before she'd left, and it provided the only light.

It was enough to see that the bed was empty.

She shoved the door open wide, heedless of the noise it made. "Rye?" There was no answer. How long had he been gone? Where had he gone? He wasn't in his room. He didn't have a vehicle, but if he'd tried to leave, he would have seen the SUV was gone. And that she was gone.

Did he think she'd run away again?

Why, oh, why hadn't she left him a note? Or woken him up? Rye wouldn't have minded going after Cody any more than she had.

She slid down onto the carpet beside her bed, her feet splayed, and tried to imagine where he might have gone. She came up empty. Rye didn't know anyone in town except her family, and they were still strangers to him. He must be hurting terribly. He must feel like she'd abandoned him, although how he could think such a thing after the way they'd made love, she couldn't imagine. She started to call him and realized this wasn't a conversation she wanted to have on the phone.

Suddenly, she realized where he must have gone. Vick scrambled to her feet and then froze. A quiet cry of despair escaped as she realized there was no way she could go after him. She couldn't leave Cody alone at the hotel, and Cody couldn't go where she knew Rye was.

Once she'd realized Rye wasn't in her room, she'd moved Cody from Rye's room to hers. She eyed her son as he slept on, oblivious to the whirlwind Vick felt swirling around her.

Who could possibly help? Who would be willing to come all the way into town in the middle of the night to watch Cody?

She turned to the one person who'd always been there for her whenever she'd needed love or comfort or encouragement. The one person who never failed to offer help when she needed it.

Vick hit the speed dial and waited. And waited. She groaned and smacked her fist against the door when the call went to voicemail. "Leah, I don't know where you are or what you're doing, but I need you to call me back. It's an emergency. My whole life depends on it."

Chapter 45

"DON'T ANSWER IT."

Leah snuggled closer to Aiden and said, "I should at least see who's calling at this hour of the night. It might be an emergency."

"Now that I have you in my bed again, and everyone knows we're husband and wife, I have no intention of letting you out of it," Aiden said. "Don't touch that phone."

Leah left the phone on the end table. She'd taken Matt's advice and told Aiden tonight that she was ready to move in with him. She had no regrets.

"I'll live with you until we get a new house built," she'd said, standing on the back porch of his ranch house as the sun was setting. "Or you can live with me. The point is I don't want to wait another moment to start our lives together."

Aiden hadn't leapt at her suggestion. He'd stood in the kitchen doorway with his hands on his hips and his mouth turned down. "What happened to waiting until King is well?"

Suddenly nervous, she'd stuck her hands in the back pockets of her jeans and said, "He might never get well."

"What happened to your plans for a big wedding?"

"Everyone knows we're married. It would be a waste of time and money." She was surprised by Aiden's interrogation, but she supposed he was entitled to question her sudden change of mind. However, his incisive questions, or maybe it was his penetrating gaze, caused her pulse to jump. Couldn't he just accept what she'd said at face value?

Leah pulled one of her hands out of her back pocket and shoved her dishwater blond hair away from her face, tucking it behind her ear. "It makes more sense to have a big christening party instead."

"What about your plans to own Kingdom Come?"

She found it significant that he'd left that question for last. "You're more important to me than any piece of property. I love you so much—"

He didn't wait for her to finish, just scooped her into his arms and carried her up the stairs to his bedroom.

It hadn't even been dark when they'd stripped off

their clothes to make love. It was after midnight, and they hadn't left his bed.

They'd talked endlessly between the three times they'd coupled, making plans, deciding where they wanted to build their house, and what they wanted it to look like.

"I'm starving," Aiden said, scratching his belly. "How about an early breakfast?"

Leah laughed. "It's the middle of the night."

"I could go for some pancakes. How about you?"

Her mouth suddenly watered. So far during her pregnancy, Leah hadn't had any cravings. Pancakes loaded with butter and dripping with maple syrup sounded delicious. "I guess I could eat a bite or two."

Aiden grabbed his jeans and pulled them on without underwear, leaving a couple of buttons undone so the denim slid down his hips revealing the concave area on either side of his belly. Leah found the panel of muscle at the center of that dip, which ran down to his sex, absolutely fascinating. She was staring, but she couldn't help it.

Leah walked toward Aiden, not bothering to grab the flannel shirt at the foot of the bed to cover her nakedness, too entranced by his muscular body to think of her own.

"Aiden," she said in a husky voice, as she laid her hand on the flesh that had caught her attention.

Aiden gasped when her hands traced the muscular indentations, sliding downward toward what was hidden by the layer of denim. His hands grasped her wrists. "Leah."

She looked up, unsure whether he wanted her to stop or keep up what she was doing. A glance at his Levi's revealed that his body was willing, even if he wasn't.

"I love your body, Aiden. I want to touch this spot . . . right . . . here."

He gave a guttural groan of surrender and released her hands.

They made love on the rug. The sex was fierce and fast and fully satisfying.

"Now I *am* hungry," Leah said when she was breathing normally again. "Are you going to feed me, or not?"

He stood and pulled his Levi's back up, this time buttoning them all the way to the top. Then he grabbed her flannel shirt from the bed and stuffed her arms into it, making sure it was securely fastened. His gaze kept slipping to her rear end, which was barely covered by the flannel tail.

"Keep that up," she said, "and I'll be expecting you to do something about it."

"Have mercy," he said, turning her and giving her rear end a loving pat as he nudged her toward the bedroom door. "I need some food to keep up my strength."

The next time Leah's phone rang, she was downstairs in the kitchen eating pancakes. She didn't hear it.

Chapter 46

VICK WAS FRANTIC. Leah wasn't answering her phone. Everyone else she could have called had babies that were likely sound asleep or lived too far away to get to her anytime soon.

She heard someone knocking at her hotel room door and raced to answer it. "Rye? Is that you?"

But it wasn't Rye.

"Matt? What are you doing here?"

Matt stepped inside her room with Nathan draped over his shoulder sound asleep. He put a finger to his lips to silence her, so she wouldn't wake him up. To her amazement, Jennie stepped inside behind Matt.

Vick's jaw dropped, and her gaze shot from one to the other.

"What are you doing here, Matt? You lost the ranch. Why are you back?"

"Leah asked me to come."

"What? Why?"

"It's late. We can discuss all this in the morning. We flew in late, and I didn't want to drive all the way to the ranch. Jimmy, the hotel clerk, told me you were staying here, and I thought I'd check with you and see whether there was some problem."

"No problem. Except I need a babysitter. Can you keep an eye on Cody while I go out?"

Matt didn't even raise a brow at the sight of the sleeping boy, and Vick decided he must already have heard about Cody through the family grapevine.

Matt glanced at Jennie, whose shoulders sagged and whose eyes looked sunken, and said, "You need to get to bed, honey. You look ragged."

Jennie grimaced. "Thanks a lot. You don't look so great yourself."

Vick had been so absorbed with her own issues, she hadn't noticed how fatigued both Matt and Jennie appeared. "What happened to make you so late getting here?"

"Mechanical problems with the jet. We didn't want to put off the trip till morning, so here we are."

"Just in time to help me out, for which I will be eternally grateful."

"Give me a few minutes to get Jennie and Nate settled and I'll be back," Matt said.

Vick paced the confines of the small room waiting

for Matt's return and hurried to the door when he knocked.

As she grabbed her coat he asked, "Where are you going at this hour of the night?"

"I have to see someone."

Matt stood with his hands on his hips, waiting for further explanation, and she said, "If you must know, it's Cody's father."

"Ah," Matt said. "The Montana rancher."

"If you've been told that much, you know things are still up in the air between us. I need to speak to him, and it can't wait till morning."

Matt gestured toward the door, grinned, and said, "Go for it."

Vick hurried out the door. She'd checked, and the Million Dollar Cowboy Bar closed at 2 a.m. She found a parking place four blocks away and ran all the way back to the bar, arriving with her cheeks pink from the cold and her lungs heaving.

Rye was sitting at a table in the bar with a drink in front of him—along with three upside-down shot glasses. She moved to the bar and slipped onto one of the saddle bar stools. "I'll have whatever's on tap."

"Drink up. We close in fifteen minutes," the bartender said as he set the beer in front of her.

Vick wasn't wearing a pair of sexy, tight-fitting jeans or a tailored white shirt that emphasized her breasts or even stylish cowboy boots. She had on a ratty sweatshirt and ripped Wranglers with her Uggs. Her hair was a mess. Her mascara was clumped and her eyeliner was smeared. She glanced over her shoulder, waiting until Rye saw her.

He froze with his drink halfway to his mouth.

She maintained eye contact for a moment too long and then smiled, giving him her very best come-hither look. Finally, she flipped her tousled hair over her shoulder and turned her back on him.

And waited to see what he would do.

Please come over and speak to me. Please give me a chance to explain. Please believe I want to be with you.

"Hello, pretty lady." His voice was rough and warm and oh, so welcome.

Vick slid off the saddle and stood facing him. "I went to pick up Cody. He had a nightmare."

"I know."

Her brow furrowed. "You know? How did you know?"

"When I woke up, I checked my phone and saw that Eve had called. I called her back, and she told me you were on your way."

"So you never thought I'd walked out?"

He met her gaze and shook his head.

"Then why did you leave?" she asked. "I came back and you were gone and I went crazy worrying what you would think. I couldn't leave Cody alone and I couldn't get hold of Leah and if Matt hadn't shown up out of the blue I don't know what I would have done."

"Matt showed up?"

"Don't change the subject," she said. "Why did you leave?"

"To see if you would follow me."

"What if I hadn't shown up because I couldn't find a babysitter," she said, exasperated.

He smiled. "I knew you would come. Knowing it wasn't easy for you to get here just makes having you here all the sweeter."

He'd believed she would come. He loved her and was willing to trust her to love him. She wasn't sure whether to kiss him or kick him. "How was I supposed to know where you went?"

"You figured it out, didn't you? Although I was getting a little worried that you weren't going to make it before the place closed for the night."

"What if I hadn't? What would you have done then?"

"Headed for the Wort Hotel, of course."

"We are *not* going *there,*" she said.

"Nope," he agreed. "We're going back to the hotel and pack our things, and when the sun comes up, we're heading home. I need to keep an eye on Mike," he continued, "so he doesn't get himself killed hunting down that poacher who shot him, and we need to get Cody enrolled in Vacation Bible School."

"And Amy Beth needs to get back to Missoula so she can finish up her exams and talk to—" Vick cut herself off, blushed, and said, "So she can finish up her exams."

"I'd like to check on Mom and make sure she's okay," Rye said.

"Is that everything?" she asked.

He shot her a wry look. "Everything except how to get you to marry me."

"You might ask."

"I love you, Vick. Will you marry me?"

"Yes."

He threw his hat in the air and gave a cowboy yell that startled the patrons in the bar. "She said yes!" he shouted.

The customers laughed and clapped and hooted and hollered while Rye scooped Vick into his arms and held her close, giving her the chance to whisper, "I love you, too."

Epilogue

THE GRAYHAWK WOMEN were both fertile and fecund. Every wife at the Fourth of July picnic being held at Leah and Aiden's ranch house was carrying a newborn or had a belly swollen with child. It had been three years since Vick and Rye were married by a justice of the peace in Jackson, with two strangers for witnesses and no family except their five-year-old son in attendance. Vick wore a smug smile. She had both a baby in her arms and another growing inside her that her husband knew nothing about.

The celebration was being held at Leah's home, instead of Kingdom Come, because you always met at your mom's place for family gatherings, and Leah had carried that burden with joy in her heart all the years King's Brats had been growing up.

Chemo hadn't worked this time on King's leukemia, and when he'd died a year ago and his will was read, Leah learned that he'd given Kingdom Come to Matt. Vick had been surprised, when she tried to console Leah, to discover that her sister wasn't at all sorry to lose the ranch.

"I was hanging on to a piece of land because it was all I had in the world. I realized it wasn't the land I wanted, it was the love and security it represented. My life now is filled to overflowing with a husband and children, and there's plenty of work at the Lucky 7 to go around.

"Besides, the house would have been a sad place with King gone," she continued. "I have a home with Aiden that I love, and with King dead and Angus living in Montana—and most of us married to Flynns—there's no need to merge our ranches to stop those two old men from fighting. The feud between our families is over and done."

Angus had come with Darcie, and Vick thought they seemed very happy together. Amy Beth had shown up this year for the first time with a boyfriend, the young man she'd been crying over all those years ago when Vick had held her and comforted her because he was getting engaged to someone else. The engagement had broken off without the young man ever getting married, and Amy Beth had made sure he noticed her this time around.

Mike had become a bitter lone wolf. No one ever saw much of him. He'd retreated to Vick's cabin in the woods and could rarely be coaxed out. He worked on the Rafter S, and did his shopping late at night so he wouldn't run into kids who would flee from the monster he believed he'd become. Vick and Rye had told Mike the scars on his face had faded, and Cody had never again reacted the same way. But nothing anybody said could change Mike's mind.

When Mike had refused for the third year in a row to come to the family picnic in Jackson Hole, Vick had decided things had to change. She was currently on the lookout for a woman who would see past Mike's scars to the man she'd come to know. It wasn't going to be easy, because the truth was the attack had disfigured Mike's face, drawing his mouth down on one side so he always looked angry. But Vick was sure the woman who could save Mike from himself was out there somewhere. All she had to do was find her.

The poacher who'd shot Goldilocks and missed had tried the same thing a year later and ended up getting badly mauled by the bear he'd shot. Once the poacher recovered from his injuries, Pete had arrested him.

Pete had a brand-new girlfriend. She was a policewoman in Kalispell. Pete had told Vick they had a lot in common—the subject of bears never came up. They were planning a trip to Hawaii together in the fall.

Leah and Aiden had built their living room and kitchen large enough to hold every one of King's Brats and "those awful Flynn boys" along with their children and the grandchildren they all hoped to have someday. Some of the men and the more pregnant women were sitting on the covered front porch in swings and rockers, while others shot off firecrackers and played flag football and other games with the kids on the lawn. The rest of the women had gathered in the kitchen to finish up the food for the picnic and were now carrying everything out to the tables that had been set up in the backyard, where a huge side of beef was being roasted on a spit.

"Hello, beautiful."

Vick felt Rye's arms slide around her waist as he nosed her hair out of the way and nuzzled her neck. She had a platter of deviled eggs in her hand and said, "Don't make me drop these."

"Put them down and turn around so I can kiss you."

"That's the best offer I've had all morning," Vick said with a laugh. She set down the platter and threw her arms around Rye's neck, enthusiastically participating as he kissed her silly.

"We need to join the others," she said, breaking the kiss. "You know how much your brothers like deviled eggs," she added with a teasing smile.

"They can wait while I kiss my wife."

"What did you do with the baby?" she asked.

"Mom is holding Tommy."

"Where's Cody?"

"He and Sawyer are pretending to be X-Men with superpowers."

"Leaving you free to come here and accost me and the baby."

"I told you the baby's with Mom."

"Not this one," Vick said, laying her hand over her belly.

It took Rye a moment to catch on, but he was a quick study. "You're pregnant?"

Vick's eyes teared with joy. "I am."

"We're having another baby?"

"We are."

Rye pulled her close and rocked her in his arms. "My beautiful wife is having a baby," he whispered in her ear. "I think I might cry."

Vick leaned back far enough to see the tears in his eyes and the grin on his face. "You're happy?"

"Over the moon. How about you? I know you would have been happy with two. Are you okay with three?"

"Are you okay with four?"

He looked stunned. "Four?"

She nodded.

"We're having twins?"

"Uh-huh."

"Are you all right?"

"I'm fine. More than fine." She laughed and said, "I'm over the moon."

"Hey!" a male voice called from outside the screen door. "Where are those deviled eggs?"

Rye slid an arm around her waist, then picked up the dish of deviled eggs and said, "Keep your shorts on! My pregnant wife needs a little help getting them on the table."

"Your *pregnant* wife?" someone yelled from outside.

"Now you've done it," Vick said.

"Vick is pregnant!" one of her sisters shouted.

Vick giggled and followed her husband, with his dish of deviled eggs, out the screen door and into the chaos and cacophony of her loving family celebrating life—and the nation's birthday—with sparklers and good food and laughter.

Acknowledgments

I want to thank Kat and Larry Martin, my wonderful writer friends in Montana (wonderful friends and amazing writers), for giving me a place to lay my head while I did research for this book.

Much thanks to Lynn Cherrington and Vic Workman, realtors at Christie's in Whitefish, for putting me in touch with Jim and Lea Ann Noffsinger. Jim was kind enough to share details of the Noffsingers' Wild Horse Ranch north of Whitefish, which became the blueprint for my fictional Rafter S.

I'm indebted to Bob Bacon and Anthony Ewell, who provided guidance and good food at Casey's in Whitefish, where the huckleberry margaritas are icy and the DJ starts the music at ten on Friday nights.

It would have been impossible to write this novel without the things I learned about grizzlies in the many books that found their way into my hands. I especially enjoyed *Mark of the Grizzly* by Scott McMillion, *Great Montana Bear Stories* by Ben Long, and *A Year in the Life of a Grizzly In Glacier*

National Park by local Whitefish author and artist Vernon Anderson.

Nancy November Sloane, owner of Rebel Marketing, provides endless assistance with all the minutiae necessary to keep readers informed about what I'm working on and what's coming next. I'm grateful for all her hard work and for being a great cheerleader when I need one.

Thanks again to my sister Joyce for being on the other end of the phone line when I'm trying to decide where a comma belongs. She's forgotten more about grammar, punctuation, and spelling than I will ever know.

I'm a better writer because of my editor, Shauna Summers, who allows me the space to let my imagination roam and puts her finger on what needs a second look with her incisive suggestions. I can't thank her enough for sticking with me through the years I've spent writing the stories of the four women I labeled King's Brats.

Letter to Readers

I might have scared myself out of the woods with the research I did on grizzly attacks for this book, the way *Jaws* scared me out of the ocean. Violent encounters between man and grizzly in Glacier National Park have gruesome results, but *Death in Glacier National Park: Stories of Accidents and Foolhardiness in the Crown of the Continent* makes it clear that you have a far better chance of drowning or dying of a heart attack (not from meeting a grizzly face-to-face, but from the altitude) than being attacked by a bear in the park. If you take proper precautions, the beauty to be found is breathtaking.

This is the final book in my King's Brats series, which includes *Sinful, Shameless, Surrender,* and *Sullivan's Promise.* If you've enjoyed these novels, you might want to check out others in my Bitter Creek series, all of which are listed on my website, joanjohnston.com. You can stay in touch with me at Facebook.com/joanjohnstonauthor, on Twitter @joanjohnston, and on Instagram @joanjohnstondinnerparties. I look forward to hearing from you!